Hollowstone

By
Dennis R. Upkins

Moxie is an imprint of Parker Publishing LLC.

Copyright © 2011 by Dennis R. Upkins
Published by Parker Publishing LLC
12523 Limonite Avenue, Suite 440-438
Mira Loma, California 91752
www.parker-publishing.com

ISBN-13: 978-1463504373
ISBN-10: 1463504373
First Edition

Manufactured in the United States of America
Cover Design by Parker Publishing Inc

DEDICATION :
This book is dedicated to Brenda Whittmore and to all of the other Ruby Scotts of the world.

And a special dedication also goes to Perry Moore. A good friend and a hero who left this world far too soon. Keep flying and thank you.

ACKNOWLEDGEMENTS:
First and foremost, I would like to thank God for giving me the faith, the strength and the skill to pen this story and the fortitude not to give up until it I saw it published.

In addition, Hollowstone wouldn't have become a reality without the help of some wonderful people. An enormous thank you goes to Todd McCaffrey for taking the time out of his hectic schedule at Dragon Con to impart a few kind words to a wide-eyed college kid and challenging him to pursue his calling.

I'll also forever be indebted to my savvy brilliant beta readers, fellow authors Anne Cordwainer and Pauline Trent aka the Mistresses of Awesome.

And speaking of awesome, I can't say enough about my extraordinary publisher Kymberlyn Reed and the fine folks at Parker Publishing who believed in Hollowstone but more than that, believe that diversity matters and that everyone deserves to have their voices heard and their stories told.

And finally thank you, gracious reader. Thank you for taking time out of your busy schedule to read this novel. Hopefully you'll enjoy it and hopefully this is a sign of things to come.

Dennis R. Upkins

Chapter One

Funny thing about the truth. No matter how deep you bury it, it's always there for someone else to uncover. I never shared with anyone about my time at Hollowstone Academy... until now. If there's one thing Caleb taught me, it's that there are some stories that must be told.

Caleb Warner. The centerpiece of this sordid saga. He was my roommate and best friend in the three years I attended Hollowstone. And while we weren't genetically related, he was my big brother in the truest sense. Though a hellion, he turned out all right in the end. He certainly deserved better than what happened to him.

They say it never snows in Newton. However it did much of that since Cal's funeral. I supposed that's what is called irony. Heavy flurries descended upon the four of us as we stood at Cal's gravesite. Father Michael continued his prayer while my roommate's weeping mother buried her face into her fiancé's chest. My grief and anger made me immune to the harsh winds.

Labored breathing and crunching snow indicated a late arrival. Turning around, my eyes widened in surprise when I spotted Vaughn Pope. Tossing his shaggy dark mane from his eyes, my classmate adjusted his thick wool trench coat. I stepped away from the gathering to greet him.

"Sorry I'm late," he said, panting heavily. "I couldn't get my car to turn over. Where is everybody?"

"This is it," I said.

"You're joking."

"I wish I were."

"They used to come to his parties by the hundreds."

"I guess they couldn't allow something as trite as a funeral to get in the way of their little luncheons. To be honest, and not that I'm not glad, but I'm surprised you came. I didn't realize you and Cal were tight."

"We weren't. I went to a few of his parties but we never really hung out. My car broke down on the side of the interstate one day. He called me a tow truck and gave me a lift back to the school. We chatted about music and stuff. He always seemed cool."

Vaughn glanced at the others present. "The parentals?"

"His mom and her fiancé."

"Any news from the cops?"

I shook my head. "They think it was a stickup gone bad. They found his wallet a few yards from the body. It was empty. They dusted it for fingerprints. Nothing."

"And this snow doesn't look like it's going to be letting up anytime soon."

"Nah. Under other circumstances it would be beautiful."

Father Michael continued to quote verses from the small leather Bible in his hands. That's when I saw him. Beyond the headstone, Cal leaned against a tree. He flashed his trademark smirk.

"What the…" I muttered.

"What is it?" Vaughn asked.

"You see him?"

"See who?"

He was gone. Of course he would be.

"Never mind."

The whirlwind of the past few months were finally taking their toll on me. All things considered, it was a miracle I hadn't unraveled sooner.

While I grew up in Atlanta, I was actually born in New Orleans. My parents were killed during Hurricane Katrina when I was 12. With no other family, I moved in with my great-grandmother, Nanna. Though the loss of my parents was hard on both of us, we found a way to make it work. She was happy to have company, especially a man in the house. She never missed an opportunity to spoil and dote on her great-grandson, despite my numerous objections. Most nights, music emanated from the Scott household. Nanna got me hooked on jazz and I turned her on to classical music. Most evenings she would rest in the den while I practiced my violin for her.

It was a typical Tuesday and I just arrived home from school. My itinerary consisted of studying for a quiz, practicing my violin and maybe watching television. Hearing voices and laughter from the kitchen, I figured Mrs. Jenkins was over for one of her weekly neighborhood gossip chats. Instead, I found Ms. Ramirez giggling with Nanna.

"Oh there he is," Nanna said.

"Hey, Noah, come join us," Ms. Ramirez greeted.

I studied my grandmother and my English teacher. Ms. Ramirez was pretty cool as far as teachers went. She always struck me as one of those fresh out of college idealistic types who thought she could change the world, one youth at a time. For the life of me I couldn't guess the reason for the house visit? I was on the honor roll and I never got into any trouble. I pulled out a wooden chair and joined the two women at the table.

"What's going on?" I asked.

"As I was telling your grandmother, I had some concerns," Ms. Ramirez said.

"If it's about that test, it's only an A- and I don't like Shakespeare," I argued.

My teacher giggled, "It's not that at all Noah. I was just telling your grandmother that she did a fine job raising my favorite student. You're very bright and good-natured. A bit quiet, but my life would be easier if I had twenty-two more like you in class. I talked to your music teacher, Mr. Baird, and he couldn't stop singing your praises. No pun intended."

"Thank you," I said. "So what's wrong?"

"To be completely blunt, I don't think the public school system is where you need to be. You're gifted and I don't want to see you lost in the system. An old buddy of mine works at Hollowstone Academy. Have you ever heard of it?"

I shook my head.

"It's in the mountains in Newton, Tennessee. It's one of the most prestigious boarding schools in the country," Ramirez said. "Some of the country's most influential figures graduated from there. They recently started a memorial academic scholarship program and between your grades, your musical background and a few letters of recommendations, I think you would be a shoe-in. And I couldn't think of a more deserving student to attend. The opportunities are endless. Graduating from Hollowstone could get you into any college and the connections you make there could set you for life."

I stared at my light brown hands.

"I know this is a lot to take in and I understand that you and your grandmother will want to discuss this, but this would be a great opportunity for you for next year. This school will allow you to thrive in a wonderful environment."

"I appreciate the kind words and the offer," I said. "I really do. It means a lot that you think highly of me but I can't abandon Nanna. I'm really sorry."

"Ms. Ramirez, why don't you let us talk and we'll give you a call," Nanna said.

"Of course," Ms. Ramirez said.

As Nanna walked Ms. Ramirez out, I spotted the faint smile on my great-grandmother's pursed lips. The very same smile that always indicated her mind was set and nothing short of divine intervention was going to stop her.

That evening I cringed when I heard the inevitable tap on my bedroom door.

"And here we go," I muttered under my breath. "Come in."

Nanna walked in with a tray of her famous warm chocolate chip cookies and a glass of cranberry juice. I had to give her credit. She pulled out the big guns.

"Thought I'd bring you a snack while you studied," she said.

"And here I was thinking that you were trying to bribe me."

She sat the tray down on my desk and walked to my dresser where she picked up the portrait of my parents and me.

"I miss them too," Nanna said. "There's not a day that goes by when I don't think about them."

"It's not about them. I just don't want to go."

"Noah, you never could lie to save your life."

"I know what you're going to say. It seems like a nice school but it's not for me. I'm just not interested."

"Then why were you looking up the school online?"

She pointed to my laptop. On the monitor was the official webpage of the school which contained an aerial shot of the large opulent campus. Busted.

"That woman came all the way down here and put herself out there like that cause she clearly sees something in you that I see every day. That should tell you something."

"I just don't want to abandon the only family I have left."

"Sweetie, you are not abandoning me."

"Aren't I?"

"Noah, you listen to me. I promised your parents that I would take care of you. And that means seeing that you get the best education and opportunities. They would want you to go."

"But what about you?"

"Boy I've been on this Earth for more years than I care to say. I'm more than capable of taking care of myself." She wrapped her small thin arm around me. "I'm gonna always be with you. No matter what. I want you to do this but only if you want to go. And whatever you decide, I'll respect."

"I guess we could give it a shot. If it doesn't work out, I can always come back home."

Nanna grinned and kissed me on the forehead. The phone rang.

"That'll be your teacher calling," Nanna said. "Right on time."

Nanna promptly grabbed the phone and answered, "Hey there. Let me switch to the other phone. Just a moment."

"How did you know she was going to call back?"

"I told her I'd talk you into going before dinner. Go on and finish studying."

I grabbed for a cookie but Nanna swatted my hand away.

"Uh-uh, it'll spoil your appetite."

Nanna grabbed the tray and made her exit.

Ms. Ramirez helped me complete the application and made certain that I submitted an exemplary essay. After the fifth revision, we both realized it was as close to flawless as it was going to get. The application packet was accompanied by two hefty letters of recommendations from Ms. Ramirez and Mr. Baird. A month later I received a packet of my own which informed me that not only had I been accepted to Hollowstone but that I would be the recipient of the Jason Finnegann Memorial Scholarship.

Nanna wasted no time telling Mrs. Jenkins and in turn half of Atlanta knew that I would be going to Hollowstone. Nanna would've been more discreet by informing CNN. But I had never seen her so happy so I forbore any slight embarrassment.

The remainder of the school year flew by in a haze. Before I realized it, I found myself boarding a bus as Nanna saw me off, waving goodbye and trying, and failing, to discreetly hide the tears. I gazed out the window. Everything I knew sped past me. The familiar urban landscape of buildings eventually faded into forestry. In four hours I would be in a new school in a new town to start a new life.

After an endless number of stops I arrived in Newton. Nestled in Monteagle, the town was an anomaly in and of itself. It was the size of Mayberry, the typical small town you saw on television. Between the clean streets and the well kept buildings, it was clear that this town had a wealthy economy. I had no doubt that the school played a part in that. It was rolling in what Nanna would refer to as "old money." An endless number of rebel flags blew proudly on top of different buildings and the statues and monuments of Confederate soldiers indicated that like most of the South, it took pride in its heritage. This of course meant that my kind wasn't welcomed.

My cab transported me from the bus station on the outskirts of town to its prized gem in the center of Newton. The school was massive. The archways indicated a Gothic influence. A fleet of polished European sports cars was found in the parking lot.

Grabbing my large blue suitcase from the cab, I silently thanked Nanna for getting the kind that came with wheels attached. Meandering, I received several glares and repulsed scowls from my future classmates. It was clear they were nonplussed about that Emancipation Proclamation business. Continuing my trek, I overheard a number of students chatting.

"Did you go to Cal's party last week?" one of the students asked.

"No I was out of town," another student said.

"You missed it! That party was insane. Cal throws the best bashes."

After getting checked in, I was escorted to my dorm room by a hyper redhead student volunteer named Cherry. The room was surprisingly spacious with desks, drawers, twin beds, and closets on either side. With the right side of the walls littered with posters of scantily clad models and rock bands, the bare left side was meant for me.

"And here you are," said Cherry.

"Cool."

"This is such an awesome school. You're going to love it here. I've been here for like three years and each year just gets better and better. Not that my first year here was bad, it was very cool but you know getting adjusted from L.A. was a bit of a change but it's very nice up here and very rustic. Of course my friends are totally the best. I met them my first year here and we had a blast. We've been tight ever since and I know this year is going to be the best ever."

I nodded and smiled nervously.

"So are you excited about being here? I'm sure you are because I know I was when I started going here and I'm still excited even now."

"It's a very nice school."

"Oh yeah totally. But we could go to like any school we want. Such is the joy of being a trust funder." She glanced at her clipboard. "Oh wait. This says you're on scholarship. Oh my God. So you're like from a public school?"

I nodded.

"That is like so badass," Cherry said. "Growing up in the hood with gang bangers and drug dealers and stuff. So what sport do you play? You're too small to be a football player. I guess you could play basketball but you're kind of short."

"What are you talking about?"

"Athletic scholarship right?"

"Actually I'm on an academic scholarship. I grew up in the suburbs. And the only thing I play is my violin."

"Oh. Well….that's…interesting. Well, we have a great musical program. I'm sure you're going to absolutely love it. Though my friend Katie, who plays the flute, says that Mr. Nolan, the music instructor, is a bit of a Nazi."

"Duly noted. Do you know who my roommate is?"

The volunteer glanced at her clipboard and gasped. "Oh my God, you are like so frikkin lucky!"

"What is it?"

"Your roommate is Caleb Warner! You're roommates with Cal."

"Who is he?"

"You don't know who Cal is? Wait a minute, of course you wouldn't. Cal is like a total legend. He throws the craziest raves around town. They're real hush-hush, but he always manages to pull them off. You're so lucky. You're about to have the craziest year ever. I'm so jealous."

I grinned wryly.

"Don't forget that there's a reception later tonight. It's basically a chance for the newbies to mingle and meet the faculty and the other students. Kind of stuffy but they're cool. And lots of great food. Feel free to look around the campus. I have to help get some other students settled. Good luck. I know this is going to be an awesome year and you're totally going to love it here."

"You drink a lot of coffee don't you?"

"Oh God no. I had to stop. One drop of caffeine and I get wired. Not a pretty sight."

I clenched my mouth shut and grinned.

"Take care," Cherry said.

Alone in the room, my curiosity got the better of me. Besides, what harm was there in "casually" observing anything that might be on the desk? There were no pictures so I had no clue as to what this guy looked like. On his desk sat a sleek black laptop, various car and sports magazines and an assortment of classic literary novels as well as Shang Tzu's The Art of War. Writer, philosopher, and legendary bad boy, he was going to be a handful.

Students tossed a frisbee back and forth on the lawn while others read under a tree. Upon noticing me, a pair of brunettes quickly clutched their purses and sped away.

"You're better than them," said a voice behind me.

I spun on my heel to face the figure. Tall and muscular, if I had to guess, he was probably a quarterback. Sandy blond hair, sharp blue eyes, he wore a disarming smirk.

"I'm sorry?" I said

"Cindy Robbins and Toni Marrett. Two of the most stuck up skanks at this school. I would know. I did them both in a hot tub last month."

I snickered, "Yeah well getting profiled is starting to get old."

"I can imagine. Don't let them faze you and don't let them convince you that you don't belong here. They tend to make pre-judgments about the unfamiliar. Give them time, they'll come around. A few of them anyway."

Completely stunned by the guy's words, all I could simply mutter was, "Thank you."

"No problem. I'll see you around."

"Hey wait, my name is—"

He was gone.

The reception was held in one of the halls named in honor of some alumnus who had donated ridiculous sums of cash to the school in the subversive hopes of having a building named after him. Trying not to look too awkward, I alternated between sipping on my glass of apple cider and loosening my tie. A hair's breath away from fleeing and hiding in my dorm, I decided to try to "come out of my shell" as Ms. Ramirez suggested and try to make the most out of the situation.

Of course things began to look brighter upon noticing another black student who stood across the room. Nibbling on an hors d'ouvre, she possessed flawless light brown skin. Catching her eye, I smiled and nodded at her. Before I could move, she rolled her eyes, turned up her nose and started away.

"And so much for that plan," I grumbled to myself.

"Enjoying the reception?" asked an older gentleman.

"Yes sir."

We shook hands.

"A firm grip," he said. "Always a good sign. I don't think we've met formally. I'm George Norrington. Headmaster of Hollowstone Academy."

"Noah Scott."

"Ah yes, Mr. Scott. You really impressed the admissions committee with your essay and your recommendations. I'm glad you'll be joining us this term."

"Thank you sir."

"If I remember correctly, you have considerable interests in music?"

"Yes sir, I play the violin."

"Impressive. Now tell me who would you say is your biggest influence."

"As clichéd as it may sound, I'm a rabid Beethoven fan sir."

"Excellent. We're certainly going to have to introduce you to Mr. Nolan. Unfortunately he's performing in London and won't be back until next week. But he's always looking for a new talent to add to the music department. Between you and me though, he's a bit on the eccentric side to put it mildly."

"So I've been told."

A woman strode up to Mr. Norrington and whispered into his ear. In turn the headmaster rubbed his eyes and shook his head.

"Not again," he said. "I'm sorry Mr. Scott but the work of the headmaster is never done. My door is always open if you need anything. If you'll excuse me."

Across the room, Cherry chatted with her friends at 5000 words a minute. I was just relieved that someone else had to deal with her ramblings. She spotted me and waved. I politely returned the gesture.

Not allowing her the chance to torture me like her friends, I promptly turned on my heel and made for the exit.

"Excuse me," a male student said. "Yes you. Could you come here for a second?"

The student stood with a group of his peers. Each of them eyeing me like a pack of jackals. The student casually waved me over like I was one of the servers. I already knew that I was going to hate this guy. I put on a fake smile—I had been doing that a lot since arriving at Hollowstone—and cautiously approached.

"Yes?" I asked.

"Perhaps you can settle a debate for us," the leader stated. "We're trying to figure out which sport you'll be playing for the school? My sister Phyllis thinks that you'll probably be a new kicker for the football team. I'm thinking you may be our basketball team's newest point guard. No offense Albert but you guys can use all the help you can get."

"What is it with this school?" I replied. "I hate to disappoint you but I won't be playing any sports."

"But you transferred in from a public school right?" Phyllis asked. "I'm assuming you're on scholarship."

"You seem to know a lot about me. Yes I am on scholarship but I'm not an athlete."

"Oh," the lead jackal said as he and minions snickered. "That's impressive. I must say affirmative action is truly something else."

"That's funny coming from the trust fund kid" said another voice. It was the guy I met earlier. "Come to think of it, I don't think your old man has ever worked for anything either. And how is the senator, Christopher? Busy ripping off honest taxpayers I imagine."

His smirk grew larger as Chris and his flunkies scowled at him.

"They haven't kicked you out of school, yet?" Phyllis asked.

"No they've been too busy dealing with that gonorrhea outbreak of yours."

"I'm gonna kick your ass," Chris barked.

"No time like the present."

Phyllis placed a hand on Chris's shoulder.

"No, Chris," Phyllis said. "This is what he wants. This isn't the time or the place. Come on let's get out of here."

Chris and his entourage departed. "I'll be seeing you around Caleb."

"Caleb?" I asked. "Caleb Warner?"

"I see my reputation precedes me."

"You could say that. Why didn't you say anything earlier?"

"I wanted to get to know my new roomie before I introduced myself."

"And what have you learned so far?"

"Your name is Noah Scott. You came here from Atlanta. You're a huge classical music buff, you play the violin. You're very close with your grandmother who by the by is a very lovely and photgenic woman."

My mouth hung ajar.

"I went through your things while you were gone."

"You what?"

"We're roomies now. Mi casa su casa and all that. You've got my back and I've got yours."

"Speaking of which, what was up with those idiots over there?"

"That's Chris and his older sister Phyllis Goddard. They're the proud offspring of Sen. Christopher Goddard."

"The ultra right-winged senator?"

"That one."

"Christ, that guy makes David Duke look like Malcolm X. Suddenly explains a lot."

"Yep and just like their daddy the senator, Chris and his kind believe that it's their God given right to torment anyone who isn't a trust funder."

"Is it that obvious that I'm not a rich kid?"

"I'm afraid it is. You're about the only person here who doesn't walk around with a silver spoon shoved up his ass."

I snickered. "Okay, I know why they hate me. Why do you all have beef?"

"Like I said before, Chris and his kind are the status quo who think they own the school. They probably would if it wasn't for a certain non-conformist whose popularity rests on the fact that he bucks the system."

"And that would be you."

He nodded. "I make no bones about the fact that I have no interest in their politics and well…conflict ensues. Chris is all bark. You just got to know which buttons to push with him. He's real easy to figure out."

"And here I was going to simply smash a plate over his head."

Cal erupted into laughter. "I like you Noah Scott. We're going to get along just fine. This sad excuse of a party is boring me. Let's get the hell out of here."

"You mind if I get some practice in with my violin?" I asked.

"Not at all," Cal answered.

"Thanks."

"If you have Nolan for a teacher, you're going to need all the help you can get."

"What is it with this guy?"

"Levi Nolan's the most psychotic teacher on campus. The local shrink loves him because he sends him so much business."

"He can't be that bad."

"Steve Zering. Played the piano. Formal training, everything. Army brat. He wrestled, played football, and could easily bench 300 pounds. By the end of the semester, that old man had Steve leaving the school in tears."

"If this guy is so bad then why don't they fire him?"

"He gets results. The school orchestra excels in competitions and is one of the most prestigious in the country. He himself is world renowned. This of course brings in big bucks from donors. So yeah, have fun Monday."

I buried my face in my hands and groaned. A bright flash filled the room. I glanced up.

"Just wanted to get a final pic of you before your brutal demise," Cal said grinning at the pic on his digital camera.

"Funny."

"Oh and by the way, as you probably can tell, I'm big on my electronic toys and gadgets. Feel free to borrow anything you like. Cameras, iPod, iPad, digital recorders, you name it, I got it."

"Thanks. You know, you're awfully generous."

"Eh. I trust you. Besides, I know where you live."

"What are you working on?"

"The usual. Checking my email, selling a few term papers to some classmates."

"Whoa-whoa-whoa. Selling term papers? School hasn't even started."

"I know. All of the teachers have to submit a syllabus and if you know a student office worker who you can charm, a few nerds for hire to write the papers, and well…you quickly become the big man on campus and a very wealthy one at that."

"You weren't kidding about the whole breaking rules thing."

"I don't break rules really. I just play by my own set."

"You've got a set all right. Aren't you worried that someone is going to turn you in?"

"I've got my bases covered. Besides everyone loves me. I'm the dealer. I get them what they want and they love me for it."

"It's good that you're humble."

"Another thing to keep in mind when dealing with this crowd. They love you as long as you can do something for them. Way I figure it, why not play it to my advantage?"

"This is going to come back to haunt me isn't it?"

"You got nothing to worry about. If things go south, it's on my head and my head alone. If anything you're the lucky one. You get to reap all the rewards with none of the risks. Any classes you want to pass without working for, let me know."

"Thanks but I'm going to try to pass them the old fashioned way."

"Suit yourself. If you change your mind, let me know. Now that the paper business has been taken care of, time to finalize the plans for the next party."

"I keep hearing about them."

"I bet you have."

"So how exactly do you pull them off?"

"I pick a deserted spot, like a warehouse or something, get the word out, charge an affordable cover and the good times roll. Oh and you're totally comped."

"I appreciate it but I'm not really a party guy."

Cal shook his head, "Noah, Noah, Noah. I see I have my work cut out for me."

"Why am I not liking the sound of this?"

"Think about it Noah. After a long hard week of school, you deserve a little play time. Dance to some awesome tunes, hang with some fun and intoxicated people. Maybe get wasted yourself. Have a little fun with some comely uninhibited girls who are looking for a good time."

"That's easy for you to say. You're forgetting that with the exception of you, no one even likes me."

"Oh that's going to change in the very near future. You're friends with me and by association, you're about to become very popular. People want things from me and will try to go through you. Many of them being of the fairer sex. Why not reap the benefits?"

"Tempting but I'm going to have to pass."

"Yeah I'm afraid I can't let you do that. I'm getting you out of your shell this year, by hook or by crook. And you will be attending one of my parties, even if I have to hire a couple of varsity wrestlers to drag you there kicking and screaming."

Cal's smirk indicated he wasn't completely joking.

"All right. I'll go to one party. If I enjoy it, I'll be a regular. If it's not for me, you won't bug me again."

"Fair enough."

He flipped open his journal and began typing on his laptop.

"That's a very nice journal," I said.

"Thanks. I like to do my creative writing in it and sometimes I transfer it to my blog."

"You have a blog?"

"Most definitely."

"I never got into the whole online journal thing."

"Well music is your thing right? Creative writing is mine. Life's a story, you know? I want to record it. All the mistakes, the adventures, everything. The stories remain, even when we're gone. The more riveting the life, the better the story. This is all we get, so make it count. And in case you were wondering, yes that was a pointed comment."

"Yeah I got that. Thanks."

It was obvious that Cal was going to be a handful. But I didn't complain. As I would come to learn, he would be the truest friend in the truest sense.

Chapter Two

Monday morning inevitably arrived and the new semester commenced. The schoolyard was filled with students who marched to class with satchels and books. A group of students were gathered around the flagpole. They recited scripture from a Bible and hoisted the flag.

A stone statue of yet another Confederate general stood proudly in the corner of the yard. I rolled my eyes in disgust as I passed by the prominently arched monument. At the corner of the building, three large jocks shoved around a smaller student. One of the athletes tripped the kid while the other unzipped his satchel and dumped his books and belongings in the middle of the yard.

"Have a good day at school, faggot," one of the jocks said.

"Stupid queer," another jock said.

I helped the victim gather his strewn books.

"Perfect way to start the first day of school," I said.

"You need to stay away from me," he said.

"Look, I was just trying to help," I said.

"You're new right?" he said. "I appreciate your help. But you don't want to be seen with me. Not unless you're looking to catch hell."

I handed him his final notebook. "What can I say? I'm a masochist. I'm Noah."

"Ryan. Thanks."

Joining the traffic, I hurried up the stairs and resumed my route to class.

"Hey you!" someone barked.

I turned around and saw an older student, probably a senior, pointing at me.

"You stepped on the insignia," he said.

"What?"

"You stepped on the school's insignia."

I glanced at my feet. Sure enough my right foot was on a plaque which contained the school's name underneath a coat of arms. I then noticed that students behind me walked around the insignia as not to desecrate it.

"That's one of the proud traditions at this school," the student barked. "You could get written up for it?"

I laughed, "Are you kidding me?"

The student's glare indicated otherwise.

"Sorry," I said. "I'm new here."

The senior scoffed, "That much is obvious. You do well to watch your step around here."

His comment a loaded one, but was sage advice all the same.

Music theory class would be my final class which meant I had the entire day to fret. My mind frantically wandered on my shortcomings as a musician. After all, my only formal training was limited to that which was provided in the public school system. No doubt most of my classmates trained with private tutors since they could pick up an instrument. What chance did I have? While I was held in high esteem by Mr. Baird, this was a whole new arena.

"You're going to be fine," Cal repeated for the umpteenth time while we waited for our chemistry teacher. "Stop worrying."

I refused to lift my head from the desk, "I am beyond dead."

"Just don't draw any attention to yourself. Blend into the background and don't stand out."

I glared at Cal.

"Oh yeah, token minority. That could be a problem. Believe it or not, you're lucky. Some people have it worse than you."

"Like who?"

"Me."

At that moment, Mr. Miller, strode into the classroom and the chatter ceased. He tossed his briefcase on his desk and proceeded to hand out syllabi. Though he appeared to be in his late twenties, his furrowed brow indicated that he meant business.

"Wallace Miller," Cal whispered in my ear, "Resident chemistry teacher and world class prick."

"How so?"

"He's notorious for playing favorites. Tries to stay in the preps' good graces because he knows their families are connected. Thinks he'll get a big payoff for being a good little pet. He's far worse than Nolan."

"I find that hard to believe."

"Oh, really? Three guesses who his favorite student is."

Cal nodded his head to the right. Sitting in the corner of the classroom and flanked by two of his goons was none other than Chris Goddard.

"Convinced yet?" Cal continued. "Nolan is a whack job but he's an equal opportunity abuser. Miller on the other hand is just like the preps. He shuns anyone who doesn't fit or conform to their little mold."

"You two butted heads last year didn't you?"

"Understatement. Ever since I clashed with Chris and Phyllis, he's taken it upon himself to be their champion and make my life a living hell. I spent the better part of last year in detention because of him. God only knows what he has in store for me this term."

That's all I needed, one more headache to worry about. Mr. Miller handed us our syllabi and delivered a fierce scowl to my roommate.

"Before we get started, I have a few announcements," Mr. Miller said. "This year I'll be serving as assistant coach for our football team."

Chris and his buddies yelped and cheered.

"Thank you, thank you," Miller continued. "The Hollowstone Knights are looking to have an exciting, successful year. We need each and every one of you to attend the pep rallies, get involved with the tailgate parties and show your support. We're also looking for some new blood for the team. On Wednesday we're having a meeting during the lunch and we want to speak with every male student about joining."

Cal scoffed.

"Is there a problem, Mr. Warner?" Mr. Miller inquired.

"No problem, sir," Cal replied.

"And tell us what is that you've contributed to the school? Are you too 'cool' to show some school spirit?"

"No mein fuehrer," Cal replied.

The class erupted into laughter.

"Enough," Mr. Miller barked. "Mr. Warner, I expect to see you at the meeting on Wednesday. And I also expect to see you in detention this afternoon. Now, class, open your books."

Chris wore a Cheshire grin. Cal tossed his pencil on the table and slumped in his chair. My roommate was right. He was about to be in for a long semester.

I didn't have Caleb to keep me entertained in U.S. History. Maybe it just as well. I wasn't sure how many other teachers held a vendetta against him.

"Now turn to page forty-three," Mr. Tyler instructed.

The door creaked open as a student quietly tiptoed in.

"Welcome, Ms. Phillips," Mr. Tyler said.

"Sorry there was a schedule mix-up," she said.

"There's an empty seat next to Mr. Scott," the teacher stated.

Tossing her strawberry blond locks, she strode to my table and sat in the seat next to me. She delivered a very warm smile and opened her notebook.

"Abby," she said.

"Noah."

Shortly after I resumed my note-taking, she leaned over to me.

"I haven't gotten my textbook for the class yet," she whispered. "Mind if I look off of yours?"

"Not at all."

"Thanks."

We followed the passage Mr. Tyler recited. The two of us inches apart, Abigail's sweet intoxicating scent made concentrating problematic. Time flew and before I knew it, the electronic bell chimed. I finished packing my satchel as my classmates flooded out of the classroom. Abigail grinned at me. Before I could say anything—

"Mr. Scott, a moment please."

She waved at me and departed. I cautiously approached the young slender teacher who leaned against his desk.

"I understand that you and I have a mutual acquaintance," he said.

"I'm sorry?"

"Helena Ramirez."

"You're the friend she mentioned."

"Yes, and she had a lot of great things to say about you. She also asked me to keep an eye on you. I know that moving to a new school and a new town can be a bit overwhelming. If you need anything, don't hesitate to let me know."

"Thank you sir."

"I hear you're a violinist."

"Yes sir."

"Have you had Mr. Nolan yet?"

"That's my next class. Any advice on dealing with him?"

He grinned, "You might want to consider pursuing other arts."

With a wry grin, I replied, "Thanks."

I trudged out of Mr. Tyler's classroom, silently praying that Mr. Nolan's passport got revoked.

"Hey Noah," Abigail greeted. "Thanks again for sharing your book."

"You're welcome."

"Hey I was thinking we could be study partners. We both have to survive Tyler's class, why not do it together?"

"That'd be great."

"Here let me give you my number."

"I'll give you mine as well."

"Thanks."

"Abby there you are!" interrupted a student. It was the girl who snubbed me at the reception. With a clipboard clenched firmly in her arms, she marched to Abigail. "I've been trying to reach you on your cell."

"Cassidy, I've been in class," Abby said. "Have you met Noah? Noah, this is Cassidy. Class secretary and president of the honor society and editor of the yearbook among other clubs."

Cassidy gave me a once over like I was discarded garbage. "Charmed. The copy center is having another crisis about the flyers for homecoming and we have a major scheduling conflict about the raffle drive."

"All of this on the first day of school?" I said.

"When you're class president, you don't get a day off," Abby said. "Let me go put out these fires. I'll talk to you later Noah."

A sappy grin etched its way on my face as I watched them rush away.

The plan was simple. Sit in the back of the room, slouch low in my chair and do absolutely nothing to garner any attention. My classmates tuned their instruments and anxiously waited for the infamous Nolan to make his grand entrance. With over thirty students in the room, the odds of me escaping unscathed were certainly in my favor.

The door slammed open and gasps were released. An older man marched into the room. Not five feet tall, his silver hair was combed back and the most defining attributes on his wrinkled face were the thick and wild eyebrows. Placing a crate behind the podium, he stood on it and faced the galley of frightened teens.

"I see some of you masochists were foolish enough to return. It also appears that a few of you brave new souls haven't gotten the memo about me," Nolan said. "This is intermediate music theory. You will attempt to play your instruments, I will cringe and then will make the futile attempt to make you great. You will be better by the time I'm through with you but each and every one of you are about to be in for a semester of hell. This class is not for the weak or for the faint of heart. We are here to study and make music. Anyone who is not willing to commit to this class 100 percent and therefore waste my time will be crying home to their mothers. And if you don't believe me, you can ask about Mr. Zering."

I slunk in my chair.

"Marvin Honnell, front and center!" Nolan barked. "Let's see if you actually bothered to practice over the break."

A student with a saxophone took his position next to the podium.

"Begin."

Marvin blew into the instrument and performed a jazz number. He was quite skilled. While I was impressed, Nolan's scowl indicated he clearly wasn't.

"Mr. Honnell, did you purposely forget how to play the saxophone over the summer just for the sake of torturing me?" Nolan asked. "Does it make you feel special knowing that you anger me with your incompetence? Have a seat and thank you for wasting two minutes that this old man will never get back. Cindy Robbins, you're next."

Cindy waltzed to the front of the classroom with her clarinet in tow. Like Marvin, her performance was impressive but the bulging vein in Nolan's forehead indicated that he was less than happy.

"Ms. Robbins, for the sake of your music and your love life, I do hope that you learn how to blow properly. Have a seat. Is there no one in this classroom that has any modicum of skill? You there."

Oh crap. Was he pointing at me?

"Yes you. The short scrawny one that's trying to be inconspicuous by slouching in his seat. Front and center."

I grabbed my violin and slowly trudged to the front. My classmates stared at me with pity, like a man walking to the gas chamber.

"Oh, no, please take your time," Nolan snapped. "It's not like I'm an old man with a few years left."

I took my place next to the podium. I decided that if I was going to face the firing squad, I would opt for a blindfold. Since one wasn't afforded to me, I simply hoisted my violin and shut my eyes. My swan song was a piece from Franz von Vecsey. Taking a deep breath, I placed my bow against the strings and sawed away. The melody flowed from my instrument. Galvanized, I played like a man possessed. I hit every note and plucked each string with perfection. I was in rare form.

"Enough!" Nolan barked. "Young man what is your name?"

"Noah. Noah Scott."

"And which private school did you transfer from?"

"I transferred from a public school, sir."

A few students snickered.

"Public school?" Nolan repeated. "Then tell me Mr. Scott, who is your private tutor?"

"I never had one sir."

The snickering continued.

"You've never had a tutor and yet you come into my class and dare put on such a performance?"

I stared at the floor.

"You know what angers me about this performance, Mr. Scott?" Nolan asked. "Everything! I have been teaching at this institution for years inundated by snotty reprobates who think they're exceptional because they've spent thousands of dollars to be tutored by hacks. And then they think they have what it takes to be taught by me. They sit in this class thinking they know the first thing about music. Then one day I receive a student with no formal training who humbly comes into my classroom and puts my entire classroom to shame. What angers me about this performance Mr. Scott is that if you are in fact the result of a public education, then clearly I've been teaching at the wrong school."

I blinked and I stared at the small man with a bewildered expression. Maybe I misinterpreted but I think he paid me a compliment.

"Take a bow Mr. Scott, you've just set the standard of excellence in this classroom. I have great plans for you and I expect to see your name on the tryout roster for the school orchestra."

"Yes, sir," I beamed. "Thank you, sir."

And with that I returned to my seat. Whispers and murmurs filled the room as my peers stared at me with shock and awe.

"Nolan's never paid a compliment," one student whispered.

"He just made history," another student added.

Maybe Nolan was insane and maybe it was pure luck that I fell into his good graces. It didn't matter to me. I took my victories any way I got them. And winning over the toughest teacher in school on the first day of class was a victory indeed. Not bad for the scholarship kid. Not bad at all.

"He said what?" Cal asked.

"He said, 'Take a bow Mr. Scott, you've just set the standard of excellence in this classroom. I have great plans for you and I expect to see your name on the tryout roster for the school orchestra,'" I repeated.

"Dude, that is beyond awesome. Your stock has skyrocketed."

Cal and I casually lounged under a tree observing our fellow students.

"How was detention?" I asked.

"It was detention. At least I got time to get some planning done for my next rave. I plan to hammer out the rest of the details while sitting in detention on Wednesday."

"You're not going to the meeting?"

"Hell no. I'm not going on principle; I've got a reputation to uphold."

"Well, luckily I've got an excuse. Nolan wants to meet with me on Wednesday. He wants to create a specific curriculum for me."

"Which basically means more work for being a good student. He should really rethink his reward system."

"I was thinking the same thing. He seemed pretty happy about me missing the football players' cult induction."

"Figures. Nolan is one of the few people who doesn't bow down to the athletic department. There was serious drama last year because he refused to serve as the band director. According to Nolan, music should serve to elevate us to a higher conscious, not serenade a bunch of trained apes tossing a ball around. Big massive blowout erupted between him and Coach Phelps. In order to save face, Norrington hired a band director solely for the athletic department."

"There's more politics in this school than at a U.N. summit."

"Tell me about—"

Abigail treaded across the lawn. My enamored roommate wore a sappy grin, much like the one I won earlier.

"Yeah, I was thinking the same thing when I met her in class," I said.

"What?"

"Abby. She sits next to me in class and is my new study partner."

Like a cat eyeing a bird, Caleb stared at me with an unnerving sneer, "Perfect."

"What do you mean perfect?"

"You, my friend, are going to help me with courting one Abigail Phillips."

"Actually, Cal, I was actually sort of interested in asking her—"

"This is perfect, I couldn't have planned this better myself and you my friend are going to help make me one happy man."

"Wait, why haven't you asked her out yourself?"

"She and I have a history. Besides there's one little complication that's stood in the way."

"And what's that?"

"Her boyfriend."

It was then that Cal and I watched Chris and Abby in the midst of a heated quarrel.

"Looks like there's trouble in paradise."

"You've got to be kidding me," I grimaced.

"Exactly. And with your help, that complication will be a non-issue."

"No," I said. "As much I despise Goddard and as much as I would love to help you get one over on him, I'm not about to get caught up in some angsty teen drama. Besides it's not fair to use Abby as a pawn. Even if Goddard is an asshole."

"This isn't about Chris," Cal said. "Don't get me wrong, if I get to burn him in the process, then yay, bonus. But Abby is something special to me and I would like a chance to show her how much so. Ultimately, it's her decision to make. If there's still something there between us, so much the better. And if not, I'll move on. You have no idea how long I've been waiting for the right moment to make my move. Come on Noah, help me out."

It was the first time I saw Cal without the cocky reassured swagger. If I didn't know any better I would've thought he was being sincere. For all the reasons I could recite as to why I was better off not getting involved, I couldn't refuse my friend's request. If in the off chance he was telling the truth and this was something resembling love, how could I refuse him? And as Caleb stated, I was doing Abby a favor.

"How much am I going to regret this?" I asked.

"That's the spirit! Don't worry, you don't have to do anything now. Just let me know the first time the two of you have to study for a quiz."

"Deal."

I placed my hands behind my head and gazed at the clouds. All things considered, my first day of class had been a victory. From the corner of my eye, I saw him. A tall gent in a billowy trench coat studied Cal and me. I turned my head to get a clearer look. He vanished.

"What is it?" Cal asked.

"Nothing. I don't think."

"Mr. Scott, the gymnasium is this way," Mr. Miller said.

"I'm supposed to meet with Mr. Nolan right now for violin—"

"You're supposed to be in the gym with everyone else," Mr. Miller said. "Mr. Nolan will understand if you're late."

So much for not incurring the wrath of Nolan. He was going to have my hide once he realized I stood him up.

"Do you know where Mr. Warner is?" he asked.

"I haven't seen him," I said. "I'm sure he's probably already there."

Mr. Miller scoffed, "Likely."

On the first row of the bleachers sat the illustrious football players. Each of them adorned their blue and white varsity jackets. I reluctantly took my seat in the top row next to Vaughn and Ryan. Vaughn tossed back his shaggy dark hair while Ryan gazed at his sneakers. Mr. Miller joined a hefty man with a protruding gut in the center of auditorium.

"What the hell are we doing here?" Ryan asked.

"Phelps caught me hiding out in the library," Vaughn said. "I figured it would be a safe bet that he wouldn't know how to spell library, much less know where one is."

"They're worse than the frikkin Gestapo," I said.

"I can't believe I used to buy into all of this crap," Ryan said.

"What do you mean?" I asked.

"Technically, I used to be one of them," he said. "I was on the baseball team. I remember everything coach used to say. The team is about brotherhood. It's about a family. That didn't last too long once they found out about me."

"What position?" I asked.

"Pitcher." Vaughn and I snickered and a reluctant Ryan joined in. "Bastards."

"All right everyone, I promise to try to keep this short," Phelps said. "Thank you all for coming to this meeting."

"Like we had a choice," Vaughn mumbled.

"I want to talk to each of you about honor," Phelps said. "Honor is something a man learns to value throughout his life. Honor in himself. Honor in his family and honor in his home. A man learns that honor and name is valued above all else in this world. Hollowstone Academy is our home and this is our family."

Chris, the football players and a few other students nodded enthusiastically.

"We're privileged to be here," Phelps continued. "And each of you have an opportunity to represent this school and defend its honor."

"I'm out of here," Vaughn whispered. "They can suspend me."

He grabbed his satchel and descended the bleachers.

"Sit down, Mr. Pope," Phelps barked. "I've known your father a long time. He would want you to hear this. Now, this year the Hollowstone Knights are geared up to have an exciting season and with our lineup we're going to go all the way. I'm giving each and every one of you an opportunity to be a part of that. This is a chance to give back to the school and join a great legacy."

The auditorium doors were slammed open. Nolan marched into the auditorium, his small legs moving in overdrive.

"Mr. Scott!" Nolan bellowed. "Much like a jealous wife, I don't appreciate being stood up so you can hang with the boys to discuss football. While I don't doubt that tossing around a leather ball and ramming your head into someone's chest is fascinating, you have a prior commitment. Front and center. Now!"

I shot down the bleachers and silently mouthed "thank you" to Nolan.

"Nolan, you are interrupting my meeting," Phelps said. "If you're done, you can leave."

Nolan stepped forward and gazed directly into Phelp's eyes. While the music teacher barely reached the coach's gut, it was clear that he wasn't the least bit intimidated by the larger man.

"Before we go, I want to make something perfectly clear," Nolan said in a low tone. "I begrudgingly accept that fact that you play a role in this school. And for that I steer clear of you and yours. Just as I wouldn't waste my time converting one of your mindless Neanderthals into refined cultured gents, I will not allow you to take my top student and brainwash him into one of your Cro-Magnons. Interfere in orchestra business again and you're going to have a promising future in opera because I will personally turn you into a soprano. Let's go, Mr. Scott."

Trying futilely to suppress the grin, I followed the short orchestra director out of the auditorium. Professor Nolan had just become my new personal hero.

Weeks passed and I slowly became acclimated with life at Hollowstone. Most of my time had been consumed with classes and music. I'd yet to ascertain how I managed to fall into Nolan's good graces but I certainly intended to remain there and that meant making certain my performances were flawless. What little time I had left was usually spent with Cal, when he wasn't in detention. Little by little life at Hollowstone began to feel normal.

"Your quiz next week is going to cover everything up to the Revolutionary War," Tyler announced. "Make sure you focus on chapters three and four when you study."

"You free later?" Abby whispered.

I nodded, "Library around four work for you?"

Snickering emanated from across the classroom. Everyone turned to the back left corner to see Ronny Garrison and Chet Hall, two of our school's fearless linebackers, guffawing like rabid hyenas.

"Mr. Garrison, Mr. Hall, I'm getting extremely fed up with the two of you disrupting my class," Tyler said.

"I was just telling Chet about something that happened during practice yesterday," Ronny said.

"I'm sure it's fascinating but it has no place in class," Tyler said. "Do I make myself clear?"

"Yes sir," Chet snickered. "Won't happen again."

"I'm glad that you think all of this is funny but the two of you are already failing this class," Tyler warned. "To date neither of you have turned in a single homework assignment and if you don't pass this quiz next week and start turning your grades around, you're going to find yourself being ineligible to play football."

"I don't think so," Chet said.

Mr. Tyler approached Chet's desk, "Excuse me?"

"I said I don't think so," Chet said. "My dad contributes tons of cash to this school. Cash which pays your meager salary. He also likes to see me play. If I don't get to do that, my dad won't be happy and you're going to find yourself facing a world of problems."

"Are you threatening me?" Tyler asked.

"Just stating facts, sir."

"Good then allow me to state a few facts for you," Tyler replied. "Fact, I don't respond to threats, specifically from a teenager whose flunking class. Fact, you and your teammates may be used to getting special treatment in your other classes but it won't play here. Fact, if you don't shape up and start doing the work, you will fail and you will be ineligible to play football. And whatever fallout may occur, you still won't get to play. If you want to keep your father happy, then I suggest you open your notebook and begin taking notes."

Mr. Tyler returned to the chalkboard and resumed his lecture. Chet's scowl indicated this battle was far from over. Part of me worried for Tyler's job. Chet wasn't the brightest sophomore but he wouldn't have made a ballsy threat like that if he didn't think he could follow through on it. The scariest thing was he probably could.

"He should've given both of them detention," I said to Cal while we waited in the library. "They wouldn't have been smirking if Tyler had given them detention and they would've had to miss practice."

"It wouldn't have happened. Norrington makes allowances for them and they know it. They can take their detention around their practice. That's assuming he doesn't overturn it outright."

"You're kidding?"

"Football is nothing short of a religion here. On top of that, they have a decent shot at winning the championship. They're not going to allow anything to interfere with that. Especially stupid little things like discipline or education or morals."

Cal anxiously paced in circles.

"You're going to burn a hole through that carpet," I warned.

"She should be here."

"It's not even four yet."

"She's not going to show."

"She's going to show. Will you relax?"

"She and Chris got into a big argument last night."

"You've been spying on her?"

"Of course not," Cal said. "…I hired a few folks to do it for me. Now do you remember the plan?"

"For the one millionth time, yes. I know what to do. It's you I'm worried about."

I scanned the area for any sign of Abby. A few students were congregated at various tables. Many of them studying and chatting. Interestingly enough, the table with the most books stacked on top of it was occupied by only one individual.

Cassidy remained hunched over her laptop. Her eyes alternated between the monitor and her classmates. The longing on her face was apparent. She suddenly began to make sense. What I couldn't figure out however was why she fascinated me. She had been a complete bitch on our two encounters and yet here I was staring at her. Maybe I was being a sap but she seemed to be—

The doors swung open.

"Showtime," I whispered.

Cal quickly disappeared into an aisle.

"How goes it?" I asked.

"Better, once this quiz is behind us," Abby replied.

"I hear you on that."

"Thank you for making time for me. I'm surprised you were free. I would think that an important musician like you wouldn't have time for the little people."

I laughed, "You're not going to let me live that down are you?"

"Oh, hey Noah," Cal said. "I'm glad I ran into you. Since you're here I had a question about…oh I'm sorry. I didn't realize you had company."

Both Cal and Abby exchanged grins.

"Abby this is my roommate Caleb," I introduced. "Caleb, this is my study partner Abby."

"We've met," Abby said, her smile still present. "Been a long time."

"That it has," Cal said. "You're looking good."

"You too."

"I'm going to go grab my notebook," I lied. "I'll be right back."

I went behind a bookcase and eavesdropped.

"I was wondering if you were ever going to talk to me," Abby said.

"Maybe I was waiting on you to make the first move."

"You've never been the shy type before."

"Didn't know where things stood. And freshmen year was crazy busy."

"Way I hear it, the only thing that you were busy with was being a whore with most of females that go here."

"Says the girl who's dating the school's biggest douchebag."

The two chuckled. Taking that as a good sign, I quietly exited. I found the pair snickering when I returned an hour later.

"Must've been some joke," I said.

"Long story," Cal laughed, wiping the tears from his eyes. "Very long story."

Abby glanced at her watch, "Oh, my God, I'm going to be late. I have to go. Noah, I'm so sorry we didn't get the chance to study."

"Not a problem." I grinned.

"You free same time tomorrow?"

"Yeah," I said.

"I promise we'll actually study this time," Abby said. "Just keep Mr. Distraction over here away from us."

"Oh, I will," I said.

"You're the best," Abby said.

"Yes, he is," Cal added. "Speaking of which, he and I need your help."

Both Abby and I stared at my roommate with bewilderment.

"Noah is in need of a date," Cal said. "He's been trying to meet some quality women but you know how it is meeting people in a school like this. And it's a shame too because he's a great catch." He wrapped his arm around me. "I mean he's smart, he's nice, he's talented, and he's oh so adorable." He pinched my cheeks. "Look at this baby face."

"Please stop," I pleaded.

"I was thinking maybe if you had any beautiful single friends who might be in the market for a certifiable stud."

"I appreciate the sentiment," I said, "but that's not necess—"

A sharp elbow jabbed my ribs.

"You know, Noah, I do owe you for basically standing you up today," Abby said. "And I think you and my friend Brianna would hit it off. I'll give her a call tonight and maybe you guys can do something this weekend."

"I've got an idea," Cal said in a rehearsed tone. "I'm throwing a party this weekend. Why don't you bring Brianna to meet Noah?"

"Oh, yes," Abby said. "Your infamous raves. I don't think Chris would be too happy if he found out I was there."

"Who says he has to find out?" Cal asked.

Abby raised an eyebrow.

"It's just a harmless get-together," Cal reassured. "And you're going to be with Brianna. I'm sure a part of you is curious to find out if all the stories are true. You two won't have to stay the whole time. Just come out for a little while and have a little fun. After all, it's for Noah."

"Well, since it is for Noah. I might be able to get away for a few hours. I'll see you later." Abigail walked away, leaving the library.

"Looks like you got a date for Saturday," Cal said.

"Just so we're clear, you just pimped me out to get a de facto date with Abby."

Cal beamed and nodded, "I'm good aren't I?"

The week quickly passed and Saturday evening arrived. We were in our room getting ready for the party. Actually I was waiting for Cal who conducted business on his cell.

"You know the score," Cal said. "I can get you and your boys some premium papers but the price isn't going to be cheap…Don't blame me, it takes a lot to keep the nerds happy…It'll be A-quality…What do you mean you can't afford it? Your dad owns a Fortune 500 company. Don't give me that crap. It's your grade on the line. Yes, you will have it by Monday. That'll work….No I am not accepting checks. Cash on delivery…Awesome. I'll see you then. Later."

"I see the criminal mastermind is hard at work."

"If I can make a profit off of those spoiled idiots then so much the better," Cal said. "But it's all good because the two of us are going to have an awesome night tonight. Especially you. Brianna Allen, smoking hot! Perfect rack and the sweetest ass. I'd so tap it in a heartbeat."

"I'm surprised you hadn't."

"I was eventually going to get around to her. But if her reputation holds true, you'll be getting some by the end of the night."

"What do you mean?"

"Word is she's quite the bad girl."

"I'm not even sure if I'm her type."

"Oh trust me, you're her type. You're breathing and you have a Y-chromosome. And all that stuff I said in the library the other day wasn't just lip service. She's going to be the lucky one. Which reminds me." Cal reached into his drawer and tossed me a pair of condoms. "Just in case you didn't have any yourself."

"Thanks but I don't think I'll be needing these tonight. I'm pretty old fashioned. I like to actually get to know a girl, spend time with her, establish a relationship before I even contemplate hooking up."

Cal scratched his chin and nodded. "Okay. You're gay. I'm cool with that. And I won't take offense if my lounging around in my boxers gets you hot and bothered. And I tell you what, I promise to give you a lap dance for your birthday."

I chucked a pillow at him. "You know I'm not gay! I'm just old fashioned that way."

Caleb snickered, "Such a good little Christian boy and everything."

I removed the thin silver cross necklace from underneath my shirt.

"I rest my case," laughed my roommate.

"What about Abby? You've made it clear that this a more than a mere hook-up. You've put way too much effort into impressing her."

"Touché."

"How did you and Abby meet?"

Cal leaned against his desk and crossed his arms, "I wasn't born into money by any stretch of the imagination. Working two jobs with a kid, my mom had to decide between paying rent or paying the gas bill. Abby was on some trip with her church youth group and was doing some charity work in my neighborhood. We met and everything clicked.

"She always wore white or cream colored clothes and she looked like an angel. I guess part of the attraction was that we were from two different worlds. She was little miss high society and I was the poor bad boy. Eventually she had to leave. We chatted and did the long distance thing but her parents got wind of it and put an end to things. As far as they were concerned, their daughter was too good for trailer park trash. Shortly after that I came into my inheritance and here we are."

"You knew she was coming to school here didn't you?"

"The school was a fresh start for me. Funny thing is she never told anyone about us or where I came from. When I came to the school, she was dating Goddard. Because she ran with the preps and dated their king, I never got a chance. So I bid my time, hoping she would've wandered into one of my raves."

That little snippet into Cal's past only raised more questions for me.

"I don't think you ever told me how you came about your inheritance."

Cal grinned, "Another story for another time. Right now, we have a party to attend."

He placed my blue baseball cap on my head and turned it backwards.

For a person who had no qualms about disclosing his underworld dealings, he was being awfully glib about his past. There was more to this inheritance business and for some reason, he didn't want to share it.

"But your mom, I take it she's doing better now that you came into your inheritance?"

"Oh yeah," Cal said. "She's better off now."

For the first time since meeting him, Cal had just lied to me. Turning to leave, they caught my eye. Two men stood outside the window. Their features concealed in shadows but like the first man I saw earlier, they both adorned long billowy dusters. I blinked. They were gone.

"Noah?" Cal called from the hallway.

"Coming," I said.

Writing it off as a trick of the light and an overactive imagination, I shut the door behind me.

Organizing the raves was a science for Cal. While the parties were infamous in the school, very few details were revealed until the last possible minute. Those interested would receive a secret invite via email. From there they would receive a second email regarding details—location, directions, cover charge—an hour before the party. A different site was always chosen for each party. Jocks from the local public high school were hired as security in case anything got out of control. Cal's parties were the few times that the locals interacted with Hollowstone students at all, much less on an even footing.

The locale of choice for this particular rave was an old warehouse on the outskirts of town. Hordes of eager attendants stood outside the building when we arrived. Stepping out of Cal's black Charger, the two of us were regaled as celebrities. Cal high-fived some and exchanged hugs. Several classmates patted me on the shoulder and hugged me as well.

Music blared from inside. Several scantily clad girls, gyrated atop barrels and crates; bills poked out of their waistbands. To my right, a group of guys cheered their buddy on as he licked salt from his girlfriend's taut belly and downed a tequila shot.

"Caleb, what the hell have you gotten me into?" I muttered to myself.

"Yo, dude, you look mellow," a tall lanky guy slurred. "Want some x?"

"No thanks," I said. "I'm good."

"Straight-edger, cool dude," he said. "I'm down with that. Long as you're having a blast. If you change your mind, let me know."

"Thanks," I said. "I'll keep that in mind."

"Catch you later bro."

Weaving through the crowd, I found Cal in a corner in the midst of a heated argument with a thin shifty guy sporting a five o'clock shadow.

"C'mon Cal, you get a cut of this and we're talking some serious bank here," the guy said.

"I already said no," Cal replied. "Not gonna happen."

"Man why you trippin?" the guy replied. "This is a huge business opportunity, man."

"Remember, Jason?" Caleb replied. "Your supplier pushes bad product and I'm not gonna have that on my conscience. I don't mind weed and a little x. No coke, no smack and no meth. Tell your boss that's my final answer."

The guy stormed off.

"Having fun?" Cal asked.

"Oh yeah," I lied. "Thanks for inviting me."

"My pleasure. Gotta look out for my boy."

"Who was that?"

"Local dealer named Burke," Cal said. "Been trying to talk me into letting him push some harder stuff at my parties. He can't take a hint that I'm not interested."

"You know life would be a lot simpler if you didn't deal in the stuff at all."

"If these kids want to blow daddy's money on a few gateway drugs, that's their choice. Besides the stuff would be getting pushed whether I wanted it to or not. At least being in on the dealing, I know the score and have a way to control it."

"And make a profit in the process."

Cal grinned and shot me a wink.

"Who's Jason?"

"What?"

"You mentioned a guy named Jason."

Cal's face went tense. "He was my old roommate. Used to help me organize the raves. Found him one night passed out in a bathroom stall. Couldn't wake him up."

"Holy crap."

"I'll never forget waiting in the hospital with his father," Caleb said. "Any other day I would be scared to be within 50 feet of the guy and there I was consoling him."

"Wait, who was his father?"

"Frank Finnegann."

"The mobster?"

"The one and the same. You should've seen him when the doctor gave him the news. The man just broke down. Turns out the coke was a bad batch."

"Wait Jason Finnegann. As in the scholarship I'm on?"

"His dad started it in his honor."

"I think I'm going to get some air," I said.

"Noah, wait!"

I ignored him and continued walking.

It was almost more than I could stomach. I had always imagined that the scholarship was named in honor of someone who passed away fifty years ago for natural causes. Only I discovered that the reason I was at Hollowstone was because a kid overdosed and a scholarship was set up in his name. It was like I was profiting off of his death. Drugs killed Finnegann and what did I do? Attend a party that was drowning in them.

The revelation probably shouldn't have gotten to me the way that it did but it didn't seem right. Me prospering over someone's death. They suffered an agonizing and painful demise and I was living it up. I was partying without a care in the world and they drowned trying to get me to safety. They? This wasn't about Jason, this was about my— a firm hand gripped my shoulder.

"God you can move," Cal gasped. "You know you are allowed to enjoy your life."

"Thanks but I think you have more than enough fun for the both of us."

"What's your deal? You act like you're Atlas and you've got the weight of the world on your shoulders or something. You're not responsible for what happened to Jason. He made his decisions. It sucks what happened but he had a lot of other problems." He placed a reassuring hand on my shoulder. "Having a little fun does not mean that you're going to become like me or wind up like Jason. You won't let that happen. Hell, I'll kick your ass before I let that happen. You're the altar boy, I'm the bad boy. That's how we roll. We can't be upsetting the balance now can we?"

"No. I guess we can't," I said.

It didn't take much to understand why Cal was as popular as he was. It wasn't because of the parties or the fact that he could get you a copy of a test or an essay. He possessed this innate ability to make you believe that the universe revolved around you and that you could weather anything it threw at you. With a smile, he could lower your defenses. Part of the source behind his power was that you knew he was being genuine.

"And looks like the fun is about to truly begin," Cal said.

I followed his line of vision where I spotted Abby and a brunette passing the bouncer at the door.

"All right buddy boy let's do this," Cal said.

Bracing ourselves, we made our way towards our dates. Cal's physical description of Brianna was dead on; dark hair, rich ruby lips, and an ample chest which nicely filled out her thin leather jacket.

"You know the stories don't do the parties justice," Abby said. "It's far more insane."

"Glad you were able to make it," Cal said.

"Thanks for putting us on the VIP list," Brianna said.

"Only fitting considering I invited you," Cal said. "Brianna, this is my roommate and good friend Noah. Noah this lovely minx is Brianna Allen."

"Nice to meet you," I greeted.

Nice to meet you? Could I be any lamer?

"So, you're Nolan's new golden boy," Brianna said. "How's that working out for you?"

"Keeping me busy," I said. "He wants me to perform a solo for the concert in a few weeks. Cal tells me you're on the tennis team. How's that going for you?"

"It's something to do," she said. "You were right, Abby. He is cute."

"Told you," Abby said.

My face was beet red.

"Hey, Abby, let's allow these two to get acquainted," Cal said. "Come on and let me get you something to drink."

Cal and Abby disappeared into the swarm of partygoers. Two drunken girls stumbled next to us.

"Cal's parties are the best," one of them slurred.

"He should have them every day," the second added. "One time I tore my skirt and I was so upset. It was Prada. Cal got my address and mailed me another skirt. Exact measurements and all."

"Some guy," I said.

"I'll say," the first girl said. "We both thanked him at his next party. We thanked him for a couple of hours."

The two drunks giggled hysterically.

"They're boring me," Brianna said.

I waved goodbye to the two ladies and led Brianna to an unoccupied couch.

"So how long have you known Abby?" I asked.

"Since freshmen year. We had algebra together. I thought I was going to hate her. She was Little Miss Perfect, student council president and all that stuff. But no, we hit it off and she's one of my best friends. To tell you the truth, she needs this more than anyone."

"Why's that?"

"Between you and me, she's planning to end things with Goddard and she's been catching grief from her parents."

"For what?"

"Same old garbage. Chris is forever trying to mold her into his little trophy wife. He criticizes every little thing she does. And on top of that she's a televangelist's kid. So her folks are always putting pressure on her to uphold this perfect image. They're the main reason she's stays with Chris."

"Why's that?"

"Chris's old man is loaded. We're talking old money. Chris and Abby's parents have been doing some major dealing. Abby's parents have been publicly supporting the senator's campaign and he's been financing some new expansion deal. If their kids are on the outs, that could complicate things."

"Well nothing complicates matters like whoring your children."

"I think that's part of the reason she came tonight. A little act of rebellion for her."

Off in the distance I watched Abby leaned against a wall laughing and nodding while conversing with Cal.

"Good for her," I said.

"I imagine rooming with Cal is quite the experience."

"He's a handful. More often than not I'm usually—"

I felt a soft hand run up the upper part of my thigh.

"You're really cute," she whispered into my ear.

Breathing heavily, I replied, "Thanks. You're quite the eye candy yourself." I seriously needed to work on my lines. "I see you you're straight to the point."

"I see something I want, I take it. And based on what my hand is feeling, you don't seem to mind."

Straddling my waist, she pushed me back on the sofa and nibbled my neck and ears. Brianna was clearly a girl who didn't believe in wasting time. And by no means was that a complaint. We would've continued making out on the couch had the loud thud from a knocked over crate not interrupted us. The doorman argued with Chris and five of his football teammates as they barged their way through. Cal and a group of bouncers were already en route to confront them with Abby close behind.

"Ah, hell," I grumbled.

Brianna and I joined the fray. The two factions stood off. The music stopped as the partygoers watched the confrontation.

"What the hell is this?" Chris barked.

"You weren't invited, Chris," Cal said. "Take your pack of inbreds and get the hell out of here."

"Why don't you make us leave," said Cliff. "See if you don't get your face pounded in."

"Your call, Cal," said one of the bouncers. "Be happy to take out these cake eaters."

"There's no need for this," Abby said. "Chris, please go home. We're not doing this now."

"What the hell are you even doing here?" Chris asked.

"I told you Bri and I were going out tonight," Abby said.

"You come here? Slumming with these fucking townies and with this piece of white trash?"

"Chris, for God's sake go home!" Abby yelled.

"I'm not leaving without you," Chris said.

"See that's where you're wrong," Cal said. "You're disappearing now."

"Abigail, get in the damn car!" Chris yelled.

"I'm not going anywhere with you," Abigail said. "Not like this."

Chris reached for her arm when Cal stepped between them.

"Get the hell out of my way," Chris warned.

"The lady doesn't want to leave," Cal said. "And seeing that you're really starting to piss me off, you're going to want to get gone."

"I'm about two seconds from kicking your ass," Chris said.

"What's stopping you?" Cal replied.

I grabbed Cal's arm. "Come on, Cal, it's not worth it."

"Why don't you go back to the hood, you little ghetto rat."

"Keep running your mouth and Cal is going to be the least of your problems," I said.

"What you gonna do, a drive-by, homey?" Chris asked.

His buddies snickered.

"These assholes are all talk," I said. "Let's go."

"Yeah, Caleb," Chris said. "Listen to your house slave."

I started for Goddard but Cal placed a firm hand on my chest and shook his head.

"You're not going to stoop to his level." He smashed his fist into Chris's nose. "I'll do it for you."

Chris recovered and tackled Cal. The two scuffled on the ground. Before Cliff could interfere, I speared him and repeatedly smashed my fist into his face.

"Talk your shit now!" I yelled.

It didn't take long for the fracas to spill over. Punches were traded back and forth between the Hollowstone jocks and the townie bouncers. Two of the townies repeatedly kicked in Ronny's ribs.

"What's up now rich kid?" one of the townies said.

A pair of arms hooked around me and yanked me off of Cliff. Thinking it was one of his cronies, I sighed in relief to see it was one of the locals. He clenched the scruff of Cliff's jacket and chucked him like a garbage bag. Cal and Chris continued exchanging blows when two of the bouncers separated the two and restrained Chris.

"I hope you're happy!" Chris screamed at Abigail.

"Get this piece of shit out of here," Cal ordered.

Cal's security shoved and dragged Chris and his friends to the parking lot. Most of them were too bruised and beaten to mount any resistance. Upon taking out the trash, they shut the doors behind them.

"Sorry about that folks!" Cal said. "It's all good now. Let's get some music back on."

The DJ resumed a track and gradually the partygoers resumed dancing and chatting about what had just happened. Brianna handed Abby a handkerchief and she wiped the tears from her eyes.

"I can't believe him," Abigail sobbed.

Cal wrapped an arm around her.

"It's not your fault," he said.

"I think I better leave," Abby said.

"You don't have to leave," Cal said. "You didn't do anything wrong."

"Doesn't mean that there won't be any fallout for this," Brianna said. "School is going to be very interesting come Monday."

"Where is he?" we heard a voice cry. "I need to find Caleb!"

"What now?" Cal grumbled.

Vaughn raced up to us, "There you are."

"What's wrong?" Cal asked.

"I just saw Chris and his boys outside," Vaughn said.

"Yeah, I bet," Cal said. "Let me guess. He was licking his wounds?"

"More like talking on his cell," Vaughn said. "I overheard him snitching to the cops. They're on their way."

"He what?" Abby said.

"Good looking out Vaughn," Cal said. "I owe you one. Come on guys. We gotta bounce."

He rushed to a nearby crate where a bouncer stood guard. Reaching underneath it, he removed a large metal box which contained the party's profits.

"Tell the others I'll pay them tomorrow, right now we gotta roll."

His next stop was to the turntable.

"Bad news," Cal said on the mic. "The cops are on their way courtesy of Chris Goddard. That's right Christopher Goddard just ratted us out because Christopher Goddard wants each and every one of you in jail."

Everyone scattered for the nearest exits.

"I can't believe Chris is doing this," Abby said.

"You sure know how to pick em," Brianna said.

"Guys this way," Cal yelled. We followed Cal to a corridor behind a door which led directly to the parking lot. There was no sign of

Chris and his cronies anywhere.

"You guys need a lift?" Cal asked.

"My car is over there," Brianna said. "We'll be fine. Thanks for a fun night. See ya slugger."

"Come on lover boy," Cal said. "Time to disappear."

I hadn't shut the door when he shifted the gear into drive and pressed the gas pedal to the floor. Cal weaved through the lanes and the other cars with considerable ease.

"Think we'll make it back to the school without getting caught?" I asked. "No offense but they see a black Charger moving like a bat out of hell from the direction of the warehouse, they're going to know we were there."

"We're not going back to the school."

"What?"

Cal reduced his speed as we entered through downtown. He turned into a dark narrow alley and shut off the lights and the engine.

"What are you doing?" I asked.

Seconds later police sirens shrieked past the entrance.

"We wouldn't make it back to the school," Cal said. "Not in this car. We'll sit here and lay low for a bit. Can't believe that bastard. I'm sorry, Noah. I know I said I'd keep you clear of trouble. I promise I'll make it up to you."

I snickered and shook my head. "Caleb Warner, I must say that for better or worse, life with you is never boring."

We guffawed.

"And my God, you got a vicious right hook," Cal said. "Cliff's gonna be spitting out teeth for days. Thanks for having my back."

"Thanks for having mine. All things considered, I think your plan worked. You and Abigail seemed to hit it off nicely. She seemed to be enjoying herself."

"If things progress, then everything that happened tonight will be well worth it."

"You've got it bad."

"Look who's talking. I'm surprised you noticed anything, the way you and Brianna were going at it."

"I never said that I'm opposed to making out with a hot girl."

"Uh, huh. Sure. And you used to be such a good little boy with morals and values and everything."

Blushing profusely, I removed my baseball cap and placed it over my face.

"You know there's going to be fallout from this at school come Monday, right?" Cal asked. "Chris and the others are going to retaliate."

"They can't do any worse than what they've done already," I said. "I say let the bastards bring it."

"You sure? You can still find another roommate."

"But then I wouldn't get in all the cool parties."

We both sat in the car and contemplated the events that just transpired and the events that would inevitably occur on Monday.

The next morning I was up and out of bed before sunrise. I stood in the mirror and adjusted my tie. A loud yawn informed me that my roommate had awoken.

"Dude, what time is it?" he asked.

"A little after seven."

"What are you doing up this early? And why are you dressed up? Is there a funeral or something?"

"I found a church I wanted to go check out."

Cal snickered, "Man you really are an altar boy. I did my time in Sunday school when I was a kid. Didn't take. There was nothing worse than having to sit there and listen to some old man drone on and on about how I needed to repent for my sins. I swore that Hell would freeze over before I stepped foot in another—"

I crossed my arms and beamed at him. Caleb's jovial smirk shifted into a frown as he remembered his promise to make up for last night's near scrape with the cops.

"You sadistic bastard," he said.

"We leave in thirty minutes."

St. Joseph's was the only Catholic church in Newton which was a shock to me; that there was one to begin with. I had to show Cal how to properly dip his hand into the holy water and to make the sign of the cross. It didn't help matters that he complained like an unruly five-year-old. Deciding to err on the side of caution, we sat in the back pews in case the church mob decided to chase us out of the building with torches and pitch forks.

"I don't understand why people got hoodwinked into this stuff," Cal whispered. "What good has it ever done for anyone?"

"Saved Nanna once," I said.

"What?"

"Nanna told me this story about when Dad was a kid, they were leaving a church food drive when they were held at gunpoint. She prayed to God for protection."

"So what happened?"

"Lightning struck the robber down right on the spot."

"Your Nanna was pulling your leg."

"I thought so too but to this day she claims that this was covered in the news and everything. I never bothered to research it. I always took her word for it, seeing as she's not one to lie."

Cal impatiently fiddled with a silver object in his hand. With the click of two buttons, he demonstrated that it was both a switchblade and a pocket lighter in one device.

"Put that thing away!" I hissed.

"Can we go yet?" Cal asked.

"We just got here."

"I can't believe you dragged me here."

"You gave me your word that you were going to make it up to me. I'm holding you to it."

"Couldn't you have just asked for my car or a kidney or something? Dude, it's church for God's sake."

"Listen, there's nothing wrong with going to the House of God to get some spiritual and moral direction. And Lord knows your soul needs more praying over than most. If you stop whining for two seconds, you might get something out of this. Now suck it up and stop your griping."

While my speech stopped Cal from complaining, it didn't stop him from scanning the room to find other ways to entertain himself.

"Dude, check out the brunette in the second row," he whispered.

She glanced back and returned a grin to my roommate.

"Forgive me Father for I'm about to sin," he said. "I think I'm going to move up there."

I punched him in his leg.

"Ouch!" he hissed.

"Sit down," I whispered.

"What? She's hot. It's not my fault God is tempting me. Besides what's the harm in a little lust? It's not like it one of the deadly sins or something."

"You do know there's a special hell reserved for heathens like you."

Mass progressed and my concentration was split between

following the service and showing Cal how and when to make the sign of the cross and how to sing from the hymnal. Aside from elbowing him in the ribs when he nodded off, kicking him in the shin when he flirted with the cute brunette or punching him in the leg when he wasn't paying attention, Cal behaved himself.....eventually.

Father Michael took his place at the podium. He adjusted his robes, and shut the Bible.

"I thought we'd do something a little different today," he said. "I thought we'd talk about what it means to be a witness for God. I've been in the ministry for well….let's just say a good number of years. And one of the biggest misconceptions that I've noticed is this notion that being a man or woman of God means that you have all the answers and that you're without fault. Unfortunately many Christians believe this too and can often be judgmental and be very un-Christlike in their behavior."

"Ain't that the truth, Padre," Cal said.

I elbowed him.

"Though it is true that we aspire to be like a being who is without fault, we have to remember that our faith doesn't mean that we are perfect, in fact far from it. What our faith means is that we are a work in progress and we are evolving through God's guidance. We will stumble, but it's how we take responsibility for those mistakes that also what defines us. And just as God shows us mercy for our flaws, we must remember to do the same for our lost brothers and sisters. We don't witness by wagging an index finger and turning up our nose. We do it through example, patience and love and an open mind. Let us pray."

Mass concluded and I nearly had to run to keep up with a dashing Cal.

"Glad that's over," he said.

"You'll be thanking me when you aren't in fire and brimstone."

"Caleb? Noah?" said a familiar voice.

With a small Bible in tow, Abby's white sweater and cream dress gave her an angelic visage.

"I thought I saw you two in the back," she beamed.

"I didn't know you went here," Cal said.

"Yeah Jason told me about this place last year," she said. "I went with him one time and I've been coming back ever since. I just feel at peace here." She waved at an older couple. "I really like it here. I can just be me. Please don't tell anyone about this."

"Uh, why?" I asked.

"I can't risk my father finding out that his daughter converted to Catholicism. As far as Southern Baptists go I might as well be a Satanist."

"This will be our dirty little secret," Cal said with a wink.

"What brings you guys here?" Abby asked.

"Even though I'm flawed man, I try to keep a relationship with the big guy upstairs," Cal said. "And I get a lot of spiritual fulfillment when I come to church. I brought Noah here today because I wanted him to have a chance to start a relationship with God as well."

I scowled at my duplicitous roommate. Special Hell: reservation for one.

"Didn't you used to hate church with a passion?" Abby asked.

"I saw the light," Cal said.

"You are just full of surprises," Abby said.

"He's full of something," I mumbled.

"Well, someone has to make sure Noah gets into Heaven," Cal said.

"And giving me hell all the way," I said.

"I assume you made it home in one piece last night," Cal said.

"Yeah," she said. "Thank God."

"I'm really sorry again," Cal said.

"You didn't call the cops on us, that would be Chris," Abby said.

"Have you heard from him?" I asked.

"Oh, yeah," she said. "He left a dozen messages on my cell. Last night and this morning. I haven't called him, nor do I intend to. I can't deal with someone who's that manipulative and spiteful. I was almost in jail last night because of him."

"How did he find out about the party?" Cal asked.

"He got my roommate Tonya to snoop around on my laptop. That's how he found the email about the party. Needless to say I've put in a transfer request for a new roommate."

"Well the important thing is that no one got busted," I said.

"Yeah. Brianna and I made it back to the school okay," Abigail said. "Speaking of which Noah, she couldn't stop talking about you. Looks like someone left quite an impression on her."

"That would be called a hickie," Cal said.

"She's never gone on about any guy before," Abby said. "You ought to call her when you get home."

"I think I will," I said.

At that moment, Father Michael approached.

"Hello, Abigail," he greeted.

"Hi, Father Michael," she said. "That was a lovely sermon today."

"Thank you," he said. "I'm glad you enjoyed it. Who are your friends?"

"This is Caleb and this is Noah."

"It's a pleasure to meet you both," said Father Michael. "It's nice to see more young people in church."

"Thank you," I said.

"Abigail, I was checking to see if you were still going to be able to join us for the food drive on Wednesday?" Father Michael asked.

"Absolutely," she said.

"Great," Father Michael said. "Unfortunately we're going to be shorthanded. Mrs. Brown had to leave town on a family emergency and probably won't be back in time and Mr. Albertson is still sick with the flu."

"That's awful," Abby said.

"Sign us up," I said.

"What?" Cal asked.

"Caleb and I will be more than happy to help out," I said.

"Noah that would be wonderful," Abby said.

"Uh, Noah, you're forgetting that I have that thing to do," Cal said. "I'm sorry, Father. I would love to help out but Noah forgot that I have a previous engagement at school. Otherwise I'd be here helping out."

"Oh, yeah," I said. "I forgot about that other engagement. He has to meet with his teachers for a project. But you know Caleb, I'm sure once you tell them that you're canceling so you can help feed the poor and spend time at the church, I'm sure they'll more than understand. We'll be there."

"Excellent," Father Michael said. "We lose two people and we gain two more. Then we're all set. We'll feed the homeless, sing some hymns and fellowship. Good times. I'll see you all Wednesday."

Father Michael waved goodbye.

"I'll talk to you guys later," Abby said. "Thank you so much."

"I figured you would appreciate the chance for some more spiritual fulfillment," I said.

Cal glared at me, "You are so walking back to school."

Chapter Three

I knew I was dreaming the second I found myself in the candlelit room. Glyphs and demonic symbols were painted on the walls and the wooden floor. Upon closer examination I realized they weren't made from paint but actual blood. In the center of the room knelt a cloaked figure who chanted to three men standing before him. Their pale skin a stark contrast to their dark attire, they were akin to vampires or some other nocturnal monstrosity.

"Our champion has made the proper offerings," one of the men said.

"He is ready," the second one added.

The chanter pushed back his sleeve. The third man placed a branding iron against the inner side of his forearm. The chanter remained silent as the skin hissed and bubbled. A demonic triangular glyph remained after the iron was removed.

"It is complete," the third man said. "You know what must be done."

The chanter bowed his head.

Whispers and murmured conversations could be heard amongst the students on Monday. Overhearing excerpts from various conversations, it didn't take long to get the gist of the gossip. While the versions varied depending on who you asked, the rumor basically stated that Chris discovered that Abigail had cheated on him and went to confront her at Cal's party on Saturday night.

"I heard he found online photos of her with three guys," one student said.

"Mitch told me there's an online sex video," another student said.

"We so need to find that website."

"She always did act like she was so perfect. Surprise, surprise, she's nothing but a world class slut."

"Poor Chris. He deserves so much better."

Coach Phelps was right about one thing. Honor and name was

everything, at least here at Hollowstone. Chris couldn't beat Cal like a man so he decided to fight dirty and there's nothing dirtier than politics and politics don't get any dirtier than those of high school. He couldn't sully Cal's reputation since his popularity thrived on being the school's resident bad boy. One could almost appreciate the Machiavellian genius of the scheme if it wasn't depraved and it didn't hurt two people I was particularly fond of.

Abby's seat remained vacant when Mr. Tyler began class. I hoped that she would eventually show up. She never did. Though I couldn't blame her, I was worried. Not just for her but for what Cal might do.

I checked the cafeteria, the library and many empty classrooms. I called Brianna's room and left a message for her to get in touch with me. Nothing. I stopped by my room to see if Cal was there. No doubt he was out looking for her as well. At least I hoped that was the case. I prayed that he didn't do something stupid like go after Chris. A few moments after I entered, the door burst open then slammed shut. Cal tossed his bag and kicked the trash can.

"I'm going to fucking kill that bastard," he growled.

"I was going to go find Brianna," I said.

"I already talked to her," Cal said. "She hasn't seen her either. You know, I knew he would retaliate. I figured he'd get his little posse together and maybe jump me or something. I've been looking over my shoulder all day. I gotta admit I didn't see this one coming. Fucking coward. And God only knows what Abby's going through."

"Cal, I think I know where she is."

For someone who had despised going to church, Cal couldn't get to St. Joseph's fast enough. Running three red lights and two stop signs, it was a miracle we didn't get pulled over by the cops. I kicked myself for not thinking of St. Joseph's sooner, though all was forgiven when we discovered that my hunch was correct. We found a sobbing Abigail sitting in the front pew, wiping the tears from her face with a handkerchief.

"I thought you were Father Michael," she said. "I was waiting for him. How did you find me?"

"Altar Boy over here figured it out," Cal said.

"I was on my way to Tyler's class and I kept getting these stares and hearing whispers behind my back," she said. "I didn't know what was going on. Then Chet showed up and filled me in. He stood there and taunted me. He called me an ungrateful slut for cheating on Chris and breaking his heart. He threw some dollar bills at me and told me I knew where his dorm room was." She resumed sobbing. "Everyone just sat there and laughed at me. People who I thought were my friends. I tried telling them that none of it was true but they wouldn't listen."

"This is all my fault," Cal said. "I should've never invited you to that damn party."

"No," I said. "If he's this hateful and would resort to this because she refused to be under his thumb then I say Abigail is lucky. At least now, Abigail, you know what type of creep you're dealing with and who your friends are."

"Noah's right," Cal said. "You did nothing wrong and you have nothing to be ashamed of."

"And you're not in this alone," I added. "We're not going anywhere."

She cracked a smile. "You don't know how much I needed to hear that."

"What do you say the three of us get out of here and grab a cappuccino?" Cal said. "My treat."

"I think I could use a cappuccino. Thank you. Both of you."

She hugged Cal and kissed me on the cheek.

"Why does he get a kiss?" Cal asked.

"I'm the one that figured out where she was," I said.

"Besides, altar boys always get a kiss," Abby added

Cal rolled his eyes in mock disgust. He draped his brown leather jacket over Abby's slender shoulders and the three of us departed.

Inevitably, we returned to school. Cal and I flanked Abby, each of us ignoring the whispers and the snickering from some of the students. Surprisingly, Abby kept a strong resolve.

"There you are," Cassidy said. "You aren't helping your case by being seen with him."

"What are you talking about?" Abby said.

Cassidy handed Abby a beige letter. Upon reading the paper, Abby's expression changed from bewilderment to horror.

"You have got to be kidding me?" she cried. "Tell me this is a joke!"

"It's not," Cassidy said.

Cal grabbed the paper.

"Fucking bastard," he growled.

"What's going on?" I asked.

"I'm being impeached," Abby said. "The student council is holding a hearing tonight to vote on whether or not I'm a suitable president. My moral character is being called into question. It seems I'm being accused of conduct unbecoming of a student body president."

"This is getting ridiculous," I said. "Can Chris do that? I didn't even know he was on the student council."

"He's not," Cal said. "His sister, however, is."

"Phyllis is the vice president," Abby said. "And no doubt she's the one leading this witch hunt. Bitch!"

"What do you want to do?" Cal asked.

"I don't know," Abby said.

"You shouldn't have put yourself in a position like this," Cassidy said. "I hate to say this but it's a good chance that you're going to be voted out of student council tonight. But for what it's worth, I don't agree with what they're doing. I thought you should hear this from me."

"You know what," Abby said. "I'm through crying and I'm through being pushed around. Let them do what they're going to do. I'll do the same."

Classroom 310 was at standing room capacity. Luckily Brianna had arrived early enough to save seats for Cal and me. The pragmatist within me suspected that the large turnout wasn't to watch the student council conduct business rather than to view the latest chapter of this dramatic saga unfold.

Abby sat at the table in front of the room, alone and surrounded by enemies. To her immediate left and right were Phyllis and Cassidy, vice president and secretary, respectively. Sitting at the end of the table were Treasurer Lacey and Student Representative Harry. Though she tried to look poised and confident, Abby's trembling hands revealed otherwise.

"Nothing like a good flaying to top off a Monday," Brianna said.

"Way to support your friend," I said. "Maybe they'll give her a fair chance."

Brianna laughed, "If they had any intentions of being fair we wouldn't be sitting here."

"I'm surprised Chris had the brains to even plan all of this, let alone pull it off," I said.

Brianna snickered, "He didn't. This is all Phyllis. When it comes to the Goddard siblings, she's the one with the brains and testicular fortitude. She's been after the presidency for a long time but Abby has always been too popular being the little princess and all. A scandal and a political coup would be the only way Phyllis would win it. Lacey is her flunky and Harry is spineless. He'll go with the winning side. Three guesses who's going to be the new president by the time this meeting is over."

Cal abruptly hopped out of his chair. Glancing at the door entrance, I saw the reason. Chris entered the room, flanked by Chet and Ronny. The smug grin on his face indicated that he relished the attention that he received from his classmates. Several patted him on the back and consoled him for being the dutiful boyfriend who was betrayed by his two-timing girlfriend.

"Goddard!" Cal barked. "You got beef with me. Fine. Take it up with me. Abigail doesn't deserve this and you know it."

Chris smiled. "She made her choice and now she'll have to live with it. Just remember that you brought this on her."

Phyllis tapped the gavel. "The meeting of the Hollowstone Academy Student Council will now come to order. Because of the urgency of this meeting, I move that we forego the reading of the minutes."

"Second," Harry said.

"We're here today because some rather disturbing reports have been made," Phyllis said. "Our president is being impeached today on charges of conduct unbecoming of a student council president. How do you respond to these allegations, Madame President?"

"These allegations are completely false," Abby said. "These lies were perpetrated by a party with a personal vendetta against me." She stared at a smug Chris. "A coward whose only recourse is to sully my reputation."

"Student council president is a prestigious title," Phyllis said. "One whose reputation and honor must be preserved at all costs. The tiniest insinuation of impropriety could jeopardize the reputation of the entire student council."

"My record speaks for itself," Abby said. "I have been a dedicated and hardworking president. On top of that, there has been no shred of evidence to validate these lies."

"We've seen the evidence," Lacey said. She held up a sealed

brown envelope. "It's all right here. And I have to say I was absolutely appalled by the pictures and the video tape."

Gasps and murmurs filled the classroom.

"That is a lie!" Abby said. "Let me see this so called proof."

"We can't do that," Lacey said. "While you've certainly made it clear that you don't mind performing in front of an audience, this meeting is not the place to show such racy material. Phyllis, Harold and I have reviewed it. There's no need for anyone else to see it."

"That's because there isn't any," Abby said. "We all know that evidence which you refuse to show is bogus."

"You have got to be fucking kidding me," Cal muttered under his breath.

"Were you not seen at a rave?" Phyllis asked. "A party in which cops were called to shut down?"

"You mean the same party your brother crashed?" Abby replied. "The same brother who I was dating until this weekend when I broke up with him for being an obnoxious jerk."

"There is no need to get personal or insulting, Abigail," Phyllis said.

"Oh I think there is," Abby continued. "This whole matter has been personal and insulting. The only reason I'm on trial is because you're carrying out your brother's vendetta."

"That is a lie," Phyllis cried. "And how dare you accuse me of being so petty."

"If I may interject," Cassidy said. "I'll be the first to say that I find some of the company our president has been keeping as of late to be less than ideal. However, you can't deny that she's done a wonderful job handling this position. And until her performance as president is compromised, I say she should retain her position."

"Being president is more than about performing tasks," Phyllis said. "It is about honor and respectability. This is a position of leadership and you very well can't respect a leader if there are allegations and scandals running about. Of course I can understand the concepts of honor and respectability being difficult for you to appreciate, Cassidy. You know, being from a broken home and all."

Before Cassidy could retaliate, Cal stood up.

"Why don't you let the student body decide?" he said. "At least this way, it'll be fair and we all get a say in the matter."

"I agree," Cassidy said. "And I make a motion we do so."

To my astonishment, a number of students nodded in agreement.

Phyllis slammed the gavel.

"You are out of order," she hissed. "Anymore outbursts and I will clear this room. It's time to put this matter to rest and vote. All those in favor of removing the president from office raise your hands."

True to Brianna's words, Phyllis, Lacey and Harry raised their hands.

With a grin Phyllis asked, "All opposed?"

Cassidy and Abby raised their hands.

"In a vote of three to two, the motion passes," Phyllis announced. "Abigail Phillips, you are hereby stripped of your title and the responsibilities and privileges that accompany them."

Abby shook her head in disgust.

In a rehearsed tone Harry stated, "Because we are currently without a president, I move that we vote an interim president in until the next election."

"I nominate Phyllis Goddard," Lacey said.

"Seconded," Harry said. "All in favor?"

Phyllis, Lacey and Harry raised their arms.

"The motion passes," Lacey said. "Welcome Madame President."

"Thank you," Phyllis said. "And as my first act as president, I want to assure each and every one of you that I promise to hold this position with the utmost honor and dignity that it deserves. For my second act, I wish to nominate my successor for the vice presidency. The person I wish to nominate is someone who has regularly been a source of inspiration. And in spite of the recent personal hardships he has endured, he has still carried himself with grace and class. I can't think of a finer person than my brother, Christopher Goddard, Jr."

Our mouths ajar, Cal and I exchanged dumbfounded stares.

"An excellent suggestion," Lacey said. "And I second it."

"All in favor?" Harry asked.

And in another three to one vote, the motion passed.

Phyllis smacked the gavel, "Meeting adjourned."

"That was fun," Brianna said sarcastically. "And now homework calls. Later."

Cal rushed to Abby's side, "You okay."

She wiped away a tear and nodded, "Yeah, I'll be okay."

Cal wrapped an arm around Abby as he walked her towards the door, but not before encountering Phyllis and Chris.

"Well at least now you'll have plenty of time on your hands to make videos, with your new boy toy," Chris said.

"That tears it," Cal said.

It took all of my strength to restrain Cal.

"It's okay, Caleb," Abby said. "You know what Chris, while it hurts losing this job, if that's what it costs to be done with you, then so be it. And a little word of advice. The next time you get dumped for being an ass, be man enough to fight your own battles instead of getting your sister to do your dirty work for you. And you wonder why I wouldn't sleep with you."

Cal wrapped an arm around her. Abby wrapped a thin arm around my neck and tugged me in. Defeated, the three of us had found solace in one another. In that solace we had weathered a brutal storm. What we didn't realize at the time was that it was only going to get worse.

Chapter Four

Abigail had become an honorary roommate in our dorm room. Not that I minded. Cal's face never lit up quite as much as it did when he was around her. The day I walked in on the two of them making out, I could see it in his eyes. He was a man in love. While she made her visits as much to see me as they were to see her boyfriend, I often opted to give the two alone time and went to practice my violin in an empty classroom. Their frequent make out sessions resulted in much violin practice. So much so Nolan frequently complimented me on my improvements in class.

Since the breakup with Chris, she also found herself in a short supply of friends. Once the ivory princess and one half of Hollowstone's super couple, she was now a pariah. The only original friend she seemed to maintain was Brianna. I wasn't sure if that was because they were now roommates or if it was simply because Brianna seemed to get a morbid thrill out of watching Abby's suffering. Brianna often tried to maintain this bad girl façade by acting disinterested in everything. I seemed to be the only one who wasn't fooled. I had to admit, I was growing quite fond of her.

The weeks passed and the infamous scandal became old news. The top headline was the success of the Hollowstone football team. Thus far the Knights had maintained an undefeated streak which ignited massive school spirit as our school slowly became the odds on favorites to win the championship. This of course elevated the football players to godhood status.

It was a week after we had taken our U.S. History test. Abby and I anxiously waited for Mr. Tyler to return our tests.

"Nice work guys," Tyler said.

Abby and I exchanged high-fives upon seeing the red A's in the top right corner.

"What the hell is this?" Chet cried.

"That would your test from last week," Tyler said. "And the big red letter on top of your test would be called an F."

"This is bullshit," Ronny said. "We're not going to be able to play."

"And whose fault is that?" Tyler asked. "I've been warning the two of you for weeks now to get your acts together. Looks like you're missing the game."

"You can't do this," Chet griped.

"I didn't," Tyler said. "You did. And now it's your problem."

Chet whispered something to Ronny and the two stared at Tyler. If Chet and Ronny were ineligible to play, there was going to be hell to pay. Unfortunately, I feared that Tyler would be the one paying.

It didn't take long for the fallout to hit. That afternoon, I returned to Tyler's classroom to ask him about a project. The yelling could be heard from outside the door.

"They're spirited boys," Phelps said. "They've got a lot of pressure on them right now. Surely you can take that into account."

"They don't do any work and they consistently disrupt class," Tyler said. "Greg, I've repeatedly come to you about them and nothing's been done. The grade stands."

"Do you know what this means if you do this?" Phelps asked.

"It means that someone in this school has his priorities straight about what's more important," Tyler said. "Last I checked education took precedent over a football game."

"Damn it, Randy," Phelps barked, "If we lose this season over your bullshit, so help me God—"

"Greg, please," Norrington said. "Now, Randy, I want you to think about this carefully and think about what this could mean to your future here at Hollowstone."

"Are you threatening my job, George?" Tyler asked. "Because I won't pass a couple of unruly kids so they can play football?"

"Think about it, Randy," Norrington intoned.

"They're going to fire him," I said. "I can't believe they're going to fire him because he won't roll over for them."

I leaned against the large oak tree and sighed. Cal stopped scribbling in his journal.

"You should know by now that no good deed goes unpunished," he said.

"It's not right."

"Of course it isn't," he said. "This isn't about right and wrong. It's about power. And at this school, if you've got enough of it, you can pretty much get away with murder. It bites but that's the reality of it…and it looks like we've got company."

"My God she's got a clipboard," I groaned. "This isn't going to end well."

Marching up the hill was none other than Cassidy. It didn't take a mind reader to know that she wanted something from either Cal or me. Whatever it was, we probably wouldn't be interested. Cassidy wasn't the type to take no for an answer.

"I've been looking everywhere for you," she said.

"Well now you found me, sexy" Cal greeted.

"Not you!" she hissed. "Him."

"What is it?" I asked.

"No doubt you know that homecoming is next week and we have a lot of events planned," Cassidy said. "I would know since I'm chairing most of the committees."

"Now this is a girl who can multitask," Cal said.

"Anyway, we're having a lavish banquet in honor of the football team—" Cassidy said.

"Because an ego boost is all they need," Cal said.

"And we need entertainment," Cassidy said. "Word has it that you're a gifted violinist and Nolan's prized student. I was wondering if you would be kind enough to serenade the dinner. Something nice and elegant. This will be a chance to showcase the best that Hollowstone has to offer in both athletics and the arts."

"Did you ask Nolan about this?" Cal asked.

Cassidy rolled her eyes in disgust. Cal grinned as he knew the answer.

"I proposed this idea to Mr. Nolan and before I could finish, the angry little man went irate," Cassidy said. "Tossing around music stands and screaming that his orchestra would not be whored out to glorified thugs. One of the reasons why I proposed a mental competency requirement for the faculty last year."

"And going behind Nolan's back and trying to snag his top protégé is just all kinds of classy," Cal said.

"Shouldn't you be planning your next rave or your future in a correctional facility?" Cassidy snapped.

"Thank you for the offer," I said. "But I'm not interested."

"What?" she asked.

"I'm not interested," I said. "My plate is already full. And the last thing I plan to be is entertainment for those jackasses. Especially after what they pulled with Abby. Not to mention what they do to Ryan every day."

"What happened with Abby was unfortunate," Cassidy said. "And if you recall I took up for her. But this isn't about that. This is about the school and doing your part."

"No thanks," I said.

"For someone who is on scholarship, you should be grateful at the chance to give back to the school."

"Look!" I barked. "I don't like to lose my patience but you're really starting to piss me off. I do plan to give back to the school and show my school spirit when I give a kick-ass performance at the concert in a few weeks. For the last time, I am not interested in any of your little tailgating parties or whatever it is you have planned for those assholes. Now will you please leave me the hell alone?"

"You know something," Cassidy said. "It is impossible to be on all of these committees, never mind my duties on the yearbook, honor society and student council and maintain a straight-A average. Nevertheless, I do all of this as well as the lion's share of most of the work and never receive the credit I deserve. Is it too much to for someone to cut me a break around here?"

"Seems to me you'd be better off not even bothering," Cal said.

Cassidy growled and stormed away.

"You know," Cal said. "She'd be smoking hot if she wasn't so uptight. Oh, who am I kidding? I'd hit it in a heartbeat. Probably what she needs to loosen up anyway. She does bring up an excellent point though. Homecoming is next week and I for one don't want to be around to see Chris acting like he's God. I think you, Abby, Brianna and me need to get the hell out of here."

"Sounds like an idea," I said. "Where were you thinking of going?"

"California. Maybe Hawaii. I'm in the mood for some surfing."

"What?"

"School is only going to be a half day for the homecoming game next Friday. We head to the airport and spend the weekend shopping, surfing and hanging out."

"I can't afford a plane ticket. Besides, I've got plenty of homework and practice to keep me busy."

"Don't worry about the expenses. The entire trip is on me since it's my idea. All you have to do is just show up and have a good time.

Sound good?"

"No. I can't let you spend that kind of money."

"Noah, I can afford it. Trust me when I say it's a drop in the bucket."

"Cal, I—"

"Look, you and Abby are the closest things I got to family. My mom and I aren't close and I don't have a father. Just a sperm donor. He made it clear that I have no place in his life. The only thing he's good for is his checkbook. Please, let me do this."

I sighed and nodded.

"Now, come on. Let's go find the girls and tell them the news."

My curiosity piqued, I perused the archives of Cal's blog, searching for any snippets about his past. It revealed none. Caleb's online journal was launched after he came into his inheritance and was awarded emancipation. And just like in real life, he didn't discuss his past before that. His blog included many pics and posts about his time abroad in Europe and many of his short stories and poetry. His talents as a writer were undeniable. His journal also chronicled his numerous—and I do mean numerous—sexual conquests. Those were some of his most vivid posts and to those who didn't want anything left to the imaginations. He clearly had aspirations of being a porn star.

There were also numerous posts and pics featuring Cal and three other guys: Jason and brothers Seth and Fenn. The four of them were a crew of sorts. With dark shaggy hair and sharp angular facial features, it was abundantly obvious that Seth and Fenn were related. Jason seemed the most out of the place of the four. Short, pudgy, his face was covered by a thick pair of glasses. According to Cal's blog entries, the quartet was at the pinnacle of popularity. Their raves were legendary and Cal was the undisputed leader of the pack. However after Jason's death, Seth and Fenn transferred out of the school and then there was only Cal.

A great number of posts were about a mystery girl who he fell in love with a long time ago. A mystery girl who was the primary reason he chose to attend Hollowstone. His more recent entries had pics from the rave and pics of him, Abby and me hanging out. As I read through the entries, one thing was for certain, he was far more complex than one would initially surmise. He certainly had his share of secrets. Of course looking back on it now, I wish I had prodded further and found out as much as possible about Cal. Had I done so, perhaps he would still be alive.

In a vote of two to one, Beverly Hills was chosen as our destination. Abby and Brianna argued for the need for shopping while Cal had his heart set on riding some Hawaiian waves. I abstained from the vote as I was more than fine with either choice. Besides, Nanna instilled in me at an early age that if a man wants to live to see another sunrise, he never interferes with a woman's shopping. There was no way I was going to risk threatening that vote and forfeiting my life.

Cal took care of all of the arrangements. Despite my repeated offers to help, he insisted that he would take care of everything. His orders for Abby, Bri and me were to be in front of the school on Friday at noon with luggage so the taxi could take us to the airport. Only the taxi never showed. Instead a black stretch limo came to a halt in front of the four of us. The chauffeur stepped out of the car and opened the door with a nod. The shocked looks on our faces was exactly what Cal had aimed for. The grin on his face indicated that our surprise was his reward.

Onlookers watched as our luggage was loaded, whispering to one another and speculating on where the four of us were off to in such a fashion. No doubt the gossip would get back to Chris and Phyllis and no doubt this was what Cal was counting on.

I could count on one hand the number of times I had been on an airplane. A private jet on the other hand was another matter. I had to admit, I could see why so many people enjoyed it and why people flew so often.

From the airport, another limousine took us to an opulent resort. The four of us would be staying in two suites which were usually reserved for celebrities according to the concierge. One thing you could say for Cal, he had style.

"Can't believe I didn't think of this sooner," Cal said as he hopped on top of his bed. "This weekend is going to rock. And just think, we would still be stuck at school listening to 'Go Knights' chants if I hadn't thought of this. Admit it. I did good."

"Yes Cal. You did good."

"You know if all goes well, this might be an unforgettable weekend for you and me."

The tone in his voice indicated clearly what he was hinting at.

"Wait," I said. "You two haven't—"

Cal shook his head. "Figured this might be the perfect place for the first time."

"And the plot unfolds."

"I'm sure Brianna might be thinking the same thing too."

"We'll cross that bridge when we get there," I said.

"That's cool. The shields are in the bathroom cabinet just in case."

There was a knock at the door.

"It's open," Cal said.

Brianna and Abigail entered.

"The room is insane Caleb," Abby squealed.

She wrapped her arms around his neck and kissed him. I closed my eyes as I felt Brianna's soft arms slide around my waist.

"Oh, get a room you two," Brianna joked.

"Look who's talking," Abby said.

"We may be using yours later," Cal said with a wink.

Abby smacked his arm.

"Tacky," Brianna joked. "I don't know about you guys but I'm starving."

"Ditto," Abby said.

"All right then," Cal said. "Let's grab a bite to eat. There's a fancy little place I heard about that I think you guys might like."

"And what do we do after dinner," Abby said.

Cal replied, "We'll play it by ear."

As was the case with the trip and the hotel, the restaurant of choice was a high class five star with a world renowned chef serving our meals. Most of the menu was in French so I allowed Abby to order for me, seeing that she was the only one at the table who I knew wouldn't intentionally order something disgusting. The four of us laughed incessantly. No doubt the other restaurant patrons suspected we were inebriated. It didn't matter. We needed the escape. To add to the obnoxious behavior, Cal snapped away with his digital camera. Brianna shielded her face.

"I don't do photos," she said.

"To a glorious weekend," Cal said as he lifted his glass.

"To a glorious weekend," the rest of us echoed.

"And here's to hoping the Hollowstone Knights get decimated at their own homecoming game," Cal added.

Following dinner, we attended a local carnival. Cal acted like a big kid—more than usual—insisting on riding every ride possible. He squealed with delight each time he and I rode the roller coasters. Of course my eyes were shut closed with my hands around my crucifix. The girls wisely waited on the safe firm earth, holding the stuffed teddy bears that Cal and I had won for them. Suffice to say I caught grief from the lot of them upon stumbling out of the acrophobic inducing rides from hell. It was a little past one when we finally made it back to our suites. Beyond exhausted, we immediately crashed.

It was still dark when I was awoken. Cal sat on top of me shaking me profusely.

"Come on guy, we're gonna go catch some waves," he whispered.

"You go," I muttered. "Me sleep."

"Come on, Noah, we're going surfing."

"I don't know how to surf," I muttered. "Me sleep now."

"I'm going to teach you. Now get up. Noah. Noah."

I kept my eyes shut and ignored him. Cal finally hopped off the bed and departed. I slowly drifted back to sleep. Minutes later, the covers were yanked off of me and a bucket of ice was dumped on top of me. I yelped and hopped out of bed.

"I'm gonna kill you!" I shrieked.

"I'll meet you in the lobby," Cal laughed.

He dashed out of the room before I could wrap my hands around his throat.

The waves were as cold as the bucket of ice my sadist of a roommate had dumped on me. We spent the better part of the morning sitting on the waves as Cal instructed me on the basics of surfing. He then handed me a disposable waterproof camera. I snapped away as he rode the waves with precision and grace. After his demonstration, he grabbed the camera and coaxed me into trying it.

For the sake of preserving some modicum of dignity, I won't go into detail as to the number of times I fell off the board and into the water or the number of times Cal himself almost fell off of his board from guffawing. Near the end I did get the hang of it and managed to ride three small waves before wiping out.

While we boys spent the day surfing, the girls spent their day shopping. When we returned to the hotel, they were only too happy to show us all of the shoes and outfits they bought.

"You do realize we won't be able to get all of this on the jet," Cal joked.

"What's Vera Wang?" I asked.

"I told you we should've dragged them with us," Brianna smiled.

"No they would've just whined the whole time," Abby said.

"Anybody want to see pics of Noah wiping out?" Cal said.

"That's not necessary," I pleaded.

"Look what else we snagged while we were out shopping," Brianna said.

Brianna removed a wide assortment of liquor bottles from one of the pink shopping bags.

"I'm not going to even ask how you two scored booze," I said.

"Brianna has her ways," Abby said.

It took my friends no time to open up the bottles. I smiled as I watched them drink and laugh.

"Come on Noah, one little drink," Abby said.

"I'm good," I insisted. "This water bottle is keeping me happy."

"Have a wine cooler," Brianna said. "There's barely any alcohol in it. You'll be fine."

"Come on Altar Boy," Cal said. "Just one wine cooler."

I've only been drunk three times in my life. The first time was in that hotel suite. I don't care what Cal and the others said, wine coolers pack more of a punch than people think. Considering that I was tipsy after the first wine cooler, much of what I remember about that night is a blur. I recall stumbling around the room and tripping over every piece of furniture there was. For some reason I had the bright idea to tour the hotel, maybe walking would sober me up. Luckily Brianna followed me and kept an eye on me. Of course we didn't get very far and somehow we wound up in her suite.

"I think I'm drunk," I slurred.

Brianna giggled as she shoved me back on her bed.

"I really think I'm really drunk," I slurred.

She removed my sneakers, "I should've gotten you wasted a lot sooner. You're so cute like this."

"You're cute too," I said. "I really like you. You're smart. Strong. You play tennis. You must make your parents proud."

"Proud," Brianna scoffed. "Mother is too busy popping pills to even know what month it is. Dad is too busy running his company. If I brought you home, they'd probably notice me then. Assuming the shock didn't kill them first."

"So sad."

"Yeah but I know something that'll make me feel better."

She lightly nibbled on my ear and promptly removed my shirt. She unceremoniously yanked my belt from its pants loops.

"What are you doing?" I asked.

She unbuckled my pants, "Getting to the main event."

"Wait. I'm not ready."

"It's okay, I'll do all the work. Just lie back and enjoy the ride."

"Hold on."

"Don't worry, I've got protection."

I pushed her back.

"What's wrong with you?" she asked. "I thought you liked me."

"I do like you," I said. "And if I wasn't so drunk I would be able to explain it better. But I like you and that's why I want to wait."

"What, I'm not good enough for your first time or something?"

I sat up, "You're perfect. You're smart, you're beautiful, you're funny and…and you know what you want. That's why I want the first time to be perfect. When I'm ready, cause I think you're worth it."

"You are such a chick," Brianna said. She shook her head and scoffed, "Of all the guys I've dated, I fall for the one guy who's a boy scout."

She planted her head against my chest and wrapped her arm around me. The two of us laid silently on the king size bed for the remainder of the night.

The three days in California felt like three minutes. Before I knew it, we were back on the jet returning to school. I didn't get a chance to find out if anything happened between Cal and Abby during the night of drunkenness, but based on the longing glances, smiles and winks the two continued to exchange with one another, something had definitely transpired.

"I take it all went well last night?" I finally asked.

"It went better than I imagined," Cal Said.

"You're glowing. And so is she."

"And what about you? I take it you finally scored."

"Oh, look at the clouds outside the window. How fascinating."

"You still have your cherry intact? There's just no corrupting you."

"Look, I'm just not ready to hook up and go all the way. Maybe that makes me less of a man but I'm just not wired that way. So go ahead and make fun of me. You know you want to."

Cal patted me on the shoulder, "No mockery here. You are who you are and I admire and respect that. Don't ever apologize for being who you are. Not to anyone. Even me. Especially me."

"So you're not going to give me grief?"

"Oh I'm so giving you grief. The grief is forthcoming along with much mockery and incessant laughing. But seriously, be you and do you. God knows my life would've been a lot less complicated if I had your philosophy. It would also be boring and miserable—"

"Hey!"

"But you get my point."

"Yeah. It doesn't matter though. Brianna's been giving off this weird vibe. I think she's done with me."

"Her loss. We'll just have to find you another hottie."

I plugged my earphones into my ears, turned on my iPod and sighed.

"Cal."

"Yeah?"

"Thank you."

"Anytime. That's what brothers are for."

Chapter Five

The concert arrived sooner than I wanted and despite all the practice I had put in, I still felt unprepared. I had performed many times before at school and a few times at church back in Atlanta. But this was different.

I had been unceremoniously labeled as Nolan's prized pupil and this concert was my debut to the world. If I choked, then this would not end well for anyone, namely me. We were on stage behind the thick red curtains, making last minute preparations. Papers were shuffled, music stands and instruments alike clattered. I poked my head out of the corner of the curtains. There were only a handful of students in the audience, no doubt only there to receive extra credit that their teachers may have offered them to attend. The seats were mainly filled by faculty, family and a few locals from town. I calmed a bit when I saw Cal and Abby in the audience. No sign of Brianna. Eventually realizing that worrying about her at the moment would get me nowhere, I adjusted my tie and got ready.

"All right, everyone!" Nolan bellowed, "Take your seats!"

Despite the petrified state that I was in, I tried my best to put on a brave front for my mentor.

"Are you ready, Mr. Scott?"

"Yes, sir. Just a wee bit nervous."

"I'd be worried if you weren't. I get petrified before each performance."

"You do?"

"But then I remember that half of the audience is too dense to appreciate my genius and that I have nothing to worry about."

"Oh. I suppose that's effective."

"You're going to be outstanding tonight. Just imagine this as one of our regular class sessions. Just relax and play. You're a natural. And just remember that if you so much as miss a note, I will put a contract out on your life. That's if I don't do the deed myself and mow you down with my Buick."

My eyes widened in terror. Nolan chuckled. Taking it as a cue that he was joking, I nervously joined in the laughter. Nolan abruptly ceased and delivered a piercing warning scowl.

"All right everyone, let's get ready," he said.

Silence fell upon the orchestra as we got into position.

"We have practiced and gone over this material," Nolan said. "Chimpanzees can perform this with ease so I'm expecting the same from the lot of you. Let's not cause Mozart to roll over in his grave. Ms. Astin, get rid of that gum! And don't you dare put it under you chair!"

"There's no trash can," she replied.

"Then do the same thing you do when you're with half of the football team," Nolan growled. "Swallow!"

The curtains parted. Thankfully the blaring spotlights made it impossible for me to see into the crowd. Nolan stepped in front of us, delivering one final warning glare. He meticulously and methodically cracked his knuckles, tapped his baton and began. We opened with a slow melodic piece. Nolan waved his small arms and we matched him note for note. Shockingly enough, no one made a single mistake. Nolan had the gift of instilling the fear of God into his pupils. More shocking was that I felt completely at ease on the stage.

Eventually, it was time for my solo. I took a few deep breaths, placed my bow against the strings, shut my eyes and sawed away. I've heard artists describe this force that overtakes them when they're performing their respective art: writing, painting or dancing. This primal force flows through them and they are in fact the instrument which its energies are being channeled through. That's exactly what it felt like when I played that night. It felt as if my soul bled from my fingertips onto the strings. Maybe that's why I felt half dead when I finished my solo.

Dead silence. Oh God. My heart stopped. A few claps echoed in the auditorium which heralded a roaring standing ovation. I sighed in relief. A beaming Nolan applauded and delivered a salute. He signaled for me to take a bow. I stood up, stepped forward and gave a hearty bow to my adoring audience.

In the midst of the applause I heard a faint yell of "That's my roommate! That's my roommate!"

Cal and Abby rendezvoused with me backstage following the

concert. Abby wrapped her arms around my neck.

"You were amazing!" Abby squealed. "I'm so proud of you."

"Thanks," I gasped, "Can't breathe."

"Oh sorry," she said.

"Dude you kicked ass out there!" Cal said.

"Thanks," I said. "I'm just glad I don't have to worry about Nolan trying to kill me in my sleep. At least not until the next concert. Where's Bri?"

My friends averted their gaze.

"I'm sorry," Abby said. "She said she was going to meet us here but she never showed. When I called her, she said she made other plans."

"It's not your fault," Noah said. I put on a hearty grin. "Besides I'm not going to let this ruin my night."

"There you go," Cal said. "Besides, you got us."

"Yeah I do."

Exiting backstage, the three of us ran passed an all too familiar group. Chris, Phyllis, Lacey, Chet and Tonya—Abby's former roommate—who was draped on Chris's arm. Both sides gave the other the once over. Opting for civility, Abby gave a sincere nod to the vipers who crucified her. She wrapped herself around Cal's arm and we continued on. Chris scowled at the couple.

"Let's treat the man of the hour to a very big dinner," Cal said.

"Sounds like a plan," Abby said.

"If it's okay, I want to go throw my violin back in the room so I don't have to drag it around," I said.

"Okay," Abby said. "I'll go freshen up in the ladies room."

"And what am I supposed to do?" Cal asked.

"You can wait like a good boyfriend," Abby said.

"Nice to see somebody isn't whipped," I joked.

"Don't you have an instrument to put away?" Cal asked.

"All right, I'll meet you guys in the parking lot," I laughed.

I meandered through the dark empty halls, in no hurry at all. I was on a euphoric high which was far more intoxicating than those wine coolers I got plastered on in California. In the distance Elias Cole, an esteemed member of our illustrious football team, crept into an empty classroom and shut the door behind him. What would a jock be doing in an empty classroom after dark? My curiosity got the better of me. He wasn't alone. He was kissing and groping someone. I stared closer and gasped as I recognized that it was Ryan. I crept away from the classroom. I wasn't sure of the dynamics but I figured it was none of my business. If anyone else deserved a shred of happiness, it was Ryan.

The parking lot was empty when I arrived. I couldn't believe that I beat the others. I didn't mind. My euphoria remained my companion. The solitude gave me a moment to gaze at the starry skies and enjoy light cool breeze. A distant sobbing finally snapped me out of my daze. Near the steps, Cassidy escorted a sobbing Dana. Her blouse ripped, hair disheveled, Dana's face and body were covered in cuts and bruises.

"Why did I let him do that to me?" Dana cried.

"This is not your fault," Cassidy barked. "That sick bastard is to blame for this! Not you!"

"What happened?" I asked.

"I need to get her to a hospital," Cassidy said. "I can't do it and keep her calm. Can you drive?"

"I got a permit," I said.

"Good enough," she said. "My car is over there."

Cassidy and I sat in the waiting room for what felt like a year. The police had yet to arrive to even get a statement from us. Part of me felt guilty. I had been so busy relishing my triumph, all the while Dana had been so viciously attacked in the most savage manner possible. I hadn't called Cal to let him know what happened. I couldn't pick up the payphone. I couldn't stomach the reality of it and having to say it out loud would force me to do so.

Dana McKaye. I really didn't know her that well. I saw her around school and it was common knowledge that she was heavily involved in chorus and drama. The few times we crossed paths in the hallway, she was always pleasant.

Cassidy rubbed her arms as she tried to generate heat in the arctic room. I removed my blazer and wrapped it around her.

"Thank you," she said, finally breaking the silence.

I took note of the slinky maroon dress she wore, "You look nice. Big night planned?"

She shook her head, "Not really. I was at the concert tonight. I saw her staggering from behind the bleachers. Fucking animal."

"Who was it?"

"Ronny Garrison."

"What?"

Cassidy nodded, "They had been dating for a few weeks. When I found her, she kept muttering his name and kept repeating she couldn't believe he did it to her. Last year Ronny dated a girl, Connie Morgan. She abruptly transferred out of the school in the middle of the term. I figured it was family problems or maybe drugs or something. Now…"

"It all adds up. We'll point this out to the cops if they ever get here. Okay, you just rolled your eyes. Why? You don't think the police are going to do anything?"

"Under the best circumstances, proving a rape is an uphill battle. Garrison comes from old money. On top of that, he's one of the best players on the football team. They're going to back him and they'll pull whatever strings they can with the police to make this go away."

"You can't be serious? For Christ's sake a girl got raped tonight!"

"Look I'm not saying it's right but that's the way it works."

"And you what, play along?"

"It's not that simple."

"It is for me or anyone who's got a conscience. But those are your buddies, the ones you work so hard to win over."

"Hey, don't you judge me," Cassidy cried. "This isn't my fault! And I am not a bad person just because I choose to be a part of the school."

"For your sake I hope you don't fall out of favor with the status quo. We see what results when that happens. Just ask Abby."

Silence resumed and the two of us sat in our seats fuming. Angry with each other and furious over what had happened to a girl who probably wouldn't receive justice. I thought the silence would continue indefinitely. Surprisingly, it was Cassidy who spoke first.

"Well, at least your heart's in the right place," she said. "I suppose that counts for something. And…thank you. For helping me get Dana here. She was hysterical and I wouldn't have been able to keep her calm and drive the car here too."

"Don't mention it."

We sat in silence for a few more moments.

"Your solo was great, for what it's worth," Cassidy said.

"Thanks."

"No doubt you're pleased."

"I was."

We both leapt from our seats to meet Dana's doctor.

"How is she?" Cassidy asked.

"All things considered, she's fine," the doctor said. "She's sleeping right now. We've contacted her sister. She goes to college in Knoxville and is a few hours out. Right now the best thing to do is let her rest. I'll check in on her shortly."

"Thanks doc," I said.

It was sometime after eight the next morning when Cassidy and I returned to campus. We waited until Dana's sister arrived. Neither Cassidy nor I felt right about leaving her alone. Though we were little more than strangers to Dana, it seemed like the right thing to do.

The police eventually arrived and took our statements. While the case should've been open and shut, Cassidy had me convinced that it probably wasn't going to be the case…or a case at all.

Shortly after entering the school, she was proven correct. Standing outside Norrington's office was the headmaster, Ronny and a man holding a notepad who I surmised was a police detective. If he was a cop, he certainly wasn't conducting an investigation as it appeared he was catching up with two buds. Paralyzed by seething rage, I curled my fists as I witnessed the spectacle before me. Cassidy shook her head in disgust and departed. No longer able to bear anymore, I headed to class.

Cal's voice could be heard outside Miller's room. As usual my roommate had found some manner to incur the chemistry teacher's wrath. Of course that usually didn't require anything more than breathing or existing on Cal's part.

"My roommate is missing," Cal explained. "No one's seen him. I've been looking everywhere for him."

"That's no excuse for being late to my class," Miller barked.

Taking that as my cue, I entered the room.

"Noah?" Cal asked. "Where the hell have you been? Is that blood on you?"

I sat down at my desk.

"Noah?" Caleb whispered. "Are you all right? What's going on?"

"Later." I told Cal. This was not the time nor the place.

"Mr. Scott," Miller called out. "I just received a note. Mr. Norrington wants to see you."

I shot back, "I bet he does."

Cassidy was already seated when I arrived at Norrington's office.

"Have a seat, Mr. Scott," the headmaster said. "I understand you and Ms. Reeves had a trying evening. You two should be commended for your actions."

"What's going to happen?' Cassidy asked.

"I've been on the phone this morning with Dana's parents. And it's been agreed that it's probably best for all involved if she finished the term at another school. This will give her a fresh change and an opportunity to cope with whatever happened."

"She was raped, sir," Cassidy claimed.

"We don't know that for certain," Norrington said. "We don't know the specifics. This is a very serious issue. Which is why I wanted to talk to the two of you. I can sympathize with emotions running high right now, but, because we don't have all the facts, I think it's best that we keep this matter discreet. The last thing we need are unfounded rumors circulating the school. We don't want to make this situation any more difficult for Mr. Garrison."

"More difficult for Mr. Garrison?" I repeated. "He's not the victim here, Dana is."

"And I for one don't feel safe with Ronny in this school," Cassidy said.

"Mr. Garrison is innocent until proven otherwise," Norrington said. "And he and I have had a discussion about what's best for this matter. His priorities right now are his classes and the football team. I strongly urge the two of you to focus on your studies and let this matter rest."

"Okay, you were right," I said to Cassidy later in the hallway. "We got to do something."

"There's nothing we can do," Cassidy said. "He made it very clear in there that if we make any waves, he'll have no problem expelling us. I can't afford to get kicked out and neither can you. I'm angry over the situation as much as you are but there's nothing we can do except let it go."

Mr. Tyler's classroom was my next destination. At that point, I simply wanted to sit in a classroom and pretend that I was immersed in my usual routine. Only I wasn't even allowed that luxury. Drawing near to the classroom, I heard adult voices emanating behind the closed door.

"An absolute outrage," Nolan said. "That piece of garbage, Miller. That's the one they should be sacking."

"What are you going to do now, Randy?" asked Ms. Blake, my British Lit teacher. "You're going to appeal right? You still have a chance to speak at the school board hearing tonight."

"I wouldn't count on it," Nolan said. "Those jackals are as crooked as they come. No wonder these brats here emulate them. You heard about what happened to that McKaye girl?"

I twisted the doorknob and entered the room. The discussion ceased. Their gazes were that of shock and pity. I remembered the blood stains on my clothing. On top of Tyler's desk sat a box filled with his personal belongings. Next to Tyler's box was a leather-bound book with golden letters emblazoned on it. It was a text on the occult. It reminded me of the weird dream I previously had.

"Let us know how it goes," Ms. Blake said.

"I will," Mr. Tyler said. "And thank you both."

"I'll see you in class, Mr. Scott," Nolan said. "For now get some much needed rest. Randy."

"Interesting book," I said.

"It's for my kid sister," Tyler said. "She's into the whole supernatural thing."

"I'm sorry I missed class. I had to meet with Mr. Norrington."

"You didn't miss class. I canceled it today."

"What's going on?"

"You guys are going to have a substitute until they've decided on a replacement," Tyler said.

"Wait, are you quitting?"

"Not exactly."

"They're firing you? For what?"

"The official answer is that my teaching methods are not conducive to Hollowstone's education. The real answer is that I refused to roll over for two spoiled jocks."

"They can't do that!" I cried. "They can't just fire you like that."

"When you get older, you'll learn that you can do a lot of things with enough money and the right strings."

"Isn't there anything you can do?"

"There's a school board meeting tonight," Tyler said. "But it's pretty much a done deal. They're pretty much along the lines with Norrington on this."

"But you can at least get a chance to tell your side," I said. "And I can speak on your behalf too. And let the board know how much of a wonderful teacher you are. I can probably get a few other—"

"No."

"What?"

"I don't want you anywhere near that meeting, Noah."

"Why not? I can at least say something."

"No! Listen. I'm a pariah and I'm out of here. But I can take care of myself. I don't want you gaining the same enemies simply for being associated with me. They may try to revoke your scholarship. I promised Helena that I would look out for you. She'd kick my ass if I let something happen."

"Maybe it wouldn't be a bad thing," I said. "To be honest I don't think I want to go to this school anymore. I have half a mind to transfer out of here."

"No," Tyler said firmly. "Whatever you do, promise me you won't do that."

"Why not? This school is corrupt as hell."

"Yeah, but this school can get you into any college and having a diploma from here will take you wherever you want to go. Play it smart. Keep your nose clean and stay off the radar. Graduate. Get into a good college. Who knows maybe one day you'll be in a position to make some changes around here."

Not able to endure any other shockers, I headed for my dorm. The plan? To crawl under the covers and wait until graduation. It appeared that the fates had other ideas. Across the yard stood Ronny and two of his cronies. The three guffawed as Ronny bragged about his attack.

"Yeah I had the bitch begging for more," he claimed.

My fists clenched, I stared at the sick bastard and thought of Dana and what he had done to her. I caught Ronny's eye. He smirked. We both knew the truth and there was nothing I could do about it.

The yank of my blazer collar snapped me back to the present. As much as I struggled Cal refused to let go.

"All right before you disappear again, you're going to tell me what the hell has been going on," he said.

"C'mon," I said.

"Fucking hell," Cal said. "I saw Connie Morgan a few days before she transferred out of the school last year. She was out of it. I figured she just had a bad break up with that asshole. Now it makes sense."

"And he's going to do it again," I said. "And nobody seems to give a damn. And if you try to do the right thing, you get punished for it."

"Like Tyler."

"Like Tyler. I don't know. I promised him that I wouldn't leave, but after seeing all this crap that's been going on, I don't know if I can stay. Part of me thinks I was better off in Atlanta."

"Whoa-whoa-whoa. You can't leave. Whatever you do, don't you do that?"

"Not you too. Is this the part where you tell me that in spite of everything I get a top-notch education and staying is for my own good?"

"Screw that, I'm thinking about me. I'm not losing one of the few decent people at this school. You leave, you're taking me with you. You know, I have a trump card that I had been saving in case I did something crazy my senior year. But it seems now as good as any time to use it."

"Do I need to post your bail now or later?"

"I'll meet you back at the dorm room. I've got a few phone calls to make and then the headmaster and I are going to have a little chat. I don't have much time but I like a challenge."

"What are you going to do Cal?"

"Ask me no questions and I'll tell you no lies. I'm going to keep you in the dark so when the shit hits the fan, you can't be blamed for anything."

"I get it. I didn't know. I wasn't in on it. I couldn't have stopped you."

"Don't worry. Everything is going to work itself out. Head back to the dorm and get some rest. You look like hell."

Upon departure, I overheard Cal chatting on his cell.

"Hey Burke," he said. "I think you and I may be able to do business after all."

Chapter Six

My alarm clock blared. On the other side of the room, Cal's bed was made and my roommate was nowhere to be found. Seeing that the earth was still rotating, I decided to go about my normal day. I didn't have to wander far in order to learn that this day was going to be anything but that.

Sirens blared as a fleet of police cruisers rested on the campus. Law enforcement officers of various agencies marched around. Canines were escorted into the gymnasium while students and faculty looked on. As I pushed through the crowd to get a view of the show, I spotted Tyler looking on with a slight smirk on his face.

"You're still here," I said.

"And it's great to see you too," Tyler said.

"You're not sacked?" I asked.

"Funny thing happened last night," Tyler said. "The board meeting was canceled. Miraculous isn't it?"

"I'll say."

Tyler stared at me suspiciously. "Uh huh."

Wanting to change the subject post haste, I quickly asked, "What happened?"

"You haven't heard?"

I got my answer as two officers escorted a handcuffed Ronny and placed him in the back of a police cruiser.

"It seems that police are here to investigate some major drug trafficking. They got an anonymous tip. And it seems they found several bricks of heroin in Mr. Garrison's locker and dorm room. And they found vials of steroids in some of the other players' lockers. Norrington has been trying to spin this all day with the media. God only knows what strings he's pulling to get this story buried."

And that's when it clicked. Burke was the drug dealer Cal argued with at the party. It was the same Burke who Cal mentioned doing business with on his cell yesterday.

"What's going to happen with the players?"

"I imagine there will be an investigation and I'm sure there's going to be drug and steroid testing. God help any of them if the results come back positive. Most of them will lawyer up and get out of any real trouble. One thing is for certain, the school's football season is shot."

They say two wrongs don't make a right and before that day I would've agreed. While I didn't completely agree with Cal's actions—and he knew I wouldn't which is why he kept me in the dark about his plans—this was one of those morally ambiguous situations where the ends justified the means. I didn't ask questions or try to stop Cal because I wanted justice for Dana and Mr. Tyler and I knew that wouldn't happen through the conventional route. Though Cal had ample reasons to stick it to the establishment, the truth is that he was acting on my behest. The only thing I was worried about now was that this ordeal was going to come back and haunt both of us.

With classes canceled I returned to the dorm. Lounging on his bed, Cal nodded hello to me as he laughed on the phone.

"Yeah, I got a girlfriend," Cal said. "But she doesn't compare to you. You just say the word and I'll leave her."

My jaw dropped.

"I mean she's great and all, but she's just a girl and I need a woman," Cal said. "A woman who knows how to keep me in line and can keep me on my toes. Oh I know you would. I think I've met my match in you. You say the word and I'll leave her and you and I can run away together. Tahiti. Italy. Yeah, you're right, Spain is lovely this time of year." Cal erupted into laughter. "You are too much for me. I know you break hearts all the time. Yeah, you're right. The world isn't ready for the two of us. Okay, next lifetime then. You and me. Bonnie and Clyde. It's a date."

"Who are you talking to?" I asked.

"Yes, just one second," Cal said. He handed me the phone. "It's your grandmother."

"Hi, Nanna. Yes, that's Caleb. Yes....he is quite a charmer. Nanna! You're old enough to be his great-grandmother! Yes, I'm doing fine. My grades are well. Yes, ma'am. Yes, I've found a nice church here. No, I am not getting Caleb into trouble and he is not innocent. Yes. I'll let him know. I love you too. Bye." I hung up the phone. "Nanna wanted me to let you know that you're invited to spend the holidays with us if you don't have plans."

"Thanks, I may just do that," he said. "So, how was class today?"

"Splendid considering it was canceled due to a drug sting. Did you have to frame the entire football team?"

"I didn't."

"What? Wait, I heard you chatting with your buddy Burke."

"Yeah and I called my lawyer and informed her that she may want to contact the federal authorities because a certain Ronald Garrison was trafficking drugs and that a few bricks might be found in his gym locker. I also told her about Dana. My lawyer was all too happy to cooperate. She helps the feds make a major drug bust, they owe her a favor down the line. I figured Norrington wouldn't have the feds in his pocket like he does the local Barney Fifes. The steroids I knew nothing about. That was just one hell of a coincidence."

"You mean to tell me that the team was doping and you inadvertently busted them by setting up Ronny."

"Pretty much."

"Okay, so how did you get Norrington to reinstate Tyler?"

"You remember when we first met that I told you how I like my gadgets and my toys?"

"Yeah."

He tossed me a pen.

"Look at it closer."

"It's a camera."

"A digital camcorder to be precise. There was a rumor among the faculty that Norrington was having an affair with one of his secretaries. As much as I was in and out of his office, planting one of these bad boys was too easy. I didn't think he'd be stupid enough to actually do the deed in his office. I'm going to save your stomach and spare you the details about what the headmaster gets into. I'll just say this much, he gives a bad name to dirty old men everywhere.

"The good headmaster and I had a good chat in his office and I showed him one of his adult videos. To spare himself the humiliation of scandal, not to mention an expensive divorce, he reluctantly agreed to reinstate Mr. Tyler and expel Garrison. I simply pointed out that a drug dealer is the last thing we need in the school, football player or not. And I also got him to put a leash on that pitbull, Miller. I gotta say, it's going to be nice to finally be able to sit in class without being Miller's punching bag."

"Well, hopefully we'll still be roommates when we get locked up."

"Sorry, Altar Boy," Cal said. "But you don't get any credit for this.

You're the good little musician. Roommates or not, no one's going to believe you had a hand in this. If I go down, it's going to be me and me alone. After all, I did all the work. Why should you get any of the credit? Norrington is too concerned about covering his ass. He's not going to do anything to jeopardize it."

"He's going to put two and two together."

"He's not that bright." He delivered one of his trademark reassuring smiles. "You gotta admit one thing."

"Oh yeah, what's that?"

"Payback's a bitch."

In less than twenty-four hours, Cal had committed drug trafficking, framing, and extortion and I was an accomplice. I thanked God he was my best friend. Because I knew I did not want him for an enemy.

For the next several days, I waited for the boom to be lowered. Thankfully it never happened. I passed Norrington in the hallways. Expecting a scowl of death, I was shocked when he gave me a warm hello. Perhaps he was simply acting and biding his time or maybe Cal was right in that he didn't think I was in on the blackmail. For the sake of my nerves, I opted to believe the latter.

Speculation was at an all-time as the school awaited the results of the steroid tests. The verdict? Over half of the players had been doping which explained the successful season the team had been having. The Hollowstone Knights were disqualified from competing for the season. Though the news was downplayed in the media, news of the scandal spread like the proverbial epidemic. Our glorious football team was now the laughingstock of the entire town and surrounding areas. Not surprising, Coach Phelps was most conspicuous by his absence. I'm sure his lawyers advised him to keep a low profile even though it was never established if he was in on the steroid use or not. But if half of your team is doping, how could you not know? No longer were the football players strutting down the hallways with their chests poked out. Most of them kept their heads slumped and averted stares and ignored the whispers from their peers.

Cal and I were on our way to class when we passed Chris and three of his flunkies in the hallway. As usual they scoffed in disgust.

"Hey Chris!" Cal cried. "Tell me, do steroids really cause shrinkage or are you just a sad little man?"

The entire hallway roared as students guffawed at Chris and the other athletes. The very student body who blindly worshipped the jocks and treated them like gods now openly mocked and ridiculed them. Chris could only make a hasty exit.

"Way to kick them when they're down," I said.

"Please, it's about time those assholes get taken down a peg or two," Caleb said. "This calls for a celebration."

"Yeah, because that worked so well last time," I said.

"Oh, Noah, raves are so last season. I'm thinking we throw a soiree. A legitimate one. Something classy, but not stuffy. The point is to have a blast. This will be the bash to end all bashes."

"And what's the occasion?"

"Isn't it obvious? We're celebrating the downfall of the Hollowstone Academy football team. It's not every day they get humiliated and we should relish every moment of it."

"You're insane," I laughed. "We'd be lucky to get anyone to show up. Especially after last time."

"You know for an altar boy, you are of so little faith. People are always looking for the flimsiest excuse to shirk their responsibilities and party their heads off. What do you say?"

The masquerade was in full swing when I arrived. Garbed in elaborate gowns and suits, the masked guests waltzed and swayed to the orchestra which played on the stage in the ballroom. I weaved through the throngs of students. I wasn't sure what I was searching for, but I had to find it. Across the ballroom, Cal was on one knee, handing a white rose to Abigail. Behind them, a cloaked silhouette emerged from the shadows. I pushed my way through the crowd, screaming to warn my friends. The Phantom brandished a scythe from underneath his cape and struck down his target.

I shot out of my bed, gasping heavily. Cal slumbered soundly. At least one of us was able to sleep these days.

The Lazarus Hotel was the sole five star hotel in Newton. Appropriately the hotel's largest banquet hall would be the setting for Cal's next party. A semi formal event, the party was by invitation only. Each of these events was a masterpiece for Cal and he meticulously made sure each detail was fine-tuned. Caleb hired a couple of art students to design the invitations. From there he repeatedly made sure that the names on his list matched the names on the invites. This was in the event that his employees decided to make an extra couple of bucks and produce a few extra copies to anyone desperate enough to pay to get into his party.

It didn't take long for word to get around school and pretty soon I found myself being repeatedly begged to talk Cal into adding them on the list. Usually, I managed to worm out of it with a simple, "I can't make any promises, but I'll see what I can do." And once again Cal's words came to pass. I found myself with a newfound popularity simply because the masses wanted something from Cal and by extension they wanted something from me. One student wasn't happy about my newfound status. Of course that student was rarely happy, if ever.

Cassidy glared at me with crossed arms.

"What you two are doing is absolutely disgusting," she said.

"No doubt you've heard about the party," I said.

"You know what happened with the football team is tragic, but rather than trying to help the school heal, you two are gloating about it and throwing a party."

"Duly noted."

I walked on. Cassidy followed.

"This whole ordeal reflects badly on the entire school," she said. "And you two seem hell bent on basking in our humiliation. I expect as much from Cal, but I thought you had a conscience."

And with that I halted in my tracks.

"Who's the vice president of the student council?" I asked.

"What?"

"Who is the vice president of the student council?"

"Chris Goddard. You know that."

"The very same Chris Goddard who tested positive for steroids? And yet he's still VP. How is that? After all, being on the student council is more than doing tasks. It is about honor and respectability. This is a position of leadership and you very well can't respect a leader if there are allegations and scandals running about. And yet no one has impeached him like they did Abby. I wonder why. Oh wait, I know. Because of his sister. And shooting steroids up your ass is far worse than attending some party. If those bastards get a much needed dose of humility, then so much the better. So why don't you do us all a favor and check your moral compass at the door. Because it's clearly broken!"

I stormed off leaving Cassidy dumbfounded. Turning a corner I found another argument in progress. Eli stood between Ryan and Chet. Ryan gathered his books from the ground.

"What the fuck is your problem?" Chet asked.

"All I'm saying is leave the guy alone," Eli said. "He doesn't bother anyone. And you guys are always picking on him."

"He's a fag," Chet replied. "And what are you his boyfriend?"

"Most of the school is pissed at all of us because you and the others let Phelps talk you into shooting up. Picking on him isn't going to make you any cooler. Now back the hell off."

"Whatever man," Chet said. "I'm out of here."

"Will you relax, Burke," Cal said on his cell when he entered the dorm. "You have nothing to worry about. I told you, I moved the stuff through the usual channels. I don't know how it wound up in that kid's locker. I don't even know the idiot. Insulting my mother isn't going to help matters. Will you please calm the fuck down? This will blow over. Just lay low for awhile and then it'll be back to business as usual. Tell your boss to do the same thing. He got his money. He should be happy. Yes I know there's a lot of heat right now. That's why I'm telling you to lay low. Tell you what. Just so there's no bad blood between me and you, I'll hook you up with another payment. Fine. The usual spot. I'll swing through tonight around nine. Later."

"Do I even want to know?"

"Oh just Burke having a hissy fit. Nothing to worry about. How was your day?"

"Cold. I think it's going to snow."

Cal laughed, "It never snows in Newton."

"What are you talking about?"

"It never snows in Newton. It's never once snowed in Newton, even though we're in the mountains. It will snow in surrounding areas. But there has never been a recorded case of it snowing in the town. Some people think it's just some meteorological phenomenon. Others think the Cherokees cursed the land or something. But yeah, that's one of the town's popular slogans, it never snows in Newton."

"Learn something new every day. What's with the clipboard?"

"Just reviewing the list for the party. Realized I need to make a few more invites. And I was also thinking of inviting a couple of more people. Any suggestions?"

"Actually, yeah. Ryan. Ryan Foster."

"Yeah, he's cool."

"And Eli."

"Eli? Elias Cole? And we would be inviting one of the preps why?"

"He's one of the few football players who isn't a tool. And he helped me out in class one day."

"You really are a bad liar, Noah."

"I have my reasons, okay."

"Fine. He probably won't even show anyway. Okay now we need to up the babe quotient. I think I've invited most of the hot girls but you can never be too sure. Hey, I know, we can invite Cassidy."

"Cassidy? Cassidy Reeves? The Ice Queen? No way in hell!"

"Yeah, she is uptight. I think that's what makes her hot."

"I did mention ice queen right? And stuck up?"

"Yeah and she likes you."

"Okay….um….one of us has lost his damn mind and I'm fairly certain it's not me."

"Dude, I know women and I've seen the way she looks at you. I'm telling you, she's hot for your ass."

"You're delusional. She treats me like crap every chance she gets."

"Noah, Noah, Noah. You have so much to learn. You know how little boys show affection for a girl they like by pulling their pigtails or throwing rocks at them?"

"Yeah?"

"Well, women do the same thing, except the pigtails and throwing rocks. Although one of my exes did throw a brick through my windshield when I refused to get back together with her."

"You're wrong about this, Cal."

"Am I? You've said it yourself, she's always pissed off at you and treats you like crap. The opposite of love isn't hate, it's apathy. If you weren't on her radar, you wouldn't be getting her hot and bothered. She may not consciously know it yet, but mark my words, she's into you."

"I don't even know why I'm listening to you."

"I think it's awesome. You got some serious options. And you've said that Brianna has been giving you the brush off."

"Ever since the trip. I rarely see her and the few times I do, she seems distant."

"There you go. It might be time for you to move on. You and

Cassidy would be one of the golden couples at the school. And considering you're the only two black students, you would be the Huxtables 2.0."

"Why am I listening to you? I'm not listening to you."

"You know I'm telling the truth. Cassidy's smart, she's gorgeous. And that uptight thing she's got going. So sexy. It's like she's just begging for someone to loosen her up, if you know what I mean. I'm telling you, if I wasn't in love with Abby, I'd be all on that. Hmmm. You know, I might be able to talk Abby into having a threesome with Cassidy. I do have a birthday coming up. Actually, I don't, but she doesn't need to know that."

I chucked my history textbook at Cal.

"Ouch," he cried. "Okay. I won't invite her. And no threesomes…..for now."

"Hey, Cal."

"Yeah?"

"I was reading your blog."

"Good boy."

"What happened with Jason?"

"I told you, he overdosed."

"Yeah. But you say in your posts that he never fooled with drugs. Why would he start out of the blue?"

Cal sat on his mattress. He grabbed the back of his neck and stared at the floor.

"Seth, Fenn, and me were tight but Jason and I just clicked. I think it was because we balanced each other out. He was the responsible one and I'm well…me. It's funny you would be asking about him. You two are so much alike. Very quiet but it's obvious you got more dimension than most people would notice." The pain on Cal's face made me regret asking. "But Jason had issues. Mental issues. He had a nervous breakdown about a year before I met him. He had to take medication every day to remain coherent. He was always fine and then a few days before he died, he just started acting crazy. Constantly talking to himself. Dancing on the ledge of a roof, insane shit. The medication just stopped working."

Cal's eyes were red. "And then I found him in the bathroom. I like to think he's in a better place and that maybe his time with me was fun." He rubbed his eyes. Placing on a brave smile, Cal said, "And on that dreary note, let's go party."

Despite the semi formal theme of the party, it didn't stop the attendants from behaving as if they were in a nightclub. Although a DJ spun tracks in one corner, a stage was set on the other side of the hall for a band to play. Cal made out with Abby in a corner. Eli and Ryan chatted near a punch bowl.

"Sup guys," I greeted. "Enjoying yourselves?"

"Yeah," Ryan said. "Thanks for the invite."

"I'm surprised I didn't get tarred and feathered the second I walked into the hall," Eli said.

"Oh, that's later," I said. "Cal didn't think you would show."

"You can either get mad about all of this or take it on the chin and make the most of it," Eli said. "Besides we deserve whatever happens to us."

"For what it's worth, no one's got anything against you," I said. "You were always the exception to the rule."

"Well, thanks," Eli said.

"Well you boys have fun," I said. I then stated lowly, "Oh and FYI, they do have available rooms here. Not as fun as a dark classroom, but I'm sure you two can manage."

They stared at me with terror. My grin assured them that their secret was safe with me. I meandered through the crowd, waving to a few familiar faces from class.

"Sup, Vaughn," I greeted.

"Hey, Noah," he replied.

Brianna casually entered the banquet hall. When I found her near the door, she was in the middle of flirting heavily with two guys. She laughed as she ran her hands across their cheeks. When I caught her eye, she made it clear that she wanted me to see it. I suppose this was where I was supposed to get angry and cause a scene.

Instead, I simply turned on my heel. Nanna always told me that if I fight to win a girl or keep her, then she wasn't worth having.

"Why the long face," Brianna asked, after catching up to me. "Everything okay?"

"You seemed preoccupied," I said. "Didn't want to disturb you."

"Oh, them. No need to get jealous. Besides I've been meaning to talk to you."

"All right. Let's find some place to talk."

"No need, this'll be quick. Look, the 'altar boy' thing was cute but it's gotten old. I've really been patient about the no sex policy but the fact is that I need a man. A real man, not a little boy."

I shook my head in disgust. "You're not fooling anyone, Bri. I see right through you."

"Oh, really?"

"This isn't about sex or me being an altar boy. This is about you being scared."

Brianna cackled.

"Your entire life, you never got any love from mommy or daddy and you've put on this whole bad girl façade to protect yourself. So the first time you actually date a guy who isn't trying to use you for sex, but actually likes you for you, what happens. You turn into a bitch, because it's easier to run him off than risk someone getting close. Seeing as I'm not your bellhop, keep your baggage."

"Is that what they teach you in Sunday school? About girls like me?"

"No I learned that from the school of walking clichés."

I didn't get very far from Brianna before an arm placed me in a firm headlock.

"You're not leaving are you?" Cal asked.

"Nope. Just getting some air."

He released me, "Everything okay?"

"I just officially ended things with Bri."

"Dude. Sorry to hear that."

"Don't be. It needed to be done. Trust me."

"Well, I have a surprise that might cheer you up. Stay right here."

Cal hopped on stage.

"Let's give a huge round to DJ Krush spinning some hot tracks," Cal said.

The DJ bowed to the roaring ovation.

"Now, I wanna thank you guys for coming out and celebrating the defeat of those glorified inbreds known as the Hollowstone Knights football team. The lost couldn't have happened to a finer group of lads."

The crowd laughed.

"Except for you Eli," Cal said. "Everybody give Eli a round of applause for being the one cool guy on the team." Cal waited for the applause to die down before he continued. "Of course, Elias, you could've spared the school some embarrassment had you simply stepped forward and told everybody that your teammates like to take it up the ass…the steroids that is."

The laughter resumed.

"Not that there's anything wrong with taking it up the ass," Cal said. "Isn't that right Ryan? I'm just joking. Ryan's a great guy and I'm glad he's here. Between you and me Ryan, I always thought you were a very good looking guy. I'm secure enough in my sexuality to admit that. If I were gay, we'd be getting a room later tonight. Hell, if I get drunk as I plan on getting, you and I might still be getting a room later tonight, regardless."

Ryan's face was beet red as he and the others guffawed and applauded Cal. Abby covered her face and shook her head.

"All right guys, I have a little surprise for you. Some very nice people decided to make a little detour on their world tour and stop here in Newton. You may have heard of them seeing as they have the number one album in the world. Without further ado, here are the Cynical Sirens!"

The crowd screamed and clapped as the five members took their places on the stage with their instruments. Donned in vintage t-shirts and jeans, the five college-aged band members epitomized the alternative rock star. The female singer, Grace, tossed back her dark red hair and stepped forward to the mic stand. She placed her guitar strap around her head.

"What's up Hollowstone," she yelled. "Let's do this."

The audience bobbed their heads and cheered as the band performed several of their songs. Once again Cal had proven why his parties were the stuff of legends. To this day I have no idea how he pulled this off, but if it were possible he outdid himself. I wasn't the only one who thought so. Cal shook hands and exchanged high-fives with Ryan, Vaughn and Eli. The audience cheered as the Sirens concluded their sixth song.

"Thank you," Grace said. "All right so the next song we're going to perform is 'We're Done.'"

The spectators hooted and cheered.

"But we need a little help with the song. I hear there's a kick-ass musician in the house; a violinist in fact."

Oh, God no. I thought. Cal didn't.

"Where's this guy at?" Grace asked.

"He's right here!" Cal yelled behind me. "Here he is!"

With a fistful of my blazer jacket, my roommate dragged me to the stage.

"I'm going to kill you, Caleb!" I warned.

"So you keep telling me." He replied.

"Hey, there cutie," Grace greeted. "What's your name?"

"Noah. Noah Scott."

"You're adorable. Got a girlfriend?"

"Not anymore."

A large "ooooooooooh" emanated from the crowd. I realized after the fact that technically I had just officially dumped Brianna for a sexy rocker chick in front of an audience.

"You and I might be meeting up after the show," Grace said. "You know the song?"

"Yeah," I said. "Backwards and forwards but I don't have my violin."

"You mean this?" Cal asked.

He handed me my violin case.

"Let's rock," she said.

The bassist strummed a few strings and the drummer pounded away. On cue, I began to play and the song commenced.

"You played your cards wanting a little fun," Grace sung. "I'm laughing last because you're on the run. It's done. It's done."

Despite my numerous stage performances, this was the first time that I actually felt like a rock star. For those five brief minutes, that's exactly what I was. All efforts to keep from smiling were futile. Despite everything I was on top of the world. At the end of the song, the band gave me an ovation as Grace gave me a kiss on the lips. The drama with Brianna was the farthest thing from my mind. As far as breakups went, that was the perfect way to end a relationship. For that matter, it was the perfect way to end a whirlwind of a semester.

Chapter Seven

I was all too excited to return to Atlanta for the winter break. It wasn't so much that I was homesick, but I was ready to return to a life that was familiar, stable and normal.

Nanna commemorated my triumphant return with an endless number of hugs and kisses. Next, came the examination where her diagnosis was that I had gotten more handsome but thinner because I wasn't eating enough, according to her. This of course would be remedied by the three course meal she prepared. As I ate, she drilled me about the school and life with the rich white kids. I told her that I had made honor roll and showed her my report card as proof. I also gave her a copy of my concert program.

Suffice it to say I omitted all of the crazy ordeals that had happened. Nanna should have only good things to say when she spoke to Mrs. Jenkins who would broadcast to the neighborhood that Ruby Scott's great-grandson was doing well at that fancy private school up in the mountains. It was good practice as I did the same thing with Ms. Ramirez when I visited her.

I spent the next several days practicing my violin. Per Nolan's instructions, I kept a detailed log of the number of times I practiced and which pieces I performed. When I wasn't practicing or being stuffed at the kitchen table by my doting grandmother, I finally caught up on some much needed sleep. For the first time in ages, there hadn't been any bizarre nightmares.

It was a few days before Christmas and I had just returned from the mall shopping for Nanna's gift.

"Nanna, I'm home," I stated as I shut the door behind me.

"We're in the kitchen," Nanna replied.

"We?" I said.

Entering the kitchen, I found Cal stuffing his face with chess pie while Nanna sipped from her coffee mug.

"Surprise," Cal greeted.

"I'll say!" I said. "What are you doing here? Not that I'm not glad to see you. But weren't you spending the holidays with Abby in Aspen?"

"Plans changed," he said. "I thought I'd take you up on your offer to spend the holidays with my best bud and this beautiful and gifted cook."

"Oh, you hush," she blushed. "I'm gonna have to watch you. And yes. You are more than welcome to spend the holidays with Noah and me. There's plenty of room and plenty to eat. Another slice of chess pie?"

"Yes, ma'am," he said.

"So, Caleb, how are your classes?"

"I can't complain, all things considered," he said. "Miraculously I skirted by chemistry with a D+, much to Miller's chagrin. I did get an A+ in creative writing."

"Yes, Noah told me that you're a writer."

"Yes, ma'am."

"Well good. I'm going to have to read some of your stuff," Nanna said. "It's good to see young people so talented. And I trust you and my grandson are staying out of trouble."

"Oh, I could tell you stories. But judging by the way your grandson is scowling at me I won't. Otherwise I'd be sleeping with one eye open. Oh, that reminds me, Mrs. Scott. I recorded Noah's concert with my digital camera. I have the DVD for you to watch later."

Nanna squealed in delight, "Oh, perfect."

That evening I found Cal gazing at a photo. It was a portrait of him, Abby, and me. Standing in front of the hotel in California, the three of us beamed while ensnared in a group hug.

"I remember that photo," I said.

"Yeah," Cal said. "Thanks for letting me hang here for the holidays."

"Hey, mi casa and all that."

Absent was his trademark smile.

"Caleb? What happened with Abby? Why aren't you in Aspen with her?"

"She left me."

"What? What happened?"

"It was a day after you left for home. Abby and I were having lunch in the cafeteria. Her parents showed up."

"The preacher?"

He nodded. "The bastard wouldn't even shake my hand. I heard them arguing as he escorted her to the car. He went on about how he got reports that she had been acting like a whore and had been gallivanting around with trash. Three guesses who I spotted gloating at the whole ordeal."

"You've got to be kidding me. Goddard? Son of a bitch. God only knows what he told her folks."

"No doubt the same lies he spread around school. I tried calling and emailing her repeatedly. She finally sent me an email saying that she couldn't be with me anymore and that she was sorry."

"That's it? Just like that?"

"Exactly what I thought. I flew out to Houston to see her. I waited until night, hopped the gate and snuck onto the grounds."

"Cal, are you crazy?"

"Don't worry. I was careful. I peeked through the window and saw Abby and her folks having dinner with Chris, Phyllis and the senator. The way Chris had his arm around her, it was all I could do not to bust through that glass and throttle the bastard."

"I remember Brianna telling me that Abby's parents were supporting Goddard's campaign. They were brokering some deal or something."

"That explains why Abby's folks are so invested in who she dates. Cause it sure as hell wasn't parental concern."

"So, what happened?"

"After the dinner, I finally caught Abby wandering around alone near the pool house. I confronted her and demanded she give me an explanation. She owed me that much."

"What did she say?"

"She stated that she couldn't reason with her parents and they weren't allowing her to see me. They even threatened to yank her out of school and cut her off. She tried to tell them about the lies Chris spread, but they didn't believe her and in fact they defended him. They said that when she acts like a whore, rumors will spread."

"They don't want anything to interfere with their precious transaction. And their kids breaking up will do that. Do you know what the deal is about?"

"Some type of funding for a land deal and some tax breaks or something," Cal said. "There's always some deal or some transaction going on with those people."

"So what happened next?"

"She told me she loved me and that this was the hardest thing for her to do. I pleaded with her and told her how much I loved her. She said she couldn't keep fighting everyone on all fronts. I told her to run away with me, to forget about school. She said she couldn't. She said goodbye."

"I'm sorry."

"Yeah. You know what's the worst thing about all of this is? I could almost live with the fact that we couldn't be together. It's painful but I could deal. It's the fact that she has to stay with that prick Goddard in order to keep the parental units happy. And Chris wins once again."

"At least you got to tell her goodbye."

"She's the reason I went to Hollowstone. I met her after I got kicked out of Mom's house."

"What happened with you and your folks?"

"Well, since I'm spilling my guts I might as well go all out. I grew up in Winridge, Minnesota; very small town and very conservative. My mom was a waitress and got pregnant with me when she was sixteen. She worked two jobs trying to provide for us.

"Single moms living in a trailer home were considered lesser than dirt. A fact we were reminded of every day. My mom was all too quick to latch on to the first creep who made a pass at her. Most of the guys she dated were losers. Drunks, deadbeat dads, ex cons, you name it. Most of them freeloaded off of her. Last guy she was with was the worst. His name was Darryl. He used to use her for a punching bag. Anytime I tried to protect Mom, I got my ass kicked too. I begged her to leave the guy. She wouldn't listen. She defended him stating what a good man he was and that we both needed to quit stressing him out.

"One night, Mom was at work and Darryl came home drunk. He started picking a fight with me. I locked myself in my room and called the cops on him. They showed up and arrested him. Turns out he had a couple of warrants on him. When Mom got home, I told her what happened. She went ballistic...on me. She said that I was being ungrateful and accused me of trying to ruin her happiness and break up the family. We got into a huge fight and I mentioned that I wish I knew who my father was because he couldn't be any worse than her. And that's when she told me about my dad.

"He was some guy who came into the restaurant one night during her shift. One thing led to another. And nine months later I arrived."

"Oh, man."

"Mom told me that she tried to contact him. But because he was married and had his vast wealth to think about, he wanted nothing to do with either of us. She was all too quick to point out how he threatened to ruin her if she started making waves and how he didn't give a damn about us because he was too busy living in his palace with his perfect family. She told me that she was going to bail Darryl out of jail and she expected me to apologize to him. I told her there was no way in hell that was going to happen. I packed my things. She told me if I left don't ever bother coming back. And I bounced. I left that trailer and I didn't look back. I crashed with friends here and there and pretty soon I found myself eating at soup kitchens and staying at homeless shelters. I had no idea what I was going to do next."

"And that's when you met Abby?"

Cal nodded, "Most beautiful girl I ever saw. She was doing charity work with her youth group, they were traveling throughout the country or something. She tried to convert me and of course I wasn't interested but I kind of pretended like I would be with enough prodding. I just wanted to spend time with her. I knew she was the one for me. I told her my story and she actually gave me the money to find my father. I wouldn't take it but she wasn't going to take no for an answer."

"So, did you find your dad?"

"Yeah. I found him all right. And true to Mom's word, he was loaded. A rich CEO who's worth billions. I won't even tell you what it took for me to slip past his security to meet him. He made it clear that he wanted nothing to do with me. He told me, and I quote, that if I ever darkened his doorstep again, he would see to it that the job would be finished that the abortionist should've started.

"I found an expensive lawyer, a real shark. She took my case. She knew she had hit the jackpot with me as a client and if I kept her on retainer, she'd rake in millions from the publicity alone if the case went public. He took me far more seriously when I lawyered up. Not wanting a scandal, he agreed to pay me. My lawyer also helped me get my emancipated minor status. So now I was a free teen with billions to burn."

"Did you ever talk to your mother again?"

"No. I sent her some money but I never contacted her. She

probably let Darryl spend it all. But, I wouldn't be where I am if it wasn't for Abby. That's why I kept my distance from her during freshmen year, when I found out she was with Goddard. I wanted to bide my time until the right moment came along."

"I had no idea," I said.

"Now, it's over. I don't know what I'm going to do now. It's going to be impossible to see her at school, after everything, especially seeing her with that ass Goddard."

"You'll survive."

"I guess."

"No. I mean you'll survive. That's what you do. You came from nothing and made something of yourself. Most people twice our age couldn't do what you did. You thought your life was over when you were homeless and look how that turned out. Sure things seem bleak right now but maybe something else is on the horizon."

The next day, the two of us decided to venture to a spoken word event being held at the Java Stop in Decatur. It took us nearly two hours to get across town. Cal's road rage kept me amused.

"Fucking traffic!" he cried. "This is ridiculous!"

I simply smiled and leaned back in my seat, "Welcome to Atlanta."

We eventually made it to the front door of the Java Stop.

"I've wanted to do one of these things for ages," Cal said. "They don't exactly have this stuff in Newton."

"You're performing?" I asked.

"Hell yeah I'm performing. I've got a new poem and everything. Finally, I get to fellowship with fellow writers, my brethren. I finally get to connect and be at one with my people. Mark my words Altar Boy, I'm going to fit in just fine."

We entered the coffee shop to find a packed house. The walls painted with green and brown earth tone patterns, the shop had a Neo-Soul décor to it. Appropriately the crowd consisted of college-aged black attendants. Most of them gazed suspiciously at Cal and myself; primarily Cal.

"Fit in with your people, huh?" I said.

"You gotta appreciate the irony," Cal said before he released a deep breath. "Nothing to fear. I'm just a scared white boy who is so out of his element, surrounded by people who look like they would love nothing more than to kick my ass."

I giggled, "Now, you know how I feel at Hollowstone. Do you want to leave?"

"Thinking about it," Cal said.

"Of course you do know that traffic isn't going to die down for another hour or so."

"Execution it is then. Besides if you're man enough to stand tall against those white supremacists at school, then I'm man enough to do this. Even if the crowd opts to kill whitey."

A petite dark-skinned woman with a maroon African head wrap approached us. With a clipboard in hand, she wore a warm beaming smile.

"Hello there sexy," Cal whispered.

"Hello," greeted the woman. "My name is Johnnie. Are you here for the spoken word?"

"We are," Cal said flashing his trademark smile. "I'm Cal and this is Noah."

"It's a pleasure to meet you both," Johnnie said. "Is this your first time here?"

Cal and I nodded.

"Cal was interested in performing," I said. "If that's okay?"

"Oh, wow," Johnnie said. "That's fine we've never had a performer so—"

"White?" Cal finished.

Johnnie giggled, "Young was the word I was going to say."

Cal and I sheepishly turned our gaze from the laughing hostess.

"It's just that we were getting the evil eye from some of the others," Cal said.

"Most of us are from Hilton College or live near the area. You guys are in what, middle school?"

"High school," Cal and I said simultaneously.

Johnnie pointed to a white cashier who grinned and waved at us.

"That's my husband," she explained. "So you see, you don't have to worry. Everyone is welcome here. And yes Cal, we would love for you to perform. I'll put you in one of the middle slots."

"I appreciate it," Cal said.

"No problem, at all. I have to go make sure everything is set up. Make yourselves at home and give me a shout if you need anything."

"Thank you," I said.

"You guys are the cutest couple."

"Couple?" I repeated.

"Yes you two remind me of my uncle and his partner," Johnnie said.

"What can I say?" Cal replied turning to me, "I just can't seem to quit you, Noah Scott."

He kissed me on the lips. I stood frozen in fright and embarrassment as Johnnie grinned and waved goodbye.

"And just so we're clear, you're the wife," Cal said.

My teeth gritted, I vowed, "I'm killing you in your sleep tonight."

"Yeah, yeah. Promises, promises."

"Let's go find us some seats."

Cal slapped my ass, "Yes, dear."

The Java Stop eventually filled to standing capacity. I was relieved, and I imagine Cal more so, when the crowd diversified: Latinos, Asians, Arabs and whites, all appearing to be in their early twenties. One by one the performers took the stage, each passionately sharing their stories and experiences about politics, religion, relationships, sorrow and joy in the lyrical form. Each poet was exceptional.

"Our next performer is definitely one of our youngest to date," Johnnie introduced. "Show your love for Cal."

Cal strode to the microphone, giving a broad wave to the applauding audience. "How are you all doing? This is a new poem I wrote. It's entitled, To the Dance:

The full moon beams brightly on this hapless night,
Lured to the den by the unlikeliest of captors,
He realizes his twilight is near.

So he dances.
He dances to surrender
He dances to forget
He dances to find the symmetry,
He dances to numb
He dances to mend
He dances for it to end,

He dances, he dances,

Mannequins stand poised, peering ahead,
Spectators in a coliseum

As lions within ravage him,
A prince among heathens,
Surrounded by them all,
He never felt so alone,

Primal is the music
Pounding him to the core
His steps those of tribal ancestors
Performing the ritual dances,
 Invoking powers from beyond,
Shocked is all,
His body galvanized,
One final stand,
Going into the night,
His departure anything but quiet,

So he dances,
He dances to surrender
He dances to forget
He dances to find the symmetry,
He dances to numb
He dances to mend
He dances for it to end,

His vision becomes focused
A charge roams throughout his skin
His time draws near,
 The Reaper's scythe
 Will greet him with a kiss,

A small kiss
A kiss that triggered all of this
A kiss that sent him spiraling
A kiss that brought reason to Faust's plight
For such a token could easily launch a thousand ships,

So he dances,
He dances to surrender
He dances to forget
He dances to find the symmetry,

He dances to numb
He dances to mend
He dances for it to end,

Images of his life speed past him
Racing to his conclusion,
And before the last call is sounded
He understands it all,

With a single tear
His heart is betrayed
And with a finger he bows,
Bidding the world ado,
The curtain falls
He exits the stage,

And so he dances,
He dances to surrender
He dances to forget
He dances to find the symmetry,
He dances to numb
He dances to mend
He dances for it to end,

He dances, he dances,

He dances to surrender
He dances to forget
He dances to find the symmetry,
He dances to numb
He dances to mend
 He dances for it to end."

Cal stepped away from the mic. He took his well-deserved bow to the deafening applause. And if I knew Cal, he was already anxiously anticipating his next spoken word.

Christmas Day turned out to be the biggest one yet at the Scott household. When I awoke, Cal was nowhere to be found. Arriving in the living room, my mouth fell open. Expecting to find a few wrapped gifts under the Christmas tree, I instead found a plethora of boxes, clothes and electronics throughout the entire living room.

"What on earth?" Nanna asked.

"You didn't know about this?" I asked.

"Merry Christmas," Cal said wearing a Santa cap. "I wanted to show you two a token of my appreciation for letting me spend the holidays with you."

Nanna shook her head, "Caleb, we can't take this—" She spotted the diamond earrings on the coffee table, "Take this with a bow on it. Those are lovely and look at how they shine."

A violin case was hidden behind the new flat screen high definition television. I opened it to find a handcrafted, chestnut varnished instrument.

"Had it imported from Romania," Cal said.

"Cal, I—"

"It's no big deal. Besides, what's the point of being rich if you can't share it with the people you love?"

Nanna sat down the earrings, albeit reluctantly. "Sweetie, let me tell you something. You don't have to buy our love. Though I appreciate the very lovely and expensive earrings, and boy you got some good taste. But anyway, you're here because we want you here. You, not your money." She kissed Cal's cheek and handed him a wrapped box. "Merry Christmas gorgeous."

Cal unwrapped the gift to find a crimson pullover inside.

"And this is from me," I said.

He unwrapped his second present to find a leather-bound journal.

"Thank you," he said. "Thank you, both."

Keeping with the Scott family tradition, Nanna cooked a humongous Christmas feast. While I was stuffed after one plate, Cal was all too happy to consume four helpings. Nanna was all too happy to stuff him.

The next morning I groggily crept down the stairs towards the kitchen.

"You know Caleb, since you've been here I haven't had to use my garbage disposal unit once," Nanna said.

"When I become a 400 pound blimp I'm holding you responsible," Caleb replied. "But there's nothing like a beautiful woman who can cook for you. You know I'm on the market."

"Boy, hush, before you make me blush…again. I'm really glad

you're in Noah's life. I think you've been a godsend for him and I hope you two always remain close."

"He's a really cool guy. He's kind of like the little brother I never had."

"Noah has definitely come out of his shell a lot since meeting you. I can tell."

"Well it works both ways. He keeps me out of trouble. You should be very proud of him."

"I am and all things considered we're really lucky."

"How so?"

"Noah came to live with me after his parents died in Katrina. My grandson and his wife."

"I'm so sorry. Noah never said anything. I figured because he lived with you, that they probably weren't in the picture, but I didn't want to pry."

"Here's a picture of them. I never saw a more gorgeous pair."

"They're both very beautiful. Noah's definitely got his dad's smile but his mother's eyes."

"Yeah and they were close, Noah being an only child and all. I know it still haunts him. He doesn't like to talk about it. He keeps it bottled up. I worry about him. He never made any close friends. I gave him his space. He just kept to himself and played the violin. His mother loved classical music. That's where he gets it from. He was always an angel. Never gave me an ounce of trouble. I think he prides himself on being the man of the house. Tries so hard to take care of me. Bless his heart."

"And he talks about me being a survivor," Cal said.

"You both are. Well I for one think your idea is great and you certainly have my permission."

Taking that as an opening, I entered the kitchen.

"What's a good idea?" I asked.

"I wasn't sure if this was a good idea to ask and I wanted your grandmother's blessing," Cal said.

"Caleb wanted to know if you'd be interested in going to Aspen."

"Actually you're both invited but your grandmother doesn't seem too keen on learning how to ski."

"I am too old," Nanna laughed. "Been done broke my neck."

"I was gonna go with Abby, but obviously plans changed. Figured no sense in letting the reservations go to waste. Great snowboarding. And I'm sure two newly single bachelors can find all types of trouble to get into."

He caught Nanna's arched eyebrow.

"I mean trouble of the non-trouble variety," Cal corrected.

"Any other time I would go, but I don't get to see Nanna often and I know she wants me to spend time with her."

"No I don't," Nanna said.

"Huh?" I asked.

"I'm grateful for the time I get to see you," she said. "But you're getting older and you have your own life to live. I'm going to help Mrs. Jenkins with the food drive at her church. You two boys go and have some fun. Just stay out of trouble."

"Yes, ma'am," I said.

"That goes double for you, blondy," she added.

"Yes, ma'am," Cal grinned.

I realized with being at a ski resort that Aspen would be freezing, but it was nothing compared to anything I was accustomed to. Being a southern lad, I was more acclimated to the heat than the cold. We have winters in the South but as I soon learned, winters in Georgia didn't compare to winters in Colorado. Hailing from the Midwest, Cal explained that the coldest winter in Atlanta was the equivalent of autumn in Minnesota. It wasn't that I didn't believe him but it was one of those instances that I had to experience it firsthand to fully grasp what he meant. I spent the better part of that trip downing hot chocolates and making frequent trips to the bathroom.

The ski lodge was crowded for the holidays, which was to be expected. Not surprising many of the other guests were vacationing high school and college students. A large number of them were female; very beautiful females, much to me and Cal's delight. We were carrying our snowboards to our room when we crossed paths with two identical black twins. They grinned and waved at us and we returned the favor.

"We're going to be grabbing some hot chocolate if you guys want to join us," one of them said.

"We'll meet you down there," Cal said.

The girls giggled and departed.

"Hello to the luscious," Cal said. "Two sexy ladies for two eligible bachelors. The gods are smiling down on us. It's been awhile since I've had some mocha anyway."

"Noah?" said a familiar voice.

Mr. Tyler stood in front of the room that was adjacent to ours.

"Mr. T," Cal greeted. "What are you doing here?"

"I could ask you two the same thing," Tyler replied.

A petite woman emerged from Mr. Tyler's room, "Who are you talking to Randy?"

"Guys this is my fiancée, Janette," Mr. Tyler introduced. "Janette this is Caleb Warner and Noah Scott."

"It's a pleasure to meet you two,," Janette said. "Randy has mentioned you both."

"They're all lies," Cal said. "Rumors meant to tarnish my good name."

"You can't tarnish something that's rusted," I replied.

"What brings you up here?" Tyler asked.

"Seemed like as good a spot as any to do some serious vacationing," Cal said.

"Exactly what we thought," Janette said.

"I suppose if I have to run into students up here, I'm glad it was you two," Tyler said.

"Ditto, Mr. T," Cal replied.

"And until we're back at school, it's Randy," Tyler said.

"So what are you two boys about to do now?" Janette asked.

"We're about to meet two lovely ladies for hot chocolate," Cal said.

"You want to join us?" I offered.

"I guess it wouldn't hurt," Randy said. "Lead the way boys."

Most students probably wouldn't invite their teachers to hang out with them in a social setting and to be honest, had it been any other teacher, I would've avoided them at all costs. But Mr. Tyler, or Randy rather, wasn't like most teachers. It was easy to forget that he wasn't that much older than us and that could easily be attributed to his no-nonsense demeanor in class.

However, outside of school he was an entirely different animal. As the six of us lounged at the table, Randy kept us entertained with a number of anecdotes. I'm sure his wit earned some points with me and Cal's dates: Kristy and Monique respectively.

"And that's when I said, 'it looked green enough to me,'" Randy said.

The entire table guffawed.

"So, how's Helena, Noah?" Randy asked.

"She's doing fine and she told me to tell you that you ought to be ashamed of yourself for not dropping her a line," I said.

"Honey, I told you to shoot her an email," Janette said.

He chuckled, "Helena and I used to date back in college."

"Really?" I asked.

He nodded, "It was brief and nothing serious. We remained very good friends. In fact, she introduced me to Janette."

"I wouldn't have guessed," I said. "Wow."

"Now that I'm finally warmed up, Randy and I were going to hit the slopes," Janette said. "You guys care to join us?"

"Yeah," Kristy said.

"Caleb here has been bragging about his technique," Monique snickered. "I can't wait to see him in action."

"We don't have to go up the slope for that," Cal said.

Monique playfully slapped his arm.

"We're in," I added.

"Great," Randy said. "I guess we'll meet in the lobby in about thirty minutes."

"Hang on," Cal said.

He dashed out of his seat and returned with a bellhop who was armed with Cal's digital camera.

"Everyone scoot in close," the bellhop ordered.

I still have a copy of that picture which I gaze at from time to time. Each time I see it, I feel a sense of sorrow. For what I didn't know at the time was that portrait would serve as a portent of the things to come. This would be the last time all of us would be together. Not all of us would be fortunate to return to Hollowstone. By night's end, one of us would be dead.

Chapter Eight

As planned, Cal and I retrieved our gear from our room and rendezvoused in the lobby with Kristy, Monique, and Janette.

"Where's Mr. Tyler, I mean Randy?" I asked.

"He said he was on his way," Janette said. "He was talking to his kid sister on the phone when I left. Of course that was about thirty minutes ago. They're real close which is sweet but they can chat for hours."

"I'll go get him," I said.

"Thanks, Noah," Janette said.

I arrived at the room and noticed the door was cracked open.

"Mr. Tyler, I mean Randy," I called from the entrance. "Are you ready?"

The lights were off.

"That's weird," I said to myself. "Randy? Are you here?"

I flipped the light switch and gasped in horror. Furniture was strewn everywhere and blood was smeared on the walls. In the center of the floor, a man in dark clothing lay dead, a knife plunged in his chest. I ran to the other side of the bed and searched for the phone. That's where I found him. My teacher's body lay lifeless in the corner, drenched in blood. His empty eyes stared blankly at the ceiling.

"Oh-God-oh-God, no!" I cried.

I quickly searched for a pulse. I felt none.

"Come on!" I cried. "Come on!"

A gloved hand clenched my throat and slammed me against the wall. It was a second man, his face covered in cuts and bruises. My vision blurred as I gasped and struggled. The man was twice my size. I reached for the small lamp on the nightstand and smashed it across his skull. He staggered backwards and I dashed for the door, tripping over his partner's corpse.

A cold grip ensnared my ankle and reeled me backwards. I turned and slammed my boot into the killer's jaw. I hopped to my feet and made another attempt for the door. My hand finally touched the doorknob when my assailant's arms coiled around my waist and flung me across the room like a piece of debris. I struggled to my feet but a sharp kick to my ribs grounded me. The killer smashed his fist into my jaw. Dazed and winded, I laid powerless as my attacker straddled me and resumed strangling me. I was on the verge of blacking out when I heard a yell.

"Noah!"

Cal tackled the assailant and delivered a flurry of punches. The larger man swatted Cal off of him and followed up with an uppercut to my roommate's stomach. While I gasped for air and attempted to recover, my attention was drawn to something metallic underneath the bed. I grabbed it. It was a gun with a silencer attached at the end of the barrel. The attacker continued to pummel Cal.

"Let him go!" I yelled.

Observing the gun trained on him, the killer released Cal.

"Get away from him!" I ordered.

The assailant sneered and limped towards me.

"You think you can pull that trigger, boy?" he asked.

"Get back!" I yelled.

"Cause I don't think you have it in you."

"I said get back!"

"I'm getting closer."

"Stay back!"

The attacker lunged for the gun. I shut my eyes and squeezed the trigger. I felt the gun go off. A gaping hole rested in the center of his torso. I sighed in relief. That relief was short-lived as the realization struck me that I was now a murderer. My body trembled.

"Noah," Cal called to me. "Noah, I need you to hand me the gun. That's it. Hand it here. There you go."

Cal gently removed the weapon from my grasp.

"Noah, listen to me," he said. "This wasn't your fault. He left you no choice. The gun just went off. You hear me Noah? The gun just went off."

"The gun just went off," I vacantly repeated.

I remained curled in the same spot until the police and ambulances arrived. The paramedics examined me and I heard one of them mutter that I was in shock. Kristy and Monique consoled a sobbing and hysterical Janette. In the background I heard Cal explain his version of events to two investigators.

"I ran back to my room because I realized I left my gloves," he said. "That's when I heard the noise in here. I ran in and saw the guy strangling Noah. I jumped in and fought the guy."

"And who shot the assailant?" one of the detectives asked.

"I did," Cal said. His eyes met mine. "He was about to kill Noah and I found the gun. I shot him. It was self defense. I told him to back off, but he tried to rush me. He left me no choice. Noah and I would've been dead if I hadn't pulled the trigger."

"Did you know Mr. Tyler had plans to be up here?" the other detective asked.

Cal shook his head, "We just happened to run into him up here. Talk about one hell of a coincidence."

"Do you know if Mr. Tyler had any enemies?" one of the detectives asked.

"No, he was a cool teacher," Caleb said. "Well. I don't think this will matter but he did irk some people at our school."

"Oh yeah?" asked one of the officers.

"They were going to sack him because he refused to pass a couple of jocks who were failing his class," Cal said. "But they couldn't fire him."

"And why not?" the first detective asked.

"I'm not exactly sure," Cal lied. "But he pissed off a lot of administrators, students and parents for standing his ground. You don't think someone would actually…"

"That's what we're going to find out," the first detective said. His cell phone rang. "Excuse us for a second."

The two detectives stepped out of the room. When they returned, both Cal and I could tell by their faces that they knew something.

"What's going on?" Cal asked. "What is it that you aren't telling us? Do you know what this was all about?"

"It's still early in the investigation," the second detective said. "We can't reveal—"

"Please!" Cal said. "We just came up here for vacation. All we wanted to do was snowboard and have some fun. Only we find our teacher, one of the few I was actually fond of, murdered in cold blood and we nearly get killed. Do Noah and I need to be worried? Can you please tell us something so we can at least have a peace of mind? We deserve that much. Please."

The first detective turned to his partner who nodded his approval.

"We just got a call from the station and they confirmed the identity of the two perps," the detective said. "Chuck Brawley and Bruno Himmer, the guy that attacked you two. They both have rap sheets as long as this room. Extortion, armed robbery, kidnapping, manslaughter. Mainly they're seasoned thugs for hire. Based on the evidence here in the room, looks like they broke in and there was a struggle. I don't think they counted on Tyler putting up such a fight. From the looks of it, your teacher managed to kill the Brawley but got taken down by Himmer."

"And that's when I showed up," I said.

"Yep," the detective said. "He must've been hiding in the closet when you arrived. And you know the rest. These guys were veterans. For all intents and purposes, you two should be dead."

And that's when my grief and trauma shifted to seething rage.

"Thugs for hire," I said.

"Excuse me?" the second detective said.

"Thugs for hire," I repeated. "Someone had Tyler killed. Someone hired those two to track Tyler up here and kill him. Someone from Hollowstone."

"We don't know that for certain," the second detective said. "We're still investigating. Anything is possible."

"The hell it is," I said. "Two seasoned hitmen don't track high school teachers across the country unless someone is making it worth their while. Someone with money. Someone at that school hired those two to kill Tyler, because he wouldn't lie down for those bastards."

We remained in Aspen for a couple of more days until the investigators informed us that they had everything they needed. I'm pretty certain Cal pulled some strings with his lawyer to keep our names from being revealed.

Not wanting to face Nanna or risk her finding out about what occurred, we decided to return to Hollowstone. The new term wouldn't begin for another couple of days and while there were a few other stragglers on the campus, Cal and I primarily had the school to ourselves. The return trip was a somber one as neither of us said anything. And while I was still fueled with rage, guilt began to seep through.

Had we allowed Tyler to be fired, maybe he would still be alive.

The local papers said almost nothing about Tyler's murder. His death was limited to a blurb in the obits. The tragedy that cut his life short wasn't even acknowledged.

"You must really hate me," Cal said.

I stopped gazing out of our dorm window, "What?"

"Can't say that I blame you," he said. "I promised you that I wouldn't drag you into any trouble and that seems to be everything I do. You wanted to stay with your grandmother and I dragged you to Aspen. If I hadn't talked you into it—"

"Tyler would still be dead," I finished. "And probably so would Janette. What happened up there wasn't your fault. You saved my life and I never once told you thank you."

"Well you did return the favor. And this isn't your fault either."

"What?"

"I know what you're thinking. And it's not your fault."

I gave Cal a puzzled look.

"You're thinking that if you had allowed him to get fired, he would still be alive," Cal said.

He was good. I had to give him that.

"You did what you thought was right. You stood up for someone who was being screwed over."

"I wonder if Tyler's family would agree with you."

"Let me tell you something, you stand by your convictions no matter the consequence. That's rare and if I was ever in trouble, I'd want you in my corner."

I nodded. He patted me on the shoulder and grabbed his jacket.

"I'm gonna go get some air."

"Bundle up, it's freezing out there."

"Yes dear."

Outside the winds howled furiously. The rake of a tree branch against the window startled me. I walked to the window and gazed into the darkness. Tyler's true killer, the one who masterminded everything, was still out there. What was worse was that it was someone from Hollowstone, meaning the killer was very nearby.

Chapter Nine

I stood in the center of the ballroom where the masquerade took place. The masked students continued their dance. Off in the corner, Cal knelt to Abby and handed her a rose. Remembering the scene from last time, I pushed my way through the crowd to reach the two. Just as Abby accepted the white rose, the Phantom emerged from the shadows and plunged his scythe into Cal's back.

I awoke with a yelp. Breathing heavily, my body was drenched in sweat. I glanced at the clock to see it was a little after six a.m. Cal's empty bed was still made. I pulled back the window curtains to find another surprise waiting for me.

The entire campus was blanketed in nearly a foot of snow. Additional flurries descended as it was clear that the snow had no intentions of disappearing anytime soon. The town would now need a new slogan. For the first time in history, snow descended on Newton.

"Cal will want some shots of this," I said.

After getting dressed, I grabbed Cal's camera and raced out of the room.

Ambulance and police lights flashed. Medics and police officers surveyed the perimeter behind the school. Large crimson stains of blood tainted the otherwise immaculate white landscape. That's when I saw him. Cal lay stiff in the snow, his torso etched with bullet holes. I continued to stare at my roommate hoping that at some moment I would wake up or somehow it would be explained that none of this was real. The reality sunk in further when a medic placed a blanket over his body.

"Cal," I muttered.

"Sir, I need you to stay back," an officer instructed.

"Cal?" I repeated. "No! No! No!"

The events were akin to an outer body experience. I attempted to rush to my friend's side but one of the officers restrained me. I screamed and struggled while the paramedics did their work. The officers finally released me when I keeled over and vomited. The paramedics carted away Caleb's body. I was powerless to act or do anything to alter fate's sadistic hand. Once again, I was alone in the world. My foundation crumbled and I was forced again to say goodbye to someone I loved.

I had never dealt with funeral arrangements before. Nanna took care of everything when my parents died. Thankfully Father Michael was gracious enough to assist me with the arrangements.

"I think it's best to let the school move on and allow everyone to deal with their grief in their own way," Norrington told me when I requested a vigil to honor the tragic deaths of Caleb and Mr. Tyler. "The new semester should be fresh beginnings all around and while such tragedies are well…tragic, this is an opportunity for us to move on and start anew."

I couldn't even pretend to be surprised by the headmaster's attitude. After all, this was the same man who attempted to fire Tyler because he wouldn't pass two obnoxious jocks. This was also the same man who threatened to expel me if I spoke out about Dana's rape. Undaunted, I posted fliers about Cal's memorial service which would be held at St. Joseph's, around campus. Tacky, I'll concede, but I figured as popular as Cal was, there would be plenty of students wishing to say goodbye to a friend and classmate.

I sat in the front pew, repeatedly glancing over my shoulder to see if anyone from Hollowstone would show up. Guilt plagued me. I couldn't even organize a proper memorial for my best friend. Save for me, the poor son of a bitch was going to be buried alone. He was right, I was the only family he had. Me and Nanna.

Breaking the news to her was one of the hardest things I ever did. Though she insisted in driving up for the service, I knew between the drive and the icy mountain roads, it wouldn't be safe and convinced her to stay home. I already had enough to worry about. Abby never called. She didn't even send a card. Cal had lived much of his life around her and in the end, this was where it got him.

The murmurs of teens stirred me from my thoughts.

"See I told you someone would be in here," said a familiar voice.

While I wouldn't have pictured Lacey and Harry at Cal's funeral, I was just grateful to see two familiar faces in attendance.

"Hey guys," I greeted. "Thanks for coming."

"Oh, hey, Noah," Harry said. "What's going on here?"

"Cal's funeral," I said. "You are here for the funeral, right?"

"Oh yeah," Lacey said. "I think I saw a flyer about it at school. Was that today?"

This led to me asking the $60,000 question, "Why are you here?"

"Oh, well we're on our way to the Branton Bragg Luncheon and we sort of got turned around," Harry said. "The weather is so crazy out there."

"I mean we'd stay but we're already running late," Lacey said.

"Anyway do you know where Tucker Street is, Noah?"

I glared at the pair and returned to my seat. In a perverse way, their logic made sense. Cal was gone and they no longer had a use for him. In hindsight it was a blessing that Cal's classmates ignored his funeral. Harry and Lacey reminded me that had they and their ilk attended, they would've used the opportunity to make his death all about them.

"Excuse me?" said a woman. "Is this the wake for Caleb Warner?"

I nodded. The woman and a bearded man slowly wandered down the aisle. It wasn't difficult to determine that the woman was Cal's mother. The similar facial features were uncanny as was their rich dark blue eyes. Faint wrinkles were etched across her otherwise young face. She gazed at her son's resting form and sobbed. The man held her and placed her head against his chest. The two sat down next to me on the front pew.

"I'm Noah Scott," I said.

"Cynthia Warner," she said. "I'm Caleb's mother."

I extended my hand to shake hers. Instead she embraced me in a hug and squeezed as hard as she could.

"I'm so sorry," she said, wiping the tears from her face. "You can imagine I've been a bit of a wreck."

"You're entitled to it," I said.

"This is my fiancé, Mitchell," she introduced.

"Honey, I'm going to go call my mother and let her know that we made it here safely," he said. "Excuse me."

I honestly had no idea how to react in this situation. On one hand, based on her history with her son, I felt obligated to avenge Cal and let her know what he thought of her and how bad a mother she had been. After all, she caused Cal so much pain and anguish. And yet it wasn't in me to do that to a woman who was using all of her strength to maintain her composure.

"Did you know Caleb well?" she asked.

"He was my roommate," I said. "And my best friend. Did you find the place okay."

"We would've been here sooner, but the flights were running bad due to the weather. I guess that's why everyone else hasn't made it yet. Because of the weather?"

I nodded and smiled. I didn't like lying to the woman, but I didn't have the heart to tell her the truth. She already suffered more tragedy than one person ought to endure.

Heavy flurries descended upon the four of us as we stood at Cal's gravesite. Father Michael continued his prayer while my roommate's weeping mother buried her face into her fiancé's chest. My grief and anger made me immune to the harsh winds.

Labored breathing and crunching snow indicated a late arrival. Turning around, my eyes widened in surprise when I spotted Vaughn Pope. Tossing his shaggy dark mane from his eyes, my classmate adjusted his thick wool trench coat. I stepped away from the gathering to greet him.

"Sorry I'm late," he said, panting heavily. "I couldn't get my car to turn over. Where is everybody?"

"This is it," I said.

"You're joking."

"I wish I were."

"They used to come to his parties by the hundreds."

"I guess they couldn't allow something as trite as a funeral to get in the way of their little luncheons. To be honest, and not that I'm not glad, but I'm surprised you came. I didn't realize you and Cal were tight."

"We weren't. I went to a few of his parties but we never really hung out. My car broke down on the side of the interstate one day. He called me a tow truck and gave me a lift back to the school. We chatted about music and stuff. He always seemed cool."

Vaughn glanced at the others present. "The parentals?"

"His mom and her fiancé."

"Any news from the cops?"

I shook my head. "They think it was a stickup gone bad. They found his wallet a few yards from the body. It was empty. They dusted it for fingerprints. Nothing."

"And this snow doesn't look like it's going to be letting up anytime soon."

"Nah. Under other circumstances it would be beautiful."

Father Michael continued to quote verses from the small leather Bible in his hands. That's when I saw him. Beyond the headstone, Cal leaned against a tree. He flashed his trademark smirk.

"What the…" I muttered.

"What is it?" Vaughn asked.

"You see him?"

"See who?"

He was gone. Of course he would be.

"Never mind."

Mitchell carried the last box of Cal's belongings out of the room. Mrs. Warner and I sat quietly on the twin beds, our eyes scanning every corner of the room, attempting to avoid the awkwardness and each other. Mrs. Warrner's fiancé was nothing like the boyfriends that Cal told me about. A middle-aged man, his polite gentle demeanor didn't ring of someone who had been in and out of the penitentiary or had a trace of malice.

"I'm going to go load this in the car," Mitchell said.

"Thanks, honey," Mrs. Warner said. "Noah, we left his laptop and his other stuff. They're yours."

"I can't take his things."

"Please. I insist. Mitchell and I know nothing about computers and I'd rather you take it. And the car is yours too. I know he would want you to have it."

"I don't know what to say."

She picked up my portrait of Cal, Abby and me.

"Was he happy?" she inquired. "Was he genuinely happy?"

"For the most part, yeah. He had his demons. He didn't like to let on, you could tell that they were there. This had been a heavy semester for the two of us. We both went through a lot, but Cal was strong. You couldn't keep him down."

Her eyes filled with tears. "I'm glad that he had at least one person in his life who looked after him."

I laughed, hoping to lighten the mood. "That was a full-time job."

"Some things never change."

"What was he like growing up?"

Mrs. Warner wiped tears from her cheeks. "He used to stay in his room and write in his notebook for hours. My beautiful little angel. He was charismatic too. People were just naturally drawn to him and he had girlfriends the second he was in kindergarten."

"That sounds like him."

"I was sixteen when I was pregnant with him. Town gossip ran rampant. Nosy old women would trash me behind my back in the store. And those were the polite ones. Others would call me a whore to my face. I had to drop out of school and work to provide for me and Caleb. I constantly struggled with bills and I didn't have anyone.

"When you're desperate, lonely and struggling to survive, it's so easy to lose your way. I got so wrapped up in me and my needs and my problems. I just let dirtbag after dirtbag use me. Cause I thought I needed a man to help out with the bills and be a father to Caleb. He tried to tell me the truth about them time and time again, but I was too stupid to listen. One night we got into a big argument and I kicked him out. I figured he'd be back the next day. He never came home. I looked for him everywhere. He just didn't want to be found.

"It was a wakeup call. I lost the one precious thing that mattered to me. Can't tell you how many sleepless nights I had. About a year ago, I get a letter with his handwriting. It said I hope this finds you well and at the bottom it told me to check my bank account. I did and I found a hundred grand had been wired to it. He didn't leave a return address or anything but I knew wherever he was, he was doing well and he was safe. It made it that much more painful. I should've been the one taking care of him. Not the other way around. I took the money and started over.

"I always hoped that one day, when he was ready, Caleb and I could work things out. They say that there's nothing more painful for a parent than losing their child. Only thing more painful than that is knowing that you failed as a parent. I'd give anything for just five more minutes with Caleb. Just to tell him that he was right and I was sorry."

"One thing you could always count on with Cal was that he was all about the grand gestures," I started. "He was always larger than life and he looked at life like one big stage and he was always performing. It drove me crazy at times, but I came to appreciate that was just his way. Life was one big adventure to him and he tried to live it to the fullest. I think, no, I know that when he sent you that letter, that was his way of saying he loved you.

"He knew that money would be what you would need to start over. And knowing him, he probably thought that one day when the time was right, he would see you again. He would've been happy that you turned your life around."

Her eyes welled up. "Boy I tell you, Caleb hit the jackpot when he got you for a friend."

"Well, I learned a lot from him, too." I handed Mrs. Warner Cal's journal.

I spent the better part of the evening getting Mrs. Warner reacquainted with her son. While it was little comfort to the fact that her child was gone, perhaps sharing memories about her son would at least bring her a modicum of peace.

I had returned to the candlelit room. Glyphs and demonic symbols were painted on the walls and the wooden floor. The cloaked figure remained knelt before the three men.

"You were wise to remove the threat," the first man said.

"But the champion still lives," the second one stated.

"And as long as the champion remains alive, so shall the herald," the third man added. "You must seek out this threat and eliminate it."

The cloaked figure lowered his head in agreement.

I awoke with a start. I was still exhausted, but I didn't want to go back to sleep. The nightmares had become more frequent and each time they became far more intense. I didn't know how much more I could endure. Glancing to my left, I released a yell. For lounging casually on Cal's bed was no one other than Cal himself. He looked exactly the same the last time I saw him alive. He delivered his trademark reassuring smile.

"Sup Altar Boy," he greeted. "How goes it?"

Chapter Ten

"For the millionth time, you're not losing it," Cal said.

I paced around the room trying to convince myself that the apparition of my dead roommate was only a symptom of post traumatic stress. It wasn't working.

"You're not real," I said. "You're dead. I saw your body. We buried you only hours ago. I was at your funeral. I did the funeral arrangements."

"And once again, yes I am dead. The best I can figure is that I'm a ghost. Don't know how the afterlife works. Never was big into religion and mostly everyone I knew told me I was going to Hell anyway so never thought to do much research. But I think somehow I'm trapped in limbo. I think you Catholics call it Purgatory."

"This is impossible. I'm not some little white kid in a Bruce Willis flick. I don't see dead people."

"It's also not supposed to snow here in Newton and oh wait a lot of powdery white stuff is outside. I think it's safe to say that there's a lot of impossible going on right now. I wonder if the two are connected?"

For the first time, I noticed that it was snowing yet again. Perhaps I was losing it because slowly the thought of reasoning with the ghost didn't seem too crazy. My logic was maybe by entertaining them, the delusions would eventually cease.

"Okay, if you're really Cal, why now? Why am I just now seeing you?"

"Ah, but, you didn't. You saw me earlier at the funeral. I couldn't figure it out. I remember waking up in the snow. The police and the paramedics were all over the crime scene. I remember seeing my body and all of the bullet holes in it. Which by the by, seeing your own corpse, really freaky! I remember trying to communicate with everyone but no one could see or hear me. Everything around me felt numb. It was like I was there, but I wasn't. I tried to touch or move something, but my hand just went through everything. And I remember seeing you show up."

"So, how is it I'm able to see you now?"

"I don't know. I was at the funeral and I saw everybody and something felt different, it was like a film around me had been lifted and I was here. And then you saw me and I can't tell you how stoked I was."

"But you vanished again."

Cal nodded. "I phase in and phase out. Kinda like a TV or a radio station with a really weak signal. For some reason, you're the only person who can see me. I still haven't figured that out."

"I must be losing it. Because as crazy as all of this sounds, and believe me this is all crazy and impossible, this is making too much sense to be a simple delusion. Okay, if you really are a ghost, then why are you still here? From what I've read, ghosts usually stick around because they have unfinished business."

"Isn't that obvious?" Cal said. "I'm still here to find out who killed me and why. Oh come on Noah, we both know that wasn't a robbery. Someone wanted me dead."

"Do you remember what happened that night?"

Cal shook his head. "After I left here, I went out to clear my head. I was walking around and I hear some gunshots ring out. Next thing I know, I wake up to find myself dead. There was no robbery. Hell that wasn't even my wallet they found."

"Do you think this has to do with Mr. Tyler?"

"I don't know, but I intend to find out."

"This is crazy. I have to be losing it."

"And we were making so much progress. Wait! I can prove to you that I'm not an illusion or a symptom of a psychotic breakdown."

"I'm listening."

"If I am a figment of your imagination, then that means I can only tell you things that you either already know or something that you can imagine."

"Okay?"

"So, basically if I tell you something that you couldn't possibly know and prove that it's right, then that means I'm real."

"All right, prove it."

"Go look behind my desk."

"What?"

"Go and look behind my desk."

I did as instructed. I leaned over and examined the narrow space between the desk and the wall.

"There's nothing—wait, what is that?"

I stuck my arm underneath the desk and recovered a small brown wallet. I opened it and sure enough, it contained Cal's driver's license, student ID, credit cards and two hundred dollars.

"Now if my wallet is right here, then whose wallet did the police find?" Cal asked.

I ran my hand over my scalp. Finding the wallet confirmed for me everything that the apparition had claimed. This also meant that Cal's murder was a premeditated one.

Chapter Eleven

The better part of the next morning was spent in the brick building that served as the Newton Police Department. I patiently waited for homicide Detective Merv Foley to arrive to work. Cal vanished shortly after I discovered the wallet and had yet to reappear.

Over thirty minutes late for his shift, when Foley did finally grace his job with his presence, I had the unenviable privilege of conversing with the slovenly police officer as he stuffed his face with a pastrami sandwich.

"I'm telling you kid, we've got enough leads, you need to leave the detective work to the professionals," Foley said.

"This changes everything," I said. "The wallet you guys found wasn't Cal's. He left his at home the night he was killed."

"Yeah, the evidence says otherwise," Foley said.

"There were no prints found on the wallet," I said. "Somebody murdered him and tried to make it look like a stickup. This evidence proves that it was premeditated murder. Have you talked to the Colorado police? This might be connected."

"What? Oh yeah, we're already looking into that possibility. Look kid. I appreciate your zeal, but you got to understand, even if this was true, your roommate had more than his share of enemies. Not the least of which was a couple of drug pushers who he had dealings with. Word has it that they may have been out for blood. Especially after that drug bust at school. Don't worry. We'll take care of this."

I closed the driver's door when I felt Cal's presence on the passenger side.

"Worthless piece of shit," he said. "That son of a bitch knows something. I'm telling you he's dirty."

"I wouldn't doubt it," I said. "He didn't even know what the hell we were talking about when I mentioned Colorado. He hasn't even bothered to look."

"He doesn't want to look. Somebody wants to keep all of this on the down low which means that this is someone who's got some serious pull."

"Foley was right about the enemies part, if it is someone from Hollowstone: Phelps, Norrington. Goddard would be my first guest."

"Me, maybe, but that doesn't explain why he would want Tyler dead."

"The more clues we find, the more questions that pop up. I need to get some answers and fast. If this does have anything to do with Colorado, I could very well be next."

"And I need you alive to solve my murder. You're no good to me dead."

"Wait a second. How did Foley know that you were on bad terms with Burke? For him to know that would require him to do his job and I don't see that happening."

"Good point. And only one way to find out. We need to find Burke."

"I don't know where he hangs."

"I do. Let's put my baby in gear and let's roll."

"Actually this is my car now."

"No, this is my ride. I'm just letting you borrow it for right now."

"Yeah, we'll see about that."

Located on the southern edge of town and away from the more fashionable buildings and homes were abandoned warehouses, trailer homes and shacks. No doubt the southside of Newton was the den to those too poor to be the working class.

Because Cal's/my car would easily garner attention from the denizens, I parked it on a dirt road behind a small patch of woods.

Several thugs wandered in and out of a battered white house, but neither Burke nor his car was present. I had no idea what I would find or if I would find anything but Cal was right in that it was certainly a start.

"You think Foley was right?" I asked while planted behind an old abandoned car. "Is it possible that Burke may have done this?"

"I don't know," Cal said. "That's what we're going to find out. To be honest with you though, something's off about all of this."

"You mean the fact that I'm sitting here spying on a drug dealer and his posse with the ghost of my best friend?"

"No, smart ass. I meant Foley's story. Burke was all mouth and all hype. He talked big, but he was just another wannabe gangsta who watched one too many rap videos. For as much trash as he talked, I can't see him doing this. It's too ballsy. What? What is it? Why are you staring at me like that?"

"It's nothing, I just noticed you're wearing that pullover Nanna gave you."

"Oh. Yeah it was my favorite. How did she take the news?"

"She took it pretty hard. I decided not to tell her or anyone else about the whole ghost business. I still don't have my head wrapped around all of this."

"Fair enough."

"Speaking of family, I got to meet your mother. You two look a lot alike."

"I saw her. I was there at the funeral and later in the room when you talked to her. I didn't get a chance to tell you this, but I really appreciate what you said to her."

"She seems to be doing well, all things considered."

He nodded.

"And Mitchell seems like he's a nice guy."

"Sucks, you know. I didn't get a chance to talk to her and set things right. Not like I probably should have."

"At least she got a chance to hear what you wanted to tell her. That's more than what a lot of people get."

"That's true. Over there!"

A red truck parked in front of the house and Burke hopped out of the driver's side.

"What do we do now?" I asked.

Cal had vanished. I reminded myself that I was there to get answers and that's what I intended to do. Placing my baseball cap on top of my head and putting on sunglasses to help conceal my identity, I was ready to investigate. Slowly, I crept to the house, my sneakers crunching the gravel and making it impossible to be stealthy. Luckily no one was outside and as far as I could tell, I wasn't spotted.

The blaring rap music from Burke's home masked any sounds I made on my end. Inside, trash and debris were all over the stained carpeted floor. A Confederate flag hung proudly on one of the walls while a music video of black rappers praising thug life played on Burke's 72-inch flat-screen television. A bunch of good ole boys pretending to be gangsters. I couldn't help but appreciate the absurdity and the irony of it all. Four of Burke's friends played cards, while they smoked blunts and drunk from an assortment of liquor bottles. Burke himself certainly seemed relaxed as he lounged on his tattered couch watching his television.

I decided to leave and return and search the house when it was empty. Turning around, I found a dual-barrel shotgun aimed at my chest.

I pulled against my bindings, but they wouldn't budge. It didn't matter. Even if I had found away to untie myself, I was surrounded by Burke and his entourage. One of whom still had a shotgun trained on me.

"Found this fucker outside," the gunman said.

"He was the one we got the tip on," said another. "He was the one at the police station."

"What the fuck were you doing spying on us?" said a third man. "Punk ass narc."

"Narc?" I asked. "What are you talking about?"

"Word is somebody has been running to the cops and diming us out," Burke said. "Word is it's you."

"I don't know what you're talking about," I said.

"Yeah keep lying," the gunman said.

"I swear to God," I pleaded.

"Then what the fuck were you doing here?" a fourth thug asked.

"Wait a minute," Burke said. "I know you. I've seen you before. At Cal's party."

I nodded.

"I didn't put the name with the face," Burke said. "So I'm going to ask you this one time and one time only. And if you lie to me, I'm going to know it. And if I catch you lying, I'm gonna have my boy Dirk squeeze the trigger. We got a tip today saying that a Noah Scott had been at the police station, telling about our dealings. You were even trying to pin Cal's murder on us."

"That's not true," I said. "Who told you this?"

"A little birdie," Burke said.

"Yeah well somebody's lying," I said.

"Then why were you snooping outside the house if you weren't spying on us?" Burke asked.

I had to pick my words wisely for they would definitely determine if I walked out of the home alive. "I'm trying to find answers, about Cal and find out who killed him. I couldn't care less about whatever it is you do."

"And you were snooping around cause what, you think I had something to do with Cal getting smoked?" Burke asked.

"Well the cops—son of a bitch!"

"What?" Burke asked.

"He played us," I said. "How could you possibly know I was at the police station today and what I talked about?"

"Anonymous tip," said one of Burke's lackeys.

"It was Foley," I said. "He's a dirty cop. He tipped you off. Don't you see, he wants you to kill me."

"You ain't buying this shit are you Burke?" one of his friends asked. "He'll say anything not to get capped."

"Think about it," I said. "You get a call telling you that I'm running my mouth about your operation, he knows I've been trying to find Cal's killer. He knows more than he's telling and doesn't want me digging and he knows that you'll do whatever it takes to preserve your business. You take me out then he's going to flip and pin both murders on you. He closes two murders, catches a notorious drug dealer and he comes out on top, all the while covering up the truth."

Burke grabbed the shotgun from Dirk, "Everybody, clear out."

He pulled up a chair next to me. The rifle rested in his lap.

"So you thought I killed Cal?" Burke asked.

"Before I wasn't sure. I mean he had his share of enemies and I know the last few times you two talked, it wasn't on the best of terms."

"I was pissed when I found out about that brick showing up in that kid's locker. That type of heat makes it bad for business. But I didn't kill him. Cal made things right. He didn't want grudges so he paid me twice the amount the brick was worth. Far as I was concerned, we were on good terms. He squared everything with me."

"Then how the hell did Foley know about Cal being involved in that drug bust?"

"Somebody must've talked. No telling who."

"No. Foley's dirty and if the cops knew about Cal, it would've been used and Ronny Garrison wouldn't still be facing legal troubles. Foley's getting his info from somewhere and I'm betting it's from somebody who's in on the dealing."

"Wasn't me," Burke said. "And I can vouch for my boys. They don't make moves like that without permission. Besides, it's not in their interest. Murder is bad for business. Draws too much unneeded attention. Besides everything was beginning to die down. Why would we wait till now to kill Cal?"

Burke had a point; a very valid one. "Cal once mentioned you had a distributor. Any chance he might be pissed at what Cal did?"

"It's possible, but considering I don't know who the hell he is, it's hard to say."

"What do you mean?"

"I never met him in person," Burke said. "He only contacts me via email or uses a voice distorter from a payphone. He also had a bunch of drop-offs which we used to exchange the money and the product."

"So, it's somebody local," I muttered to myself.

Burke removed a knife and slashed my bindings. "Like I said, I can't speak for everybody else but Cal was all right with me. Watch where you stick your nose, kid. Next time you might not be so lucky."

It wasn't until I was back in the car car that I finally allowed myself to breathe.

"Well that was bracing," Cal said.

"Yeah nothing says bracing like nearly getting your head blown off."

"Those were some nice moves on your part. How'd you figure it out?"

"You'd be surprised how inspired you get when the barrel of a shotgun is lodged against your skull. These guys are low class thugs. They can't even afford a decent house. I don't see them having police informants on their payroll. I never told anyone I was going to see Foley. Considering his reaction when I showed him the new evidence, it just made sense."

"So, Foley is working for whoever had me killed?"

"Then there's Mr. Tyler's murder? We haven't determined if there's a connection between your deaths or just one hell of a coincidence...the dreams."

"What dreams?"

I explained the recurring dreams.

"I thought they were just a bunch of crazy nightmares. What if that was a warning? And I didn't say anything and..."

"Don't. I wouldn't have listened anyway. There was no way for us to know. But if they aren't just regular dreams, then that means they could be connected to me being here and everything else."

"One of the men in the dreams mentioned threats. He had to mean you and Tyler. So we just have to find the person who had a lot to gain by wanting both of you dead."

"Well, at least Burke's off the list."

"Yeah but his boss isn't whoever the hell that is."

"So, what now?"

"We definitely know Foley is dirty and probably taking orders from whoever is pulling the strings. I think a little stakeout is in order."

"You're planning to spy on a cop? A bit ballsy aren't we?"

"Not me. The ghost who can't be seen by anyone except for me."

"Plan's sound. You think we're going to find anything?"

"Foley's gonna get sloppy and hopefully we'll find a clue. I'll drop you off at the station and you can tail him from there."

"Not that I haven't appreciated your newfound resolve, but you do realize that this is only going to get worse and probably more dangerous."

"Whoever killed you and Tyler might be after me next. I need answers and it beats sitting around feeling helpless."

While facing death would've turned away wiser men, I was now more determined to get to the truth and see this through to the end, no matter what that meant.

Chapter Twelve

The new semester brought many changes. With tougher classes and no friends, I immersed myself in my studies. The only constant was Mr. Nolan and me maintaining my status as his golden pupil.

The new semester saw the departure and arrival of students. One student transferring to another school was Brianna. The official word was that she got accepted into a school with a more prestigious tennis program. The unofficial truth was that her parents came out of their workaholic and pill-induced stupors and remembered they had a daughter after some drug-related trouble on a holiday trip in Ibiza.

For the first time ever I was truly alone at Hollowstone. A specter going through the motions until my sentence was up and I could graduate with that diploma which would open doors and set me for life. I faded into the masses and made it a point not to draw any attention to myself. It wasn't hard as most students avoided me anyway.

Sitting alone in the cafeteria, I tried to ignore the occasional whispers I heard about the guy whose roommate was murdered. The most boisterous tables were that of the preps where Chris and Abby sat as the royal couple.

Neely Daniels, one of the semester's new transfers, was one of the few souls who dared to be openly original. Between the pink streaks in her mousy blond mane, the maroon corduroy jacket and her stylish brown boots, she certainly had no qualms about announcing to the world that she was an individual.

Unfortunately such confidence brought about the wrong kind of attention. Phyllis and her pack made no attempts to hide their pointing and snickering at the new girl. Neely strode across the cafeteria, her steely resolve impervious to the verbal slings from her critics. I had resumed chomping on an apple while reading The Great Gatsby for American Lit. So, I was more than startled when I heard a tray clank down at my table.

"This seat taken?" Neely asked.

I shrugged my shoulders. Behind her, I spotted Cassidy walking towards the table. When she saw Neely, she turned and stormed away.

"I thought my last school was bad about the politics," she said.

I shrugged my shoulders and continued reading.

"Gatsby eh? I love that book."

"Listen," I said. "You seem really cool, but I'm not really up for small talk."

"You're Noah Scott aren't you?"

"What?"

"I heard about everything that's happened."

"Of course you did." I grabbed my tray and prepared to leave. The last thing I needed was to deal with some nosy new student looking to get the juicy gossip about everything that transpired.

"I'm sorry," she said. "I didn't mean to offend you. Look, I'm just trying to make some friends here. And you seem to be one of the few kids in this school that doesn't have a silverspoon shoved up his ass."

It was the same thing that Cal said to me the first night I met him. I placed down my tray.

"It's not you," I said. "As you've probably learned by now, you have to be on your guard here."

"I've noticed. For all its faults, I was perfectly content at my old school. But no my dad, the General, thought this school had the ideal conservative values that I so desperately needed. He wasn't fond of my ex."

"What was wrong with him?"

"My ex? Nothing. Except that he was a she."

"Oh! Lesbian."

"Actually, I'm bi. I'm an equal-opportunity romantic. But it's cool. Hannah and my thing had run its course and she's living in Madrid. She emails me every once in a while."

I nodded.

"You know, Noah, this is going to sound weird, but I sort of knew who you were when I first saw you."

"Why because I'm one of two black kids in the school?"

"Well, yeah that too, but it's your aura. It's emanating a peculiar energy."

I shot her a wry look. "And what type of energy is my aura emanating?"

"Death," she said. "You're being haunted."

"Well, death can be haunting," I said. "Especially when your roommate gets killed."

She leaned closer, "No. You're literally being haunted. Maybe you've seen something or someone that you shouldn't be seeing."

"I don't know what you're talking about."

"I'm willing to bet that you do."

"All right," I said. "For the sake of argument, let's say you're right. Let's say some weird stuff has been happening to me. What now?"

"I have some books and can do some research. There's usually a reason why these spirits remain in limbo. Something needs to be resolved in order for them to move on. I want to help."

"Why? What's in it for you?"

"I'm a Wiccan. This stuff is an obsession of mine and I want to help. Besides, you look like you've got a lot on your shoulders and could use a friend. And to be completely honest, if I'm going to be stuck in this hellhole, I need to do something to pass the time."

"I don't want to talk about it here," I said. "Too many prying ears. I have to go into town later and run some errands. I can call you when I get back. We'll meet up later and I'll tell you everything then."

While in town I spotted a wanted sign in the window of Wong's bookstore. Working at a bookstore wouldn't seem like really strenuous work and it would be a much needed haven away from Hollowstone. And I could always use a few extra bucks in my pocket.

An elderly Asian man—who I assumed was Mr. Wong—was stationed behind the counter with a short woman in her thirties who appeared to be his daughter based on their resemblance.

"Hello," Mr. Wong smiled.

"Hi," I replied. "I was wondering if you were still hiring?"

"Absolutely," Mr. Wong said excitedly. "Lydia, get this nice boy an application."

"Sure, Dad," Lydia replied.

"So, tell me about yourself, young man," Wong said.

"My name is Noah Scott. I'm still in school and I'm just looking for a part-time job."

"What school do you go to?"

"Hollowstone Academy, sir."

A deep scowl appeared on his wrinkled face.

"Forget it," he said. "You're not welcome here."

"What the—"

"You bastards have made my life a living hell long enough and now you think I'm going to hire you? You can get out and tell your buddies to find some other store to terrorize."

"What are you talking about?"

"Get out!"

"Dad!" Lydia cried.

"He's from that damn school!" Wong said.

"I don't think he's one of them," Lydia said. "I'm sure he had nothing to do with it."

"What about my school?" I asked. I turned to Lydia. "What's going on?"

Wong rolled his eyes in disgust.

"You must be new to the school," Lydia said.

I nodded.

"Well, several of your classmates have made it clear that they aren't fond of our kind," Lydia explained.

"Born and raised in this country," Wong ranted. "I've got every damn right to be here."

"They used to ride through here egging the store and spraying graffiti on the walls," Lydia said.

"Not to play devil's advocate here, but how do you know these morons were from Hollowstone?"

"How many other teens around here drive Ferraris and Porsches?" Lydia asked.

I shrugged my shoulders and nodded.

"The police wouldn't do anything and this garbage continued," Lydia said. "We even went to your headmaster and he all but laughed in our face. One night someone threw a cocktail through the window and set everything on fire. Thankfully, we got the fire out in time. It was only then that the cops began to take us seriously."

"Did they ever catch the guys who did it?"

Lydia shook her head, "And there haven't been any problems since. They seemed to have had their fun."

"And I'll be damned if I'm letting one of those bastards work in this store," Wong said. "So what happened rich boy? Why do you really need a job? Mommy and Daddy cut your allowance. They make you work for a living like the rest of us?"

"Actually my parents are dead," I replied. "They were killed in Katrina. And no I wasn't born with a trust fund. I'm on a scholarship."

Wong's anger seeped away from his face. He glared at the counter not wanting to betray the remorse his expression began to show.

"Noah Scott?" Lydia asked.

"Yeah?" I said.

"I thought I recognized that name," Lydia said. "You were Caleb Warner's roommate?"

I nodded.

"He was the one who got killed at the school," Lydia told her father. "Remember I told you about the story." She turned back to me. "I work at the newspaper."

Wong picked up the application, "The job is yours if you want it."

He went into his office and shut the door behind him.

"I apologize for that," Lydia said. "He's not normally like this, but that garbage with that school has taken its toll on him. Even though we got the worst of it, it's not just us."

"What do you mean?"

"You really are new. Those kids come into town all the time rubbing their money in the locals' faces. Of course we can't do anything about it. No one should have to deal with that type of nonsense."

"Trust me," I said. "I know exactly what you mean."

She nodded, "I bet you do."

"When can I start?"

"Thursday work for you?"

"Thursday will be good. I'll see you then."

In spite of all of that I wanted that job. I felt that I had some type of obligation to make things right with the Wongs.

"Noah," called a familiar voice.

Abby fidgeted and repeatedly looked behind her to confirm that we were the only two on the promenade.

"What do you want, Abby?"

"I just wanted to see how you were."

"Couldn't be better. Excuse me."

"Noah, wait."

"Abby, I really don't want to get into it with you about this."

"I didn't want to break up with Cal. I loved him."

"You got a funny way of showing it. You didn't even go to his funeral. Hell you didn't even send a card."

"You think I wanted to break up with Cal? That was the hardest thing I ever had to do?"

"Then why did you? And to go back to Goddard?"

"Dad told me that if I insisted on acting like a slut and being with trailer park trash, he would disown me and put me on the streets. I know my father. He would do it. I tried to be strong. But I couldn't. I didn't have a choice."

"Why are you telling me all of this Abby? Why now? What do you want?"

"I don't want you to think that I'm a bad person."

"Why do you care what I think?"

"I just…"

Her eyes wailed up with tears and she departed.

I quickly locked my door before I found myself in the middle of any other dramatic maelstroms.

"Where the hell have you been?" Cal asked.

So much for that idea.

"What's wrong?" I replied.

"Got news," he said. "Foley. And man let me tell you that guy is a slob."

"What did you find?"

"He took this bag of cash and dropped it off in the middle of nowhere. I stuck around and hours later a woman came and picked it up."

"Do you know who the woman was?"

"No. But then I followed Foley back to his office. He was talking to his chief. Seems that they're looking for Phelps."

"Phelps?"

"And here's where it gets even better. Phelps has skipped town. He's nowhere to be found."

"If he somehow found out that you got the team busted with the steroids, that certainly gives him motive."

"And he wasn't too keen on Tyler standing his ground in regards to his jocks."

"The pieces are starting to fit. Did the police find anything?"

"No, they ransacked the house. Nothing, and no one has seen or heard from him. I'm thinking we should go sleuthing. Check out his pad."

"Two things. One, breaking and entering. Two, if the cops didn't find anything what are we going to find?"

"Hello?" Cal said. "We're talking about the Newton police. Not exactly the brightest bulbs. Besides, we might notice something they wouldn't think to look for. The place is abandoned."

"You got a point. All right let me just call my friend and let her know that I won't be able to make it."

"Neely?"

"Yeah, how did you know?"

"She left a message earlier. She's not going to meet you, something came up."

The answering machine was indeed blinking.

"She sounds hot," Cal said.

"She is."

"What's her story?"

"She sees dead people. And she's bi."

"I like her already."

Breaking into Phelps's place proved to be no problem at all. Someone else had already done it. The police tape had been ripped down. We crept behind the house and discovered the kitchen door was ajar.

"I don't like this," I said.

"Yeah something's off," Cal said. "Only one way to find out what that is?"

Furniture was upturned every which way. Carpet was ripped and the sofa was upside down and ripped open. There was a huge hole in the center of the television.

"What the hell?" Cal asked.

"This wasn't the police," I said. "Someone else wants Phelps. I'm going to check upstairs."

Arriving at the top step, I caught something out of the corner my eye. I turned just in time to see a boot collide with my face. The blow sent me tumbling down the flight of stairs. The back of my head smacked the hardwood floor. Everything went blurry and faded to black.

"Noah?" said a voice. "Noah."

I'm not sure how long I was out. I was still groggy when I came to. I opened my eyes and found two figures kneeling over me. The first figure I quickly made out as Cal. His arms crossed, he shook his head in disgust.

"Can't believe you just got your ass kicked by a girl," he said.

"Shut up Cal," Neely said.

"Huh?" I muttered. "You can see him?"

"She can see me," Cal answered.

"I told you I can see dead people," Neely said. "He's been catching me up while you were out. Are you okay? Noah, I'm so sorry."

"Neely, what happened?"

"I sorta drop-kicked you down a flight of stairs. My bad. I thought you were one of the guys who ransacked this place coming back."

"What are you doing here?" I asked.

"I'm afraid I haven't been completely honest," she said.

"You don't say," I replied.

"Uh guys," Cal said. "We got company."

Cal vanished. Two men slowly entered the room. I was still too groggy to even sit up, much less run. One of the men was short and lanky with thin dark hair. His burly partner looked like a fullback.

"Date's over kids," the thin man said. "Mr. Heard would like to have a word with you two."

"I would love to but we have a curfew," Neely said. "Besides I don't talk to strangers."

"Don't get cute, girly," the larger man said. "You're coming with Paulie and me. Let's not make this difficult."

The larger man opened his blazer to reveal the gun resting in its holster. Neely raised her hands in defeat and approached the men.

"You too small fry," the larger man said.

"He fell down the stairs," Neely said. "He might have a concussion. He's going to need help getting up."

The larger man bent over to pick me up and Neely quickly shoved Paulie into him. Both men tumbled to the floor.

"Shoot her, Carlos!" Paulie yelled.

Carlos scrambled off the ground and drew his gun. Neely kicked the weapon from his grasp and landed a sidekick on his nose. Paulie lunged at the blonde, swinging wildly. Neely parried his attacks, before she landed a right cross. She vaulted and connected a spin kick across Paulie's jaw. Neely reached for the poker in the fireplace.

"Hey!" Carlos cried.

He pulled back the hammer on his firearm.

"What are you waiting for?" groaned Paulie. "Shoot the bitch!"

Carlos licked away the trickle of blood from his lip. "All right, blondie. You're a badass. I'll give you that, which is why I'm going to try this one more time. Our boss Mr. Heard would like to have a chat with the both of you. If we wanted you two dealt with, we would've already done it. Now, Mr. Heard just wants to talk. Answer his questions and I'm sure he'll send you on your way. Now how are we going to do this?"

Neely tossed the poker.

"Still should've shot her," Paulie grumbled.

"You're just mad she kicked your ass," Carlos replied.

Carlos lifted me into a fireman's carry and carted me out of the house with Neely and Paulie following suit. We were placed in the back of a dark SUV.

"All right, Buffy, you got some explaining to do," I said. "First of all, where in the hell did you learn how to fight?"

"My brother."

"Who in the hell is your brother, Jet Li?"

"Randy Tyler."

And with that revelation, Neely knocked me down another flight of stairs.

"Randy Tyler?" I repeated. "My teacher was your brother?"

"Half brother, technically," she said. "Same father, different mothers."

"What are you after?"

"I think the same thing you're after. That's why you were at the house, right? You're trying to find out who murdered my brother. Someone sent those men up there to kill him. And I think it was someone from Hollowstone. I heard about what happened in Aspen. You and Cal nearly got killed fighting the men."

"Why didn't you just tell me truth?"

"I didn't know how you would react. I didn't know if you were trying to put everything behind you and move on. But when I saw your aura, I knew there was more to this. If I had known you were looking for answers too, I would've told you everything from the get go. I'm really sorry."

"I probably would've done the same thing. Your brother was a great teacher. He always looked out for me."

"He mentioned you a lot. You were one of his favorite students."

"All right, the psychic stuff. Were you always this way?"

"No. When I was six I nearly drowned in a pool. After that I was able to start seeing things. Randy was the only one who believed me."

I then recalled the occult text that was on Tyler's desk the day I visited him. The book was for Neely.

"What do you think is going to happen with this Heard guy?" she inquired.

"I don't know," I said. "But if he's got some questions for us, hopefully he'll have some answers as well."

I wasn't exactly sure what I was expecting when we met Carlos and Paulie's boss, Herman Heard. What I can tell you is that he turned out to be nothing like anything I would've imagined. Upon taking our seats in the office of Heard's Flower Shop, Neely and I found a small man in a pastel purple suit arguing with a striking brunette regarding a bouquet of roses she held.

"Honey, honey, no this is a just a hot mess," Heard said with a long southern drawl. "If we showed up with this, the Templetons would never forgive us nor should they. Use the pattern we used at the Smith wedding last month."

The woman exited and Heard sat behind his desk.

"I apologize for that," Mr. Heard said. "I love my wife to death but the poor thing knows nothing about ambiance."

I pressed the ice pack Carlos gave me against my head.

"Tsk, tsk, tsk," Heard said. "Looks like somebody was a naughty lad. I hope my boys weren't too rough with you." He noted the cuts and bruises on Carlos and Paulie's faces. "But it looks like you put up one heck of a fight."

"Actually, it was Xena over here who did all of the damage," I said.

"Well, Mama always said men were the weaker sex," Heard said.

"Why are we here?" Neely asked.

"I'm trying to track down the whereabouts of Coach Phelps who seems to be M.I.A.," Heard began. "I had Paulie and Carlos keep an eye on the house in case Phelps decided to go back or sent someone like two of his students."

"I'm not his student," Neely said. "Actually, I've never met him before."

"If that's true then what were you doing in his house?" Heard asked.

"We're trying to find him," I said.

"We think he may have had my brother killed," Neely said. "And his roommate."

"Oh my," Heard said. "I wouldn't have thought of him as the violent sort. But then you know what they say about desperate people."

"Why are you trying to find him?" I asked.

"Your coach has a bit of a gambling problem," Heard said. "And unfortunately he has amassed quite a bit of debt. We gave him some time to balance his books. He started making progress by betting on your football team."

"The same team he was supplying steroids to," I said.

Heard smirked. "That last game was going to be his biggest payoff and then his dirty little secret got exposed. So why do you think Phelps had your loved ones killed?"

"They weren't football fans," Neely said. "He may have thought that they were responsible for exposing him."

"And that's why he hired hitmen to have them killed," I added.

"Wait," Heard said. "Hired hitmen? You kids and your stories."

"It's true," I added. "I was in Colorado when it happened. They nearly killed me. Look it up online if you don't believe me."

"I'll do one better," Heard said. "Sit tight and I'll be back in a spell."

Heard exited the office. Neely turned to me for answers and I simply shrugged my shoulders. We waited. Carlos read the sports section of the newspaper while Paulie alternated between rubbing his swollen lip and glaring at Neely. Heard eventually returned.

"I just had a long conversation with some associates," Heard said. "You were absolutely right, young man. You're also completely wrong."

"I don't follow," I said.

"That makes two of us," Neely added.

"Two men were hired to kill your brother," Heard said. "No one knows who hired them, but top dollar was paid for them. From what I heard, they weren't counting on your brother being such a tough mark, but I see now that it runs in the family. Your brother killed one of the men before he was finally done in. And then word is two pesky boys showed up and killed the second hitman. I take it that was you and your roommate. Those hitmen were two of the best. Someone must've been praying hard for you young man, because for all intents and purposes, you shouldn't be alive."

"You said I was wrong about something," I said.

"Oh, yeah," Heard said. "I can see why you thought Phelps was the one behind this dreadful business. But he didn't have your people murdered."

"What makes you so sure?" Neely asked.

"Simple, sweetheart," Heard said. "He couldn't afford to. The amount of money it costs to hire those men for a job is more than twice what Phelps made in a year. To put it simply, they were out of his league. Between me, the cops and a couple of angry ex-wives hunting him down for back child support payments, your brother and your roommate were the least of his problems. Whoever had your loved ones murdered is still out there."

Neely and I exchanged glances. It was clear by her worried face that she was thinking the same thing I was. While another suspect had been eliminated from the list, we were back to square one.

It was nearly an hour later before Neely and I returned to campus. We strolled silently through the promenade, when I grabbed her arm.

"What is it Noah?" she asked.

"You might want to sit down," I said. "There's something I need to tell you."

I explained the series of dreams I had and how I thought they might be connected to Cal. Neely listened intently as I also explained how Cal and I saved Tyler's job and perhaps our interference is what got him killed.

"This wasn't your fault, Noah," Neely said.

"Wasn't it?" I asked.

"No, it's not. Even though he couldn't figure out how, Randy thought you somehow had a hand in saving his job. He decided to leave the school anyway. He was going to finish out the year. He already had a job lined up. He had given Norrington his notice."

"So, if he was going to leave anyway, then Norrington had no reason to have him killed. The football season was shot and his issues with Tyler were moot at that point."

"So, what happens now?"

"I'm going to find out who murdered Cal and Tyler. And I could use some help. Anything you can figure out about Cal's ghost might help us figure out who killed him and your brother."

"Well, partner, I guess we got a lot of work to do."

"Later. Right now. I'm going to take some aspirin and go to bed."

"Again, sorry about that."

"Noah!" Ryan cried. He raced to us carrying his opened laptop.

"Have you seen this?"

"What is it Ryan?" I asked.

The three of us watched the newscast on Ryan's laptop where a male reporter stood in front of the police station.

"We're expecting an official statement later," the reporter said. "But it has been confirmed that a suspect has been arrested in Caleb Warner's murder. Two hours ago, 43-year-old Lawrence Favreau was apprehended by police in conjunction with the homicide of the Hollowstone Academy student. We will continue to follow this breaking news as it continues to develop."

I watched in disbelief, all the while one question continuously plagued me. Who in the hell was Lawrence Favreau?

Chapter Thirteen

"I'm telling you, Noah, I've never seen this guy before in my life," Cal said. "Or in my death either."

We sat in one of the aisles at Wong's, staring at the mugshot on the front page of the newspaper.

"And trust me," Cal said. "I would've remembered a face that gruesome."

"According to the paper he's confessed to killing you," I said. "His only excuse is that he thought he was doing the Lord's work in punishing the wicked children."

"By blowing a hole through my chest?" Cal asked. "No, something isn't adding up here."

"I plan to go talk to this guy and get some answers."

"Which will probably lead to more questions."

"Yeah that tends to happen a lot."

I read the story for the umpteenth time. Hoping to find some morsel of a clue that I may have overlooked.

"Hey, Noah," Lydia greeted. "You're shocked by the news, no doubt?"

"That would be one way of putting it," I said.

"Well, I can tell you that no one was more shocked than Kelley," Lydia said.

"Who's Kelley?" I asked.

"That goofy looking guy from work my daughter has a crush on," Wong interrupted.

"I do not have a crush on him," Lydia said. "And he is not goofy looking. I think he's kind of cute."

"Who's Kelley?" I asked, again.

"Kelley Vance," Lydia said. "He's the one that wrote the article."

I spotted Vance's byline underneath the headline.

"He's been following this entire story since it's broke," Lydia said. "I've never seen him dig into a story like this one before."

"Has he found out a lot of stuff?" I asked.

"From the stories I've copy-edited, it looked like it," Lydia said. "Unfortunately a lot of his stuff hasn't been allowed to get printed."

"Why not?" I asked.

"The publisher is a spineless idiot," Lydia said. "A lot of connected people with ties to Hollowstone want this ordeal buried. The publisher's been putting pressure on Kelley to kill the story. Only problem is Kelley's not the type to compromise his principles."

"Who doesn't have a crush on him again?" Wong asked.

"Will you stop," Lydia said.

"Do you think he'd be willing to talk to me?" I asked.

"I'm sure he would," Lydia said. "In fact, I remember him mentioning that he tried several times to contact you, but your headmaster threatened to have him arrested for trespassing."

"Why am I not surprised?" Cal asked.

"I think I'm going to have a chat with Vance," I said.

"I think he'll be happy to see you," Lydia said.

"My daughter has the lousiest taste in men," Wong said.

"Yeah," Lydia replied. "I clearly get that from my mother."

The Newton Press newsroom was in complete bedlam. Employees hurried from cubicle to cubicle. In the corner of the office, Kelley Vance typed feverishly at his desk. His concentration unfettered by the bustle of his surroundings. Appearing to be in his forties, he was a thin man with sharp angular facial features.

"Excuse me, Mr. Vance," I said.

He ceased typing and gazed at me suspiciously.

"My name is Noah Scott," I continued. "You've been doing the stories on Caleb Warner's murder."

"I was," he said. "Not any longer."

He scribbled on a sheet of paper.

"I wanted to talk to you about what you found," I said.

"Did you hear what I said?" Vance replied. "I'm not at liberty to discuss my stories with you. They've caught the murderer, case closed."

"Sir if you could just—"

Vance hopped from his seat and grabbed my arm.

"Hey!" I protested.

Everyone in the newsroom watched as he escorted me to the outside steps of the building.

"And if I see you around here again, I'll call security," he warned before returning inside.

"What the hell?" I cried.

Cal stood next to me on the steps.

"Check your back pocket," Cal said.

"What?" I asked.

"Either he slipped a note in the back of your pants pocket or he was grabbing your ass to cop a feel," Cal said. "Possibly both."

I reached into my back pants pocket and removed the handwritten note Vance scribbled at his desk.

"Huh," I said.

"What does it say?" Cal asked.

"He wants me to meet him in the park later tonight," Noah said. "Looks like he's got information for me."

It was nightfall when I arrived at the park. Fortunately, it was deserted and I surmised that's what Vance wanted. While waiting in the car, I phoned Neely and brought her up to speed.

"I'll call you after I finish meeting with him," I told her. "No, I don't think he would be going to this much trouble if he didn't have a good reason. Hey, I gotta go. I see a car pulling up. Later."

The red Honda Accord parked next to my car. I stepped out to meet with Vance.

"Nice ride," Vance greeted.

"Thanks," I said.

"Sorry about the stunt at the office earlier," Vance said. "My boss is looking for a reason to fire me. He wants this story to disappear and he's not too fond of me digging around. Thanks for meeting me."

"No, thank you," I said. "Lydia told me you've been catching a lot of heat."

"Oh, you know Lydia?" he smiled. "She's really...great."

"Anything you can tell me about this case would be greatly appreciated."

"Maybe it'll help if you tell me what you know."

"Okay."

"You mind if I record this?"

"Uh, sure."

Vance sat the recorder on the hood of his car. He listened and occasionally nodded as I told everything that took place, more or less. I omitted Cal's involvement with the football team scandal as well as the supernatural business.

"I've covered some bizarre cases before but this one takes the cake. Up until a few days ago one of my sources on the force told me that the cops were looking for Phelps in conjunction with Tyler and Warner's murder. All of a sudden this Favreau guys comes out of nowhere."

"I had a chat with Herman Heard," I said.

"Newton's resident bookie?"

"Yeah, Phelps owed him a lot of cash. He doesn't think Phelps was behind it. Heard thinks he had too many problems and even he wouldn't be smart enough to pull off two murders."

"Which brings us back to Favreau."

"Who is he?"

"He's a local. Had several scrapes with the law. Bad checks, shoplifting, drug possession. Nothing like this. It's not adding up. And he hasn't said squat about his partner."

"What? Partner?"

Vance opened his manila folder and removed a set of photos.

"There were two sets of footprints found in the snow," he said. "There were two people present when Caleb was murdered. Notice the pattern of the second set of footprints. They're smaller and they coincide with the killer's."

"So, someone smaller was with the killer that night. An accomplice or something."

"Exactly."

"Have you interviewed Favreau's family or friends?"

Vance shook his head. "I'm afraid my boss has me on a tight leash. He finds me snooping around, I could lose my job. I don't want to press this matter until I got all of the evidence. What doesn't add up is the motive. Only thing I can think of is that he was so distraught over his daughter that he just lost it."

"Wait? His daughter?"

Vance reached into his folder and removed additional photos. The first was that of a teenage girl in a cheerleading uniform. The second was a picture of Favreau kissing a tall plump woman on the cheek. I felt Cal peering over my shoulder, studying the pics.

"Son of a bitch," Cal muttered. "It's her. The woman. That's the one who picked up that drop-off of cash Foley left! Noah, tell him about Foley. He might know something."

"This woman?" I asked. "Who is she?"

"Belinda Jackson," Vance said. "Favreau's live-in girlfriend and the mother of his daughter, Lawretta. Why do you ask?"

"Now, I remember her," Cal said. "She was in a hit and run last year."

"Lawretta," I said. "Was she in a hit and run?"

"Yeah, she was," Vance said. "Last year. Is still on life support. Doctors say she won't ever wake up again."

"And there's your motive," I said. "Sort of."

"What are you talking about?" Vance said.

"Cal...I mean I...saw Det. Foley," I said. "I've been trying to find information on the case and I knew he was hiding something."

"Foley's involved," Vance said. "Shouldn't be surprised. He's as dirty as they come."

"So, I tailed him. He made a drop-off with a lot of cash and Belinda picked it up."

"Wow, and I thought I was the investigative reporter," Vance said. "All right Bernstein, so you think your roommate had something to do with that hit and run?"

"I didn't," Cal said. "I don't know anything about it. Other than what was reported."

"Only thing is that he didn't," I said.

Cal and I watched the reporter ponder.

"What is it?" I finally asked.

"Reporter's instinct is kicking in," he said. "All of the pieces fit nicely but it's just a little too off. The payoff, the lack of a connection between the victim and the suspect. This is getting dirtier by the second."

"You think Favreau's taking the fall?" I said.

"It's the only theory that makes sense," Vance said. "A lot of powerful people will do anything to make this matter disappear. That's how that school has worked for years. Something bad happens, they cover it up. Think about it. Why now? Favreau might be a criminal but he's a petty one at best. Why wait until now to kill Caleb, especially so closely after Tyler's murder."

"So, whoever is behind Tyler and Cal's murder is offering a fall guy to help cover up the matter."

"A fall guy that the powers that be are all too willing to accept," Vance said.

"Whoever is behind this has plenty of money to throw around."

"If they're affiliated with your school, that doesn't exactly narrow down the suspects," Vance said. "My next plan was to meet with March Steinberg, Caleb's attorney. She's in town. However she hasn't returned any of my calls and if my boss finds out I'm still snooping—"

"I can talk to her," I said. "Besides she might not be so guarded and might let something slip talking to a teen as opposed to a reporter."

"Good point. She's staying at the Lazarus Hotel."

"I'm also going to have a chat with Favreau."

Vance shot me a puzzled look.

"Same reasoning," I said. "He might let something slip."

"All right," Vance said. "But I need you to be careful. Someone's going through a lot of trouble to bury this murder. If they find out you're snooping around…"

"I know. I'll watch myself."

"Keep me posted."

"I will."

Vance departed.

"So, what do you think?" I asked my ghostly partner.

"We're definitely making a little progress," Cal said. "Of course I don't know whether to be flattered or disturbed that someone wanted me dead this badly."

"Burke said his supplier did drop-offs."

"So the mysterious drug dealer is behind your murder and Tyler's. And if they're doing all this cloak and dagger, that means they're leading a double life."

"Which goes back to them being connected to the school."

"Hopefully, your lawyer will be a bit more forthcoming."

Cal wore a worried expression, "You're going to see her first?"

"Yeah, I figured I should talk to her before drilling Favreau. The more information I get the better. What's wrong?"

"Nothing," Cal said. "Come on, let's get out of here."

And for the second time ever, Cal had lied to me.

There was something Cal didn't want me to uncover. Something at the expense of solving this murder. The only other time he had reacted like this was when I asked about his family. And that's when it hit me. His lawyer knew the truth about whatever it was Cal was trying to conceal from me.

There had been no sign of my roommate that entire morning.

Whether it was because he was hiding from me or had simply phased out again, I wasn't sure. Part of me was grateful because I suspected he would've tried to convince me not to see Steinberg.

I spent the better part of the morning staking out the Lazarus Hotel lobby. Luckily I thought to look her up online. Upon seeing her profile pic on her firm's website, I immediately saw why Cal had chosen her as an attorney. Of all the lawyers in the world, leave it to him to choose the one that looked like a lingerie model.

Steinberg was in her late thirties; her key features were her dark red hair and her thick glasses. The daughter of prominent attorney Ned Steinberg, March had emerged from her father's shadow and now owned one of the premiere firms in the country. Nanna had an old saying regarding lawyers. Whenever you're dealing with them, always bring a recorder and a revolver; a recorder to keep them accountable and a revolver to keep them honest.

The elevator opened and my target strode into the lobby holding a briefcase in one hand while chatting on her Bluetooth.

"Doris, make sure those files are faxed over by the end of business tomorrow," March said. "I don't want to give them any legroom."

"Excuse me, Ms. Steinberg," I said. "My name is Noah Scott. I need to speak with you. It's about Caleb Warner. He was my roommate."

She studied me for a second and flashed a predatory grin, "Doris, I'm going to have to call you back. How can I help you?"

"It's about Cal's murder," I said.

"Didn't you hear?" March said. "The police caught his killer."

"He didn't kill Cal," I said. "Whoever killed Cal is also responsible for Randy Tyler's murder."

"Your teacher. Yes, I had to pull some strings to keep you and Cal out of that mess."

"I also think that this may somehow tie in to Cal's past. Anything you can tell me would be a big help."

"You do know there's this thing called attorney-client privilege."

"I'm not asking you to testify or go on the record. Just point me in the right direction and I'll find the rest on my own. Please. Cal's killer is still out there."

"I think I'm going to need a drink," March said. "And I don't drink alone. Come on."

March and I found a corner booth in the empty hotel bar. She sipped on her gin and tonic while I nursed a glass of water.

"I suppose you could say that I owe Cal everything," she said. "He's the reason I am where I am today."

"How so?"

"His case was the one in a million jackpot that set me for life. I wouldn't have my own firm if it wasn't for him."

"How did you meet him?"

"I had just graduated from Harvard Law and was working in my father's office. Cal showed up in our lobby. He looked like he had been surviving on the streets and just barely. He claimed he had the case to end all cases. There was something about him. He was cute but there was something else. So young and yet…he had these deep eyes. You could tell he had a poet's soul and that smile could just melt—"

"You slept with him didn't you?"

March took a sip, "Repeatedly. And let me tell you something. When it comes to technique, innovative doesn't even begin to cover the things he did. You would never get bored with him."

"That's more than I needed to know."

"Hey, you wanted to learn about Cal."

"Fair enough. Go on."

"Cal claimed that not only could he prove paternity, but he had some incriminating files on his old man."

"I'm sure Mr. CEO wasn't expecting Cal to lawyer up on him."

"CEO?" she looked confused.

"Cal's father, he was some CEO of some Fortune 500 company. Wasn't he?"

March grinned, "Oh sweetie, someone told you a fib. Cal's daddy owns several companies."

"Who's Cal's father?"

March giggled, "You really don't know do you?"

I slammed the door to my dorm and tossed my satchel in a corner.

"CAL I KNOW YOU'RE HERE!" I yelled. "GET YOUR INCORPOREAL ASS IN HERE NOW!"

I turned around saw my roommate with a solemn look on his face. He walked to the bed and sat down.

"I take it you caught up with March," he said.

"Sure did. I learned quite a bit. I learned that Harvard has a great law program, lawyers like to drink very early, and oh yeah you're Sen. Goddard's son. Which makes you Chris and Phyllis's brother!"

Chapter Fourteen

"You lied to me," I said. "YOU LIED TO ME! Chris and Phyllis, they're your brother and sister."

"Half-siblings."

"What difference does it make?"

"I didn't want you to find out this way."

"You didn't want me to find out period."

"No. I guess I didn't."

"What the hell is going on?" I demanded.

What I reveal next is based on what Cal shared with me. His situation with his mother was true enough as was his meeting with Abigail. Shortly, after Abby had given him the money, Cal tracked down the senator to his mansion.

It was a Saturday afternoon. The gates were open and security was lax due to the birthday bash taking place. Because teens ran around the grounds, it was all too easy for Cal to slip in unnoticed.

He meandered through the home past the series of statues and portraits of who he presumed were images of his relatives. Upstairs he peered through a cracked bedroom door and spotted Phyllis alternating between devouring lines of coke and devouring a shirtless boy toy.

"This is some really good stuff," the guy chuckled. "Where did you get it?"

"My dealer at the school has a killer hookup," Phyllis said. "Take another hit."

Phyllis's lover snorted another line. She straddled him and Cal left the two to their debauchery. His trek concluded in an empty study.

Cal perused the numerous titles resting on the bookcases. Underneath the desk he spotted a small external hard drive attached to the desktop. The door creaked open.

A returning Senator Christopher Goddard Sr. found Cal staring at a painting of the Goddard family in a corner across from the desk.

Cal took in the sight of his father. Though powerful in reputation, his body told another story. His emaciated frame was riddled with wrinkles and liver spots. His thinning white hair barely covered his scalp. A far cry from portrait which hung overhead, the haggardly man personified all of the rot and evil of his two offspring.

"What are you doing up here?" Sen. Goddard asked. "The party is downstairs, young man."

"Actually, sir, I'm here to see you."

His father grinned, "Ah, I see. Need a letter of recommendation. I'm always happy to help a friend of my children."

"I don't need a letter, sir. I did want to ask you about the last time you were in Winridge, Minnesota."

"Son, I'm a politician. I've traveled all over the world many times over."

"This was a specific visit. About fourteen or fifteen years ago."

Sen. Goddard's eyes narrowed, "I'll be damned. So, what is that you want?"

"I just want to talk."

"I see. And by talk do I need to get out a blank check?"

"I just want to know what happened."

"You mean why didn't I claim my illegitimate son? You were hoping what that I would tell you that I didn't know about you and now that I've seen you standing here, you're expecting to bond and make up for lost time. Maybe you and I could go play catch in the park."

"Mom was right. You really are a bastard."

"You're one to talk. You want the truth, son? Have a seat and I'll tell you how I met your mommy. I remember your mother. Pretty little thing. Could tell she was still a virgin. Working in some grease spoon diner. Too dense to appreciate a man of my position was taking an interest to her."

"She was sixteen."

"She also didn't seem to understand that I'm a man who doesn't take no for an answer."

"You mean....you?"

"Your mom was a feisty one. Definitely a screamer. I told her she was better off getting an abortion. She was also advised that life would be problematic if she began making any waves. You clearly weren't given the message."

With his fists clenched, Cal bore a glaring hole through his father.

"The pup wants to defend his mother's honor," Sen. Goddard said. "Looks like you've got a lot of fight in you too."

"Why?"

"Why? Because I can. Do you know how powerful I am? Of course you do, that's why you're here. Well, I have news for you, son. I'll be damned if I'm going to spend one hard-earned cent on some worthless piece of poor white trash."

Two security guards chucked a beaten and bloodied Cal onto the pavement. Clutching his side, my roommate remained motionless on the asphalt while Sen. Goddard stood over him.

"Take a good look at this mansion," Sen. Goddard said. "And take a good long look at me. This is the last family reunion we're ever going to have. If I ever lay eyes on you again, I'm going to perform that abortion, your whore of a mother should've had."

The large steel gate shut behind a departing Goddard and his entourage. Though beaten, my roommate was far from broken.

A couple of days later, March stepped out of the elevator and found her newest client waiting in the lobby. His bandaged ribs didn't deter him from pacing anxiously.

"What's going on?" March asked.

"This gentleman here said that he desperately needs a lawyer," the receptionist replied.

March strode to Cal whose eyes lit up.

"I'm March Steinberg, how can I help you?"

"Are you a lawyer?" Cal asked.

"Yes, I am. What seems to be the problem?"

"If you take me on as a client, I promise to give you the case to end all cases."

Cal found himself face to face with his father yet again. The two sat directly across the table from each other in of the meeting rooms in the Steinberg law firm. While March served as Cal's sole legal champion, the senator was flanked by a team of lawyers.

"Even if you manage to find a judge willing to order a test for paternity, we are willing to file an injunction and will tie this matter up in court," Sen. Goddard's head lawyer said. "By the time this case gets a date, your client will be drawing social security."

"Do you think you'll be able to file an injunction on statutory rape?" March asked. "I'm sure Mr. Family Values wouldn't want this matter going public."

The head lawyer smirked, "The senator is a respected leader. We're confident that the media will point out that this is another scheme for a bunch of opportunists looking to cash in on a free meal ticket."

"Your client isn't the victim here," March said.

"I'm sure the media will say he is," the head lawyer said.

"You're going to buy off the press too?" Cal asked. "That's rich."

A smirking Sen. Goddard sat poised in his chair.

"I'm going to be frank with you Ms. Steinberg," Goddard's head lawyer continued. "Christopher Goddard is one of the most revered and—no disrespect sir—feared senators in office. Do you honestly think you can hope to find a judge who would be willing to go up against him? Bottom line is my client isn't paying a cent. Next time send your dad, because you're clearly out of your depths, Ms. Steinberg."

"I guess we'll see you in court," March said.

"No, you won't," the head lawyer said. "We're done here."

Sen. Goddard and his legal entourage stood.

"I was afraid something like this might happen," Cal said. "Before you go Daddy, allow me to give you a little word of advice. You should be careful where you misplace things. Something valuable could mysteriously disappear or worse yet fall into the wrong hands."

"You thieving prick," the senator growled. "You stole my hard drive when you were in my study."

"I didn't steal anything," Cal said. "That's just preposterous and against the law. Let's hope that hard drive doesn't reach the light of day or that could be very…what's the word…problematic?"

"I'd like to have a word alone with Mr. Warner," Sen. Goddard said.

The head lawyer objected, "I don't think that's a good—"

"Out!" Sen. Goddard ordered.

The entourage of lawyers filed out of the room. March turned to Cal who nodded.

"I'll be right outside," she said.

Father and son gazed at one another.

"You know I think I have your nose but the rest of my looks I get from Mom," Cal said. "Thank God. I figured those files on your computer looked important and I'm sure whoever took them thought the same thing."

"You may have the hard drive but those files are encrypted. You have nothing."

"Funny thing about the cyber-age, hackers are a dime a dozen. All too willing to prove their mettle and get their kicks out of hacking corporate and government mainframes for little more than $20, a beer and a porno mag. Your little hard drive would be a cakewalk. If I had it of course."

"You son of a bitch. Who in the hell do you think you're dealing with? You think I'm going to get sandbagged by some worthless puissant—"

"That's your problem, Dad. You keep underestimating me and yet here we are."

"What do you want?"

"Here's what's going to happen. You're going to sign over a third of everything you own. No more, no less. That's what I'm entitled to anyway. In exchange I keep mum about everything. You maintain your picture perfect image and it's business as usual. It's certainly better than the alternative."

"Which is?"

"I go public with everything including the contents on the hard drive. You won't be worth a dime when I'm done with you. So you can either pay what you owe and lose a third of your vast fortune or not pay and lose everything. And one more thing, anything happens to me or Mom, the files go public. I have at least twelve people on standby who know everything, four of them work in journalism."

Cal propped his feet on the table.

"You must be really proud of yourself," Goddard said.

"For kicking your ass? You betcha and you should be too. After all, it seems that I'm my father's son."

And the senator's next gesture was the most surprising. He smiled and nodded, conceding Cal's point. "Yes. I suppose you are."

"It was the damnedest thing," Cal said to me. "The way he looked at me. It was like admiration and respect."

"And Chris and Phyllis?"

"I didn't meet them until I came here. Definitely no love loss with those two. Not sure how much the old man told them, but they made it clear that they knew I was their long lost sibling. Neither of them wanted that news getting out either."

"Christ," I muttered. "I'm sorry. I shouldn't have been angry that you didn't want to share."

"I should've told you the truth. You've nearly gotten killed trying to find my murderer. The least I could do was tell you everything. I owed you that much. It was just hard to bear what I did. If I had any idea what he had done to Mom I would've never…"

"You're not to blame for what happened to your mother."

"Aren't I? I'm the reason she had it hard and it wasn't like she was given a choice. And I repay her by…"

"This isn't your fault, Cal. There's no way you could've known. And even if you did, there isn't exactly a manual on how to deal with this sort of thing. You did the best you could. Well we finally know who your killer is."

"It's not the old man."

"Why not, because he's not capable of doing something heinous? I think the evidence says otherwise."

"Think about it. Why now? He has more to lose than anyone. If he was going to kill me, why didn't he do it before he signed over my inheritance?"

"Maybe someone else found out about those files. So what was on that hard drive?"

"Beats the hell out of me," Cal said. "I never could decrypt it."

"What? You mean you bluffed him?"

"Pretty much. I figured if he had those files encrypted in his own home they must've been important and probably weren't on the level. My suspicions were confirmed when I saw the fear of God in his face when I mentioned the hard drive. The rest was cake. Besides, the old man paid so I didn't bother. I just gave it to March to hold onto it for safekeeping."

I grabbed my satchel and removed the small silver hard drive.

"How in the hell did you get it?" Cal asked.

"Well you're not the only one who can blackmail."

I held up my cell and hit the playback on the recorder function.

"So young and yet…he had these piercing deep eyes," repeated March's voice from the phone. "You could tell he had a poet's soul and that smile could just melt—"

"You slept with him didn't you?" my voice said from the cell.

"Repeatedly. And let me tell you something. When it comes to technique, innovative doesn't even begin to cover the things he did. You would never get bored with him."

I stopped the recording. "Let it not be said that I don't listen to Nanna. I threatened to go to the bar if she didn't hand over the hard drive. And did you have to sleep with her too?"

"It was that damn mini-skirt she wore. March must've been pissed that you blackmailed her."

"Strangely enough, no. In fact she said that I had the makings of an excellent attorney. She gave me her business card and told me to give her a call if I ever wanted to go into law. First thing's first, we need to find out what the hell is on that hard drive."

"And to do that," Cal said. "We're going to need a hacker."

That afternoon Neely and I met up underneath one of the seldom-used stairwells. It was her idea as she too was overly cautious about prying eyes and eavesdropping ears. Considering that the murderer could be on campus and the multiple brushes with danger, I chastised myself for not being more careful. I brought her up to speed on everything that happened with Steinberg, Cal's revelation about his father and the mysterious hard drive.

"Holy cripes," she muttered. "And Cal is certain that his old man isn't behind his murder."

"He seems to think so. His dad would have the most to lose with a scandal and whatever the hell is on those files."

"So, we need to find out what's on that hard drive."

"Only problem is that the files are encrypted. I'm not a hacker and I don't know where to find one."

"Actually, I may be able to help."

"Don't tell me you're a hacker, too?"

"No, but I know someone who might be willing to help. But considering what you went through to get that hard drive, I understand if you don't want to part with it."

"It's not going to decrypt by itself."

I retrieved the hard drive from my backpack and handed it to her.

"This explains why someone would want Cal dead, but I can't figure out how this connects to Randy's murder," Neely said.

"I was thinking about that too," I said. "For now we're only grasping at straws. Did you talk to Janette again?"

"Yeah. She's still not doing too well. Whatever was going on with Randy at work, he never mentioned it to her. But she said something was definitely serious. She said the vibe she got was that Randy was having an issue with a colleague. Did he have a lot of enemies on staff?"

"Not really. Aside from Phelps."

"And Phelps had enough problems to worry about. Avoiding the cops and Heard the bookie florist. Which brings us back to this Favreau guy who's taking the fall."

"I'm going to go see him today."

"You think he's going to talk?"

"No, at least not intentionally. Someone's paying him to take the fall. I'm hoping he'll let something slip. Have you found out anything else about ghosts lingering behind?"

Neely shook her head, "Most of the stuff is pretty standard. Ghosts have unfinished business here on this plane, they have an exceptionally strong soul to linger on the mortal coil. However there was something interesting I found."

"What is it?"

"I was doing some research on the town. This area has got a very rich history. The Cherokees steered clear of this territory as they considered it cursed. This place is a hodge podge of demonic energy. After the European settlers arrived, many warlocks met here and practiced the dark arts in secret. The warlocks went underground when the Salem Witch Trials hit but that doesn't mean there still isn't a supernatural presence here. They could be attributing to your dreams and Cal remaining after death."

"That cloaked figure I keep dreaming about. He's got to be the killer and if all of this is true, then—"

"This might be bigger than two murders."

"I so don't like where this is going." I glanced at my watch. "I'll call you after I leave the jail."

"Noah. Be careful."

Chapter Fifteen

I waited anxiously in the visitation area of the jail. I wasn't sure if I could get Favreau to talk, but at this point any modicum of information could prove useful.

"Do you know how you're going to play this?" Cal asked.

"Not yet, but I'm working on it," I said.

"Here we go."

Cal disappeared. The door opened and a guard escorted Favreau into the room. He stared at me curiously while taking his seat across the table.

"And who the hell are you?" he asked.

"I'm Noah Scott," I said. "I'm the roommate of Cal Warner. The guy you allegedly killed."

"You come to tell me how much of a scum I am for killing that little shit?" Favreau asked. "Save your breath. I ain't interested."

"Well good because I wasn't going to say any of that. Truth is I know you had nothing to do with Cal's murder."

Favreau laughed, "I guess you ain't been reading the papers."

"Yeah, well you shouldn't believe everything you read. Sometimes you should find things out for yourself which is what I've been doing. Someone's paying you to take the fall."

"You're crazy."

"Maybe, but I'm also right. Who's paying you?"

Favreau crossed his arms.

"Got nothing to say?" I asked. "Good. Let me do the talking then. I'm sorry about what happened to your little girl, but Cal didn't have anything to do with that hit and run and I think you know that. You're taking the fall for this so you can get paid which I assume is to cover your daughter's medical expenses. I get that. But whoever is paying you off might be the same person behind my best friend's murder. So you're going to tell me everything you know or I'm going to take this evidence to the cops."

"You're wasting your time."

"Really, I know there were two sets of footprints in the snow," I said. "The killer had an accomplice whereas you're taking the credit for the crime all by yourself. I've also got pics of Belinda picking up money from the drop-off." I watched Favreau's eyes widen in terror. "Now, you can play this two ways. You can keep mum and I can go to the cops and tell them what I know and hand over the evidence. It may not help them catch the killer, but they'll release you and well there goes your payoff. Or you can tell me what you know, I build a case against the son of a bitch who murdered Cal, and you get your payoffs in the meantime."

"I used to watch these commercials and the actors were always like 'you should pay for health insurance'," Favreau said. "You should always have health insurance. They used to say it with that attitude of if you get sick and you can't afford to pay hospital bills it's your own damn fault for not having health insurance. It's my fault I can't pay my little girl's hospital bills.

"You try paying for health insurance when you're only making three bucks over minimum wage trying to support a family. All of these Fortune 500 companies making more and more money and getting corporate welfare and bailouts. They don't pay their employees nothing, no benefits, nothing. They rake in all the profits and then cut jobs. Folks always wonder why I been in and out of jail my whole life. Well I ain't no saint, but I ain't never done a crime I didn't have to do to feed myself. You want to find real criminals. Go to Wallstreet or some corporate meeting. Those rich pricks do more dirt than anyone, but because they do their shit in a suit and tie, it's called big business.

"Ain't no such thing as the American Dream. The system don't give a damn about you if you're poor. Ain't nobody coming to save you. Not the government, not God, not nobody. You do what you gotta do to survive.

"When my baby girl was born I said I was gonna do better. I wasn't gonna walk out on her like my old man did. I was gonna do right by her. No more hustling, no more scrapes with the law. Belinda and I weren't perfect and God knows we fought, but we both did what we could for Lawretta. She worked two jobs and I worked three. Lawretta was always happy, always had a funny joke to tell. So what happens? Some rich son of a bitch runs her down in some fancy ass car like she's an animal. Some asshole from your school.

"You uppity motherfuckers sit up there in your big fancy school thinking you're better than us. Cause you were born with money, the rest of us are dirt. And you can mow my little girl down like she's trash. Well my baby ain't trash! I saw my chance here. Nobody offers that kind of money to pay for someone's comatose kid. I don't give a damn about you or your roommate."

I couldn't do it. He was a man in hell and what's worse was that he didn't deserve to be there. I slid my chair back and prepared to leave.

"I'm sorry about your daughter," I said. "I'll ask around. If I find out anything, I'll let you know."

"And what, you want something in return?"

I shook my head, "No. You've been through enough."

"The guy's voice was masked," Favreau said.

"What?"

"I got a phone call. The guy's voice was distorted. He told me that if I took the fall for Cal's murder, he would provide for Lawretta. He left the gun and the first payment at a drop-off. Some alley. It was all cloak and dagger shit. He never uses the same drop-off twice."

"Thank you," I said.

And once again everything pointed back to the Dealer.

"I can't believe you," Cal said.

"Will you let it go," I pleaded.

I swept one of the aisles in Wong's bookstore trying my best to ignore the ghost of my pestering roommate.

"No, I'm not going to let it go," Cal said. "What the hell is wrong with you? She's fun, she's hot and she's bi. She's the perfect girl."

"I am not sleeping with Neely."

"Why the hell not?"

"She's the first friend I've made since…well….everything that's happened and I'm not going to ruin that."

"Fine then do it for me."

"No!"

"It's so unfair. Why do I have to be the dead one?"

"Scott!" Wong bellowed. "Get over here."

I raced to the front counter to find my boss holding a piece of paper in his right hand.

"What is this?" he asked. "What is this B+ about?"

"It was trig," I exclaimed. "It's a very tough class."

"I don't want to hear any excuses," Wong said. "No more B's."

"I'm sorry Mr. Wong. Wait a minute. Why am I apologizing? And why are you holding my report card? Why are you snooping in my backpack in the first place?"

"Making sure you're staying away from the drugs."

"Thank you for your concern. Now will you please stay out of my things?"

"Don't be offended," said Lydia emerging from the office. "It's just Dad's way of showing how much he thinks of you as his own son. He used to snoop through my things all of the time. It drove me crazy."

"Used to?" Mr. Wong laughed. "Whoever said I stopped?"

Lydia glared at her father, "Have a good a day Noah."

Mr. Wong's overbearing nature would pale in comparison to the next headache that entered the store. With her nose turned upwards, Cassidy gingerly ran her tiny hand over the rim a few previously owned books, clearly not wanting to risk having an allergic reaction to second-hand items. She finally decided on picking up a copy of an Octavia Butler novel. Until this point, the bookstore had been my haven from Hollowstone as the elite wouldn't dare matriculate with mere mortals. As had been the precedent in previous encounters, Cassidy's presence was an omen that problems were about to ensue. Hoping to elude her, I silently started to hide until she vanished.

"Hey there," she called out.

Damn it.

"Hi, Cassidy."

"I heard you worked here. How blue collar of you."

"Did you need help with something?"

"I have a proposition for you."

"Not interested."

"You haven't heard it yet."

"I don't have to. It has something to do with the school that you're hoping to rope me into. I'll save you the trouble in making a pitch and tell you no right now."

"Hey," said a returning Wong. "You're supposed to be working. Not socializing with your friends."

"She's not a friend," I pleaded. "Feel free to kick her out or better yet call the cops."

"Oh, you're funny," Cassidy said.

Wong turned to me, "She's a cutie. She your girlfriend?"

I scowled at the old man.

"Excuse me, sir, I need to borrow Noah for a few minutes," Cassidy said.

"I'm busy working," I said.

"Yeah, because you're so busy with the one customer in here," Cassidy said. She turned to Mr. Wong. "Sir, how much do you pay Noah, ten, twelve dollars an hour?"

Mr. Wong guffawed so hard that he had to wipe a few tears from his eyes, "You're hilarious. I like you."

"I'm standing right here!" I snapped.

Cassidy reached into her purse and removed a few bills from her wallet. "Here's $50," she said. "I only need Noah for an hour."

"I'm not some piece of meat for sale," I said. "And I can't be bought."

"The hell you can't," Wong said flipping through the bills. "He's all yours."

"Judas!" I cried.

"Thanks, I'll bring him back in one piece," Cassidy said.

Cassidy pulled me outside of the store.

"You're not used to being told no, are you?" I asked.

"Not really."

"What do you want?"

"I'm sure you've heard about the Atticus Johnson Cotillion. Big snooty event. Parents show up and give money and rub elbows with each other while we all get presented and showcased."

"Yeah, what about it?"

"I was planning to attend the event and decided that it probably wouldn't be a bad idea to procure an escort."

"No one's asked you out, huh?"

Cassidy dodged my glance. "I'm sure they will, but why take chances? I figured if you were going, why not go together?"

"Thanks, but I wasn't planning on going."

"Well, you're planning to now. And don't worry I promise to make it worth your while."

I raised an eyebrow.

"In your dreams stud. I'm willing to pay you $500 for the night to be my escort. Just for the event."

I had to admit, I didn't see that one coming, "Um, I'm flattered, but why me?"

"Well you're not repulsive and you seem to be a decent guy and I know you're single. That skank Brianna is gone and as far as I know you're not dating that weirdo you hang out with."

"You mean Neely? No, but she is a very good friend of mine and she's not a weirdo. Thanks, but I'm not interested."

"Do you not have a suit? That's okay. I can front you the money to get you something."

"Cassidy, I'm flattered, but I have no interest in going. I don't really care for that type of crowd and classes notwithstanding, I try to avoid them as much as possible."

"You know this superiority complex of yours is getting old."

"Excuse me. What?"

"You think because you're poor that you're better than the rest of us because you're pulling yourself up by your own bootstraps. Problem is you're so prideful that you're missing out on a lot of great stuff including earning some cash, that you obviously need, to take out a very sophisticated, smart—and in case you're blind—smoking hot girl. That's why you have no friends save for the one and you're miserable. Honestly, you seriously need to get over yourself."

Had Cassidy been a man, I probably would've slugged her.

"Get over myself?" I said. "You're one to talk. You're involved in every extra-curricular activity there is just so people are forced to give you the time of day. You're so obnoxious that you have to pay men to take you out on a date. Why don't you take that $500 and buy yourself a clue!"

It felt wonderful to finally put Little Miss High and Mighty in her place. At least it would have if her eyes hadn't begun to water behind her glasses. At a loss for words, she simply sobbed and raced away. That brief gratification quickly turned to guilt.

"So let's review," Cal said. "Of all the guys she could've picked, she chose to bribe you in a not-so-veiled-attempt to ask you out on a date. Real smooth, Casanova."

"Drop dead!"

Following work I met up with Neely in the library. I thought discussing the investigation would take my mind off of the argument with Cassidy. It didn't.

"Here was everything I could find," Neely said, sliding a file and a stack of books across the table. "I called all of my contacts who are authorities on the occult. There are some theories in that file and in some of the highlighted books but nothing definite."

"What did you find?"

"Well…at the risk of sounding like a loon….they talked about some major dimensional shifts in this region."

"Dimensional shifts?"

"As in upheavals on a supernatural plane. I'm not sure how it pertains to Cal specifically, but it is a possibility."

"Not to be a cynic, but you got to admit this is a bit far-fetched."

"Says the guy who sees ghosts."

"Touché. I'll read it and see if something clicks. Thanks."

"I managed to get into Randy's email account. Unfortunately, I wasn't able to find anything."

"You hacked your brother's email account? I thought you weren't a hacker?"

"I'm not," Neely said.

Vaughn approached our table. He and Neely exchanged a quick kiss.

"We're dating," Neely explained.

"Yeah, I gathered," I replied with a shocked expression.

"Weirdest thing," Vaughn said. "On my way here, I saw Cassidy crying."

"Um, honey, girls tend to do that a lot. What's the big deal?" Neely declared.

"Hollowstone's resident Ice Queen shedding a tear?" Vaugh said. "That's unprecedented. I wasn't even sure she was human. Something brutal must've happened to rattle her like that."

"Or someone," Cal said.

Neely's suspicious gaze alternated between Cal and me. I slunk in my chair and covered my shame-ridden face.

"Any luck with the hard drive," Neely inquired.

"I've got a few programs I'm running now," Vaughn said. "I'll keep you posted."

We gathered our things and made our way to the exit.

"Neely and I were going to go grab a bite," Vaughn said. "Want to join us?"

I never got the chance to answer. In the hallway, we witnessed Eli and Ryan in the midst of a heated argument with Chet and fellow thugs Trevor and Owen.

"What the hell is your problem?" Eli asked the three jocks.

"What the hell is your problem?" Chet asked. "You've been ditching your boys just to go hang out with this fairy."

"Maybe I'm sick of you guys being complete pricks to everybody," Eli said. "And it's none of your fucking business who I hang out with."

"They're not worth it," Ryan told Eli. "Just ignore them."

"Shut up, faggot," Trevor said.

He shoved Ryan backwards and Eli rammed his elbow into Trevor's nose and kneed him in the gut. A rabid animal, he instinctively decked Chet with a right hook, pounced on top of Owen, pummeling him and slamming his head into a locker. Chet yanked Eli off of his friend and in return he caught a left hook and was repeatedly stomped on. When Ryan finally managed to restrain Eli, Chet lay sprawled on the ground, blood trickling from his mouth.

"Taking up for your boyfriend?" Chet asked. "What are you a fag now, too?"

"Yeah I am," Eli cried. "And I just kicked your asses, so what does that make you three?"

Eli shoved his way through the murmuring crowd as Ryan followed suit.

The nightmares became more frequent and more intense after Cal's death. I long dreaded going to sleep. Unfortunately the demands of a job, school, music practice and investigating murders led to inevitable exhaustion.

I knew I was dreaming when I found myself in the middle of a political rally, but for the life of me I couldn't wake myself up. Weaving through the mob of supporters, I made it to the front to identify the speaker as Cal. Only it wasn't Cal, at least not the version I was familiar with. Certain facial features were slightly different and his hair was strawberry unlike the natural sandy blond that my roommate possessed.

"Change is never simple," the speaker bellowed. "To not at least adapt to change means to be lost in history. And to not learn from the past means to damn the future. Doing what's right is rarely easy which is why it's often the road less traveled. However, if each of us does our part, we will have a future and a legacy that we can take pride in."

The crowd erupted. One thing was certain, he possessed Cal's charm and charisma. The masses cheered him on with the fervor of a rock star as opposed to a political leader.

The winds picked up. The skies turned dark. The others continued to praise the speaker, but I was the only one who was aware of the sudden climatic shift. Time seemed to slow for me.

Thorny vines erupted through the wooden planks of the stage and ensnared the speaker. The crowd screamed and scattered while the speaker struggled to break free. By the time I reached the stage, the roots drug the speaker into the gaping maw in the earth.

"Grab my hand!" I yelled.

The speaker's eyes turned black. He released a guttural reply, "It's all connected."

The crack of thunder awoke me. I was drenched in sweat; my heart beating rapidly. Cal stared absently out the window. Torrents of rain descended and the lightning flashes illuminated the night sky.

He stated, "The storm is only going to get worse."

I forgot the actual date of the Atticus Johnson Cotillion. It was probably my subconscious's way of alleviating my guilt from my blowup with Cassidy. This is why it took me a minute to figure out why students and adults congregated outside one of the banquet halls while I was en route back to my dorm.

My curiosity getting the better of me, I peered through a window to view the festivities. The usual suspects were in attendance. Phyllis and Chris Goddard beamed as they graciously conversed with classmates and parents. It was interesting that their daddy, the senator, wasn't present. No doubt wasting our tax dollars in Washington.

Mr. Norrington shook the hands of parents and potential donors. Standing near the refreshment table were Cassidy and a tall slender dark-skinned woman who could only be her mother.

"I do hope you're not planning to stay here all night stuffing your face," Mrs. Reeves said. "I thought you said your date was going to meet you here?"

"He is," Cassidy said. "He's just running late."

"Right and is this date real or imaginary like all of your friends at this school. Sad, even your imaginary date doesn't take you seriously enough to show up on time. And for God's sake will you stop slouching. You are embarrassing me. Such lousy posture. No wonder you can't get a man."

The guilt I felt the day I lost my temper with Cassidy returned with a vengeance.

"Don't just stand there Altar Boy," Cal said. "There's a damsel in distress who needs some serious rescuing."

Needing no further prompting I dashed to my dorm with the same speed as Clark Kent racing to the nearest phone booth. The moment I reached my closet, I ripped open my shirt in the same vein as the Man of Steel. Minutes later I flew back to the banquet hall.

Not much had changed when I returned.

"I'm so sorry I'm late, Cassidy," I greeted as I kissed her on the cheek. "Nolan wants to make sure that Brahms piece is flawless for the concert."

Both Cassidy and Mrs. Reeves stared at me with utter shock.

"And you must be Mrs. Reeves," I continued, shaking the shocked woman's hand. "Cassidy talks about you all the time."

"She-she does?" Mrs. Reeves stammered.

"Absolutely," I said. "She won't admit it, but I know you're the reason she's the successful overachiever she is. She clearly wants to emulate her mother. And might I add Mrs. Reeves that you may want to be very careful."

"Excuse me?" Mrs. Reeves asked.

"It's just that I see where your daughter gets her beauty from and if you're not careful, you're going to have legions of love-struck teenage boys chasing you around."

Cassidy's eyes shifted back between me and her mother, her brain still hadn't registered that the scene in front of her was actually happening.

"Would you excuse us?" I asked, wrapping my arm around Cassidy's waist. "There's been a change in plans with some friends of ours and we need to go catch up with them. It was a pleasure meeting you."

I promptly escorted Cassidy out of the room, leaving Mrs. Reeves in a dumbstruck fugue.

It wasn't until we arrived at the promenade that Cassidy finally emerged from her shocked state.

"That has to be the first time I've ever seen my mother speechless," she said.

"I could say the same about you."

"You bailed me out. But why? Oh yeah. A deal's a deal and better late than never."

"What?"

She reached into her purse and removed several $100 bills.

"Cassidy, will you please put your money away. I didn't do it for that. I kind of owed you one. What I said to you at the bookstore, it was harsh."

"Yes, it was very hurtful." She sighed. "It was also the God's honest truth." She sat down on a nearby bench. "It's like no matter how hard I try, I just can't seem to get anything right and people just hate me. And I really try so hard to be perfect at everything and I just seem to repulse people. I don't get it. I'm smart, really smart. I'm top of our class. I'm involved with most of the school clubs. The ones that matter anyway. I'm interesting and look at me, I'm very hot. If I was a guy I would so do me in a heartbeat."

"Well, you can be a bit intimidating."

"Why, because I'm a strong, confident black woman? If people have a problem with that then that's their issue not mine."

"So what part of that wasn't your mother?"

Cassidy grinned. "I've gone to schools like this my entire life. Elite schools with rich spoiled brats, most of them all too quick to point out that I'm the stupid dirty black girl. I remember coming home from school in tears. My mother just scoffed at me and told me that if I was that pathetic at school, no wonder I was being ridiculed. I just realized that the only way people are going to respect you is by being better than them at everything. I thought maybe if I brought home straight-A's, if I got thin enough, maybe I could please my mom. Leave it to her to find some other flaw."

"No one should have to do that for a parent."

"Yeah, well, you're lucky. Your parents are dead."

"Nice, Cassidy!"

"Noah, that's not what I meant. It's sad your parents are gone and I know it hurts for you, but you're lucky. At least you know your parents loved you. You didn't have a father that walked out on you when you were a kid. The only relationship I have with him is the court-ordered child support. And you don't have a mother who constantly puts you down so she can feel better about herself. I know people think I'm a bitch, but when you've got the whole world against you, you tend to be a bit on the hostile side."

"I think the problem is that you try so hard to be perfect that you're not being yourself."

"And what would that be, the weak weeping sap?"

"No. The part of you that is smart, confident, strong and very sexy and not so frosty."

Cassidy turned to conceal her grin, "You're really sweet." She sighed, "I really don't want to have to go back in there."

"Who says you have to?"

"Night is still young, I suppose I can get some studying done. Well, thanks again, Noah. Good night." She stood up.

"Hey Cassidy?" I moved closer to her.

"Yeah?"

"Since it is a Saturday night and it's still early, you want to grab a bite to eat and catch a movie? My treat."

"Thanks, but I've had enough pity thrown my way for one night."

"Believe it or not it could be something other than just pity."

Cassidy smiled. "I suppose it wouldn't hurt to skip studying for one night. You want to catch that new movie, Z: The Demon Hunter? It just came out and I've been dying to see it."

"I never pegged you for the comic book fan."

"What can I say, I'm full of surprises."

"So, I'm learning."

Flurries of snow descended.

"This town is definitely going to need a new motto," I said. "Hey, Cass?"

"Yeah?"

"All right something's been bugging me so I just have to ask. Just out of curiosity. How many other guys did you try to bribe into escorting you? You can't tell me a girl like you didn't have any other takers."

"Funny thing. You were the only person I asked. I have a very hectic schedule and I didn't get a chance to ask anyone else."

Note to self, never question Cal's expertise on women.

Chapter Sixteen

Things were different and for the life of me I couldn't understand why. Nothing changed. No progress had been made with finding Cal and Tyler's killers and yet things were different. While I still felt burdened about everything, it felt as if the weight was lighter somehow. I couldn't figure out where this was coming from. Or perhaps the answer was literally staring me in the face.

Across the cafeteria Cassidy smiled at me while waiting in line. I beamed back at her.

"Earth to Noah." Neely said.

Still grinning I turned to my table-mate. "What?"

"What is with you?"

"Nothing. I'm fine."

She shifted in her chair, "Oh my God!"

"What?"

"Oh, my God! You two!"

"I don't know what you're talking about!"

"You're such a lousy liar. It's all over your face. You sly dog you." She chucked a fry at me. "And you didn't tell me, jerk! You and the Ice Queen. I thought she's been smiling a lot more in class. Now I know why. Vaughn said he spotted you two outside the cotillion the other night. I want details now."

"It's no big deal," I said. "We've gone out a few times and she's kinda nice."

"Uh huh." Neely said. "It's nice seeing you smile for a change."

"I smile."

"No you don't. You're always so serious and sullen. I'm happy for you."

"Thank you."

"You're welcome. Hey, Cassidy."

"Hey, Neely," Cass greeted. "Noah, I was just checking to see if you wanted to still catch that movie this weekend. If you didn't already have plans."

"Hold that thought," Neely said.

Vaughn hopped in the seat next to Neely.

"Hey, guys," he greeted. "Oh, hi, Cassidy."

He shot Neely a puzzled look who in turn grinned and nodded her head.

"Your timing is impeccable, honey," Neely said. "We were just talking about plans for the weekend."

"I had talked to Neely about this and she was going to ask you, Noah," Vaughn said. "I was thinking if the weather permits, we could go camping this weekend. I know this perfect spot."

"That'd be cool," I said.

"What about you, Cass?" Vaughn asked. "You in?"

"I don't want to impose," Cass said.

"Don't be silly," Neely said. "It could be a double date."

Cass turned to me and I nodded encouragingly.

"Yeah," Cass said. "Sounds fun, though I know nothing about camping."

"Don't worry," Vaughn said. "You'll be fine. I'll pick you guys up Friday after class."

"And, honey, try to have the car cleaned out before then," Neely said.

"Don't you start," Vaughn said.

"I have to go," Cass said. "Yearbook committee. I'll talk to you all later."

Waiting until Cassidy was out of earshot, Neely turned to Vaughn.

"Any luck with the hard drive?" she asked.

"Not yet," he said. "But I got a few more tricks up my sleeve."

While Vaughn explained the intricacies of some of the hacking programs he wrote, I spotted Abigail picking at her lunch at an empty table. Her eyes red, it was clear she had been crying. With an incorporeal arm draped around her, Cal consoled her as best he could. I couldn't decide who was more pained. Abby for whatever turmoil she was experiencing or Cal for not being able to assuage the hurt of the woman he loved.

Friday afternoon arrived and I couldn't leave school fast enough. Little wonder that I was the first to have all of his things packed neatly in Vaughn's SUV. His old car finally died on him. The weather was perfect for camping too. Only in the South can it reach the low sixties in the dead of winter. Cal and I sat on the steps and watched the others load their gear. I mindlessly played with the switchblade-lighter that belonged to Cal. I hadn't seen much of him that week for obvious reasons.

"Did you find out what's going on with Abby?" I asked him.

Cal shook his head. "I've never seen her that upset before. She doesn't talk to anyone. And it looks like she's on the outs with Goddard, which thank God for small favors. Still though, I'm worried about her."

"When we get back, I'll talk to her and see what's going on."

"Thanks."

Cassidy assisted Neely in placing another large satchel into the back of the SUV.

"Shouldn't you be helping them?" Cal asked.

"Nah," Noah said. "Vaughn kept telling the girls to keep the luggage to a minimum otherwise they would have to lug it. He and I both agreed that if they over-packed, they would have to deal with it."

Cal chuckled, "Nice."

Cassidy flashed me a nervous grin and I waved at her.

"I'm happy for you, Altar Boy," Cal said. "She's good for you."

"Everyone keeps saying that."

"Because it's true. You were never like that with Brianna."

"That's because I was always worried about her biting my head off after we mated or something."

"Hehehehe. That's true. Do me a favor."

"What's that?"

"Appreciate every second you get with her. Never take a moment for granted. Don't end up like me and Abby."

I turned to respond, but he was gone. Cassidy took his seat on the steps. She wore a worried look on her face.

"Hey, Noah, I was thinking that maybe I should just hang back and let you three go on," Cass said.

"What? Why?"

"Well I have some homework I can do and there are things I need to take care of for student council and I'm really more of a city girl and you know I don't want to—"

"What's really going on?"

Cassidy sighed. "What if they don't like me?"

"Who? Neely and Vaughn? Don't be ridiculous. They invited you, they totally like you."

"What if they don't? Usually that doesn't bother me. If someone doesn't like me, I'll just intimidate them but they're friends of yours so I can't do that and if they don't like me—"

"You think I won't like you. Cass, you have nothing to worry about. And trust me, once they get to know you, they're going to love you as much as I do. Okay maybe not as much as me, but pretty close."

"I know how stupid I sound. I'm just not good with people. I never had many friends growing up. Actually, I never had any. Generally, I have very little use for them and I—"

I held the side of her face and kissed her passionately. Ten seconds passed before she pulled away.

"That's not really helping," Cass said.

I sighed and shook my head.

She grabbed the back of my neck, "I didn't say stop."

We resumed until Neely's arrival prompted us to break for air.

"You two lovebirds ready?" she asked.

Cass and I nodded.

"Thanks for inviting me, Neely," Cassidy said. "And that's a very lovely jacket too. And the pinks stripes in your hair are also very creative."

"Uh….thank you?" Neely replied.

Satisfied with her attempt at being human, Cassidy beamed. A bewildered Neely turned to me for an answer. I could only cover my face and shake my head.

"C'mon, guys," Vaughn said. "Let's roll before the girls find more luggage to hold us up with."

"Oh, don't you start," Neely said. "We would've already been on the road if you had cleaned out that pigsty of a car like I told you too."

"My car is not that bad," Vaughn protested.

"Vaughn, I found your boxers in the backseat!" Neely countered.

"Hey!" Vaughn returned. "You know exactly how my boxers got back there so I don't want to hear it."

The otherwise laid back computer hacking hipster became quite the taskmaster in regards to sticking to our itinerary which was interesting because I didn't realize we had one. The two gas stops were limited to fifteen minute breaks for restroom use, buying snacks and stretching our legs. Upon arrival, we immediately hiked up the trail. Cass and I were thoroughly entertained by the endless barbs between Vaughn and Neely who threatened to bitch slap him senseless if he barked one more order.

But to Vaughn's credit, once we reached the peak of the trail and gazed at the view of the mountains and forestry, we understood why he was in such a rush to show us.

"It's beautiful," Neely gasped. "Wow. I wish I had a camera."

"I have one," Cassidy said. She removed a small digital camera from her purse and snapped away. "When did you come up here, Vaughn?"

"Last year in Miller's geology class. That trip was hell. Chet bitched the whole time about the hike. Miller was constantly griping at Jason and Fenn. Chris was being a world class prick while his sister was flirting with Miller."

"Are you serious?" Cassidy asked.

"I exhibit no surprise when it comes to that walking STD," Neely said.

"Wow, where did that come from?" I asked.

"What you didn't know?" Vaughn said. "I nearly had to stop her from kicking Phyllis's the other day at school."

"That's because she and her little posse were hassling Ryan," she said. "We LGBTQs have to stick together. Especially against the Goddards of the world."

"She's no worse than her brother," I said.

"Chris is just a scared little boy trying to act like a man," Neely said. "His sister, is a different breed of bitch entirely."

"Hey guys gather in, I want to get a shot of all of us," Cassidy said.

She set the timer on her camera. We huddled together and grinned as the camera flashed and snapped a shot of all of us together.

Stepping out of my tent, I noted the clear starry night, illuminated by the moon's effulgent glow. The cool breeze was refreshing. Cassidy sat in front of the campfire, turning the page of a graphic novel.

"Where are the others?" I asked.

"Neely went with Vaughn to get some wood."

"I bet she did."

"So, I guess it's just the two of us."

"Yeah, I guess it's just the two of us."

"So?"

"Yeah? Oh screw it."

The book hadn't fallen by Cassidy's side when I pounced on top of her. I cupped the small of her back while she unzipped my jacket and unbuttoned my shirt.

"Oh, yeah," Cal said. "Things are finally getting interesting. Bow-chick-a-wow-wow!"

I chucked my jacket at him.

"NOAH!" Neely screamed. she emerged from the woods, doubled over and panted heavily.

"Neely what's wrong?" Cassidy asked.

"Where's Vaughn?" I added. "Is he all right?"

"He's fine," Neely said. "You need to come with me now. There's something you need to see."

The foul stench grew stronger. Vaughn sat under a tree, horror etched across his face.

"It's over there," he pointed. "Cass, you might not want to look."

I slowly peered over into the ditch. "Oh God!"

I wasn't sure how long the corpse had been there. While one question had been answered, a dozen more were now raised. In the center of the ditch was none other than the remains of Coach Phelps.

Nearly half an hour had passed before the cops, the paramedics and Vance arrived.

"What the hell is going on?" he whispered.

"Your guess is as good as mine," I said. "You may want to pay Herman Heard a visit."

Det. Foley strolled up, smoking a cigarette with a cocky sneer on his face.

"Mr. Scott," he said. "Why is it every time there's a murder, you seem to be involved somehow?"

"Couldn't tell you," I said.

"You want to tell me how you just happened upon your old coach's corpse?"

"We were camping and my friends found it," I said.

"Right, so when did you last see Phelps alive?" Foley asked.

"Late last year, right before he got fired," I said.

"Uh huh," Foley said. "And what was your relationship like with the coach?"

"What are you getting at?" I asked.

"Funny, how all of these murders didn't start until you rolled into town."

"What the hell?" I asked.

"For God's sakes Foley, that coach has been dead for days probably weeks. Anybody can see that," Vance interjected.

"Maybe the kid here dumped the body here and brought his friends back not to cast any suspicion."

"And how in the hell was I able to lure him out into the middle of nowhere?" I asked.

"Even if he did, the guy was like three times this kid's size," Vance said.

"Those were bullet holes in that coach's chest," Foley said. "Isn't that what you banger types like to do in Atlanta? Bust a cap in someone?"

"I'm not sure," I said. "Talked to Burke lately?"

"Maybe I should take you downtown," Foley said. "For a little game of twenty questions. See if we can hold you for forty-eight hours until I find something, maybe longer."

"And maybe internal affairs will get a sneak peak of tomorrow's top story, police officers indebted to local bookies," Vance said. "How much you still in the hole with Heard, Foley? Ten, fifteen grand?"

Foley scowled at both Vance and me.

"We're not done," Foley said to me. "Not by a long shot."

The slovenly pitiful excuse of a cop waddled off.

"Thank you," I said to Vance.

"Don't mention it," he said. "Get the hell out of here before he comes back for round two."

"Quick question," I said.

"Shoot."

"Heard. Does he deal in drug trafficking?"

Vance shook his head, "He never messed with the stuff. He always said that it invited too much attention from the cops."

"So it's not him," I said to myself.

"What?"

"Nothing. Thanks again. Keep me posted."

"Likewise."

The masquerade was in full swing when I returned to the

ballroom. With a quick glance at the grandfather clock, I knew I had to find Cal before the Phantom struck. Grace and the other Cynical Sirens performed on stage with an accompanying orchestra. Like the guests, they adorned, suits, gowns and masks. I weaved through my waltzing classmates, peering for any semblance of Cal.

In a corner, Vaughn nibbled on Neely's neck. I started for them when Chet and Owen hooked my arms and drug me to a bench. The two stood guard in front of me. I slid around on the bench and crept away. I didn't get far when Phyllis and her gaggle surrounded me, each rubbing their hand across me before they flurried off. Ahead, Eli and Ryan exchanged kisses and weaved to the band's music.

In the center of the floor stood Cassidy. In a long silver gown, she looked absolutely stunning. I was drawn to her and powerless to turn away. She placed a soft gloved hand against my face. I leaned in to kiss her when I spotted the shadow. The Phantom had arrived. Cal was on the balcony with Abby. This dream was different from last time. I pushed my way through the crowd to reach the two. Just as Abby accepted the white rose, the Phantom emerged from the shadows and plunged his scythe into Cal's back.

The sun slowly set as I continued my trek through the cemetery. I somberly passed the row of tombstones. It was then I noticed the names: Jason Finnegann, Randall Tyler, Caleb Warner, Greg Phelps. I came to a halt upon spotting the name on the last tombstone: Elias Cole. I read the name again.

"What the?" I muttered.

Jason stood behind me, "It really is all connected."

I awoke in the back of Vaughn's SUV.

"Noah you okay?" Cassidy asked.

"Does anyone have Eli or Ryan's number?" I asked.

The others shook their heads.

"What's wrong, Noah?" Neely asked.

"You're scaring me," Cassidy said.

"Vaughn, how far are we from the school?" I asked.

"About twenty minutes out," he said.

"Make it five," I said.

"Noah, what's going on?" Neely asked.

"I'm not sure yet, but I hope to hell I'm wrong."

Unfortunately, I got the answer I was dreading the second

Hollowstone came into view. Ambulances and police cars were camped in front of the school.

"What the hell is going on tonight?" Vaughn asked.

Racing to the scene, I arrived in time to watch the paramedics place a beaten and bloodied Eli into the back of an ambulance. He was still alive…barely. The overheard whispers from onlookers informed me of what transpired. Someone found a half-dead Eli in the parking lot. Though names weren't mentioned, I knew which group of thugs was responsible.

"My God, Eli," Cassidy said. "Who would do this to him? Noah, how did you know that something had happened? Noah? Noah?"

I spotted an ominous figure beyond the crowd of spectators. Ryan stood transfixed. His grey pullover stained in blood. His fists curled, his jaw clenched with rage. He pulled his hood over his head and disappeared into the dark of night.

Chapter Seventeen

His name was Raphael. I saw him briefly at school with Cal. The duster and the fiery red hair were unmistakable. A prophetic dream would be my second encounter with him.

He descended from the heavens and landed on the rooftop of St. Bartholomew's Cathedral. His expression was a pained one. He passed by me, clearly oblivious to my presence. Whatever this dream was, I was meant to observe. The angel closed his eyes to meditate but a buzzing fly clearly had other plans. It buzzed near Raphael's face, nimbly evading his swatting hands.

"That tears it," he growled.

With clenched fists, Raphael soared into the air and unleashed a massive lightning bolt at the insect. The fly dodged the blast and departed. Raphael descended to the rooftop and ran a thin freckled hand through his fiery red hair. He gazed at the gray cloudy sky.

"Heavenly Father, I have been your devoted son for many an eon," he said. "I have never faltered on an assignment. But now I am frightened. For some time now there has been a rage festering within me and…and you saw what just happened. I am frustrated, Father. I have done everything in my power to deliver your message to the humans but no matter how many souls I try to reach, they seem intent on obliterating one another and allowing the Destroyer to win. However, I am now wondering if perhaps it's me. Maybe I am not qualified and perhaps I am simply not worthy of serving you.

"Father, I desperately need an answer. I do not want this rage to corrupt me. Please Father, I need some direction."

The winds intensified. The angel's green eyes scanned for some semblance of a Heavenly sign. It never manifested. Raphael sighed in defeat. At that moment everything shimmered and the entire scene shifted.

Weaving through droves of pedestrians on a crowded street three days later, Raphael happened upon a news report shown on a widescreen television in a store display.

"And authorities are still astonished by the bizarre occurrence that transpired on Tuesday," the female reporter stated. "According to police, Ruby Scott and her 8-year-old grandson Isaac were leaving Mass at St. Bartholomew's Cathedral when they were held at gunpoint by 39-year-old Jarvin Jones. Jones threatened both victims when he was struck by a bolt of lightning."

The angel gasped. The screen cut to Nanna who looked only a few years younger. Next to her was my eight-year-old father. Nanna always said that I resembled Dad. It wasn't until I saw him on the television that I fully appreciated what she meant.

"He was going to shoot us," Nanna said. "I just prayed to God to send his angels to protect my grandbaby."

"Jones remains hospitalized and in police custody," the reporter said. "Though meteorologists are baffled by the strange phenomenon, Scott maintains that this was divine intervention."

"God is always there guiding and protecting us, even when it feels like we're alone," Scott said.

Having received his answer, Raphael strode away from the display with a grin on his face. Nanna was telling the truth about the robber being struck down by lightning. Who knew.

The scene shifted once more. Raphael and I stood on the roof of a trailer home. Only this time, Raphael was flanked by three other angels. I recalled previously seeing the two male angels on campus, outside of my dorm. The pair appeared to be in their early twenties. The female angel, Nasira, was the most captivating of the four. Arabic, the young dark-skinned beauty stood as a contrast to her pale peers. Below we watched Cal sling a tote bag on his shoulder, departing the trailer park for the last time.

"And there he goes," Sylvester said.

"And so it begins," Richard added.

"Which is what I fear," Raphael said.

"The portents are still there," Nasira said. "The herald is in grave danger and could be lost if action isn't taken."

"I know and we must do something immediately," Raphael said. "Time is running out and too much is on the line."

"Poor child," Richard said. "He's entering the gates of Hell and doesn't even know it. That entire town is bridled with demonic energy. Of all the schools he could've picked, why that one?"

"Love," Nasira said. "Love will make fools rush in where angels fear to tread."

"That school would be better off being struck down," Sylvester said. "Hey, Raphael, you should have at it. Granted it's not a fly, but even you can't miss a target that big."

"Richard, you and I are going to have a long chat about keeping one's mouth shut," Raphael said.

"Oh, don't blame him," Sylvester said. "He can't keep a secret from me, not one that big. You should've known better."

"Everything rests on the herald," Nasira said. "If he dies, the world will be submerged into further darkness."

"We can't interfere," Sylvester said.

"Sylvester is right," Richard replied. "The other side doesn't know about the herald yet and any interference on our part could tip them off. They would no doubt kill the herald or worse, corrupt him. We have to let these events unfold as they're meant to."

"Perhaps," Raphael said. "Just because we can't intervene directly doesn't mean that we can't intervene at all."

"Ralph, what are you planning?" Sylvester asked. "I don't like that smirk on your face."

"No one said that the intervention had to be divine," Raphael said.

"And what is that supposed to mean?" Sylvester asked.

"The herald needs a champion," Raphael said. "I think I know where we can find one."

Everything shimmered and this time I found myself in a very familiar setting. The angels and I were in the front lawn of my home in Atlanta. I remembered the scene taking place through the living room window. It was a week before Ms. Ramirez stopped by the house. Like many nights, Nanna would rest in her brown recliner while I serenaded the house, practicing my violin.

"The boy?" Nasira asked. "That's your champion?"

"He'll be the one," Raphael said. "I'll make arrangements to have him attend the school where he will protect the herald."

"Him?" Sylvester asked. "That scrawny little thing? What is he going to protect?"

"Hey!" I protested, none of them hearing me.

"You should never judge on appearances Sylvester, for things aren't always as they appear," Raphael said. "After all, that boy's great-grandmother, a frail elderly human, changed my life in a most profound way."

"But what about the boy?" Richard asked. "You know what has occurred at that school. You send him there and you could very well be sending him to his death."

"If his grandmother has instilled in him a fraction of the wisdom and strength she possesses, he will be more than capable of protecting the herald," Raphael said.

"How will the boy know his purpose?" Richard asked.

"We'll equip him the necessary tools," Raphael said. He turned and stared directly at me. "When the time is right, I'm sure he'll realize how this is indeed all connected."

Lifting my head from my desk, I groggily rubbed my face. I needed some air.

I found Abby sitting alone in the promenade, crying.

"You've been doing a lot of that," I said.

She nodded, "You have no idea. I've been meaning to talk to you."

"What's going on?"

"I got no one to turn to. And I've never been so scared in my life."

"Abby what's wrong?"

"NOAH!" Cassidy cried. She rushed to Abby and me, breathing heavily to catch her breath. "I thought that was you. Hi, Abby."

"Cass, what's wrong?" Abby asked.

"I just heard about Eli," Cassidy said.

"What is it?" I said. "What happened?"

The pain and sorrow on Cassidy's face told me everything. Abby covered her mouth and sobbed.

"I don't understand," I said. "He had stabilized. He was even getting visitors. What could've happened?"

Cassidy's averted glance indicated there was more.

"Cassidy," I said with trepidation. "What happened?"

Abigail and I were petrified with disbelief horror as Cassidy gave us the tragic details pertaining to Eli's death.

Chapter Eighteen

Ryan Foster is what you would call a tragic protagonist. He was a sad soul who spent most of his life apologizing for his very existence. The youngest of four brothers, Ryan's home life was less than ideal. While his older siblings won the adoration of their parents through sports, the introverted Ryan was loathed as the proverbial runt of the litter. The rebuke from his parents and the abuse from his brothers became the daily norm as much as chores and homework.

He was elated when his parents finally shipped him off to boarding school. Though he surmised they were doing so out of embarrassment, he was ecstatic just the same to be away from the daily hell that was his home life.

His objective was simple. Blend in with the masses and not draw any attention to himself. Because of this, few people knew very little about the real Ryan. Few people knew he was an amazing photographer or that he was a rabid comic book fan. Though brilliant, he kept his grades just above average so he wouldn't be bullied for being a brain. He even joined the baseball team his freshmen year. His logic was that if he was a jock, he wouldn't have to worry about being one of their targets. His freshmen year was heavenly. While he kept his distance and avoided making friends, he had no enemies and for the first time in his life, people actually treated him decently. It came to a crashing end thanks to one nosy roommate.

While Ryan was in class, a bored Christopher Goddard decided to entertain himself by rummaging through Ryan's things. Goddard discovered a gay magazine tucked away in a bag hidden in Ryan's closet. The gossip spread like an outbreak and before the day was over, Ryan was branded Hollowstone's resident homo.

His hopes and plans were all for naught. Daily he dreaded the inevitable taunts, the trips and the garbage chucked at him. Of course the jackals never gave Ryan the remotest chance of a fair fight. For when they pounced, it was always in packs. The teachers did nothing, neither did Norrington. Leaving was certainly not an option less he be remitted back to the hard time that was life at home with his family, so he did his best to ignore the abuse at school.

His hope was that eventually the bullies would get bored and would move on to another target. It never happened and the attacks continued. Ryan merely bid his time and counted the days when he would be able to graduate.

However something unexpected happened in Mrs. Blake's British Lit class. Ryan was paired with Elias Cole for a class assignment which blossomed into a forbidden romance. It wasn't long before Eli's friends caught wind of the relationship. However unlike Ryan, Eli had no qualms about standing his ground and he did so by pummeling three of the bullies in front of the school.

Feeling betrayed by their friend and humiliated that they had just been beaten by a gay, Chet, Trevor and Owen gathered bats, lead pipes and tire irons to exact revenge. They used Tonya to lure Eli to a deserted part of the stadium. From there they attacked him and beat him mercilessly. He survived, only barely. He made it as far as the parking lot when someone finally spotted him. Unfortunately for Eli the physical assault would pale in comparison to what lie ahead.

His parents were incensed in discovering their son's orientation. Recuperating from his near fatal injuries, Eli was forced to endure the endless barrage of threats and denigration from his mother and father. Eventually they took their toll. While his parents were in the cafeteria, Eli snuck out of the hospital. His body was found hanging from the noose of a chord in the nearby woods.

But Eli wasn't the only victim.

I made repeated attempts to track down Ryan but he didn't want to be found. No one knew where he was and no one remotely cared. Ryan Foster was indeed the quintessential tragic protagonist who spent the better part of his life apologizing for his very existence. However, it would be on a fateful Saturday that Ryan would stop apologizing once and for all.

. My practice session with Nolan was sheer crap. Expecting to be read the riot act, I was shocked when he simply ended practice early and kindly told me to get some rest. Though he never broached the subject, I suspect he knew why I kept screwing up on the Vivaldi pieces. I was surprised at how hard Eli's death had hit me. Maybe it was because another good soul had been lost to this school. We weren't close but I always held him in high esteem

"I know what you're thinking," Cal said. "You couldn't have done anything to help Eli."

"I knew about him and Ryan before anyone did," I said. "I saw them making out in the classroom the night of my concert. Maybe if I had tried to reach out to him and been a friend or something. Maybe if I had made myself available for him to confide in, maybe he wouldn't have felt alone and would've tried to—"

"Noah, there was nothing you could've done. What happened to Eli was fucked up but…"

I glanced behind me. Sitting on the window ledge, Abigail stared absently at the campus lawn.

"How goes it?" I greeted.

"Hey, Noah," she smiled.

"What happened to your arm?" I asked.

She raised her bandaged forearm. "Oh this? I was crossing the street and this drunk driver nearly mowed me over. I barely got clear."

"I'm sorry," I said.

"I'm fine," she said. "What about you? You doing okay?"

"Not really," I said. "I'm sorry I didn't get a chance to talk to you. Eli's death just really—"

"I know. We were friends. He was always kind. His passing put a lot of things in perspective. I'm glad I got to see you one last time."

"One last time?" Cal said.

"One last time?" I repeated.

"I'm leaving Hollowstone," Abby said.

"I don't understand," I said. "Why?"

"There's nothing left for me here," she said. "I can't stay here. And the past few days I had to make some tough choices."

"Is it your parents again?" I asked.

She smiled, "Not anymore. I am finally free of them."

"Where are you going to go?" I asked. "How are you going to support yourself?"

"I don't know," Abby said. "And I don't care. I'll figure something out. I'm going to be free. I think the only reason I stayed this long was because of Cal. It's weird, but sometimes I think I can feel him around."

"You can?" Cal asked.

"You can?" I repeated.

"Yeah, I think that's why it was tough for me to leave and that's why I put up with Goddard for so long. I mean at least I could still see Cal when he was still alive."

She rubbed her small soft hand down the side of my worried face.

"Altar Boy was always the perfect name for you," Abby said. "You're a sweet guy, Noah. Ever since the first day of Tyler's history class, I always got the impression that if Cal hadn't been in the picture, maybe you and I would've…"

I nodded.

"Wait what?" Cal cried. I briefly forgot he was still present. "You and her? You had a thing for her? What the hell?"

"When are you leaving?" I asked.

"Today," she said. "The sooner I get out of here, the better. Oh, boy."

Chris and Chet strode up.

"Abby, we need to talk," Goddard said.

"Damn it, Chris, it's over," Abby said. "Will you please leave me the hell alone."

"Why are you doing this?" Chris asked.

"To get away from you," Abby said. "Don't you get it? I want nothing to do with you."

Abby started to leave when Goddard grabbed her arm. I shoved his hand away.

"Get your hands off of her," I warned.

"Stay out of this," he snarled.

"The lady wants to be left alone," I said. "So take a hint."

"You are two seconds away from getting your ass kicked," Chet said.

"What's stopping you?" I asked.

A fifth individual joined the fray. Wearing a dark hoodie, and black jeans, the disheveled hair and the rings under Ryan's eyes revealed that he had been without sleep for days.

"Hello, Chet," Ryan said. "I've been looking everywhere for you."

"Oh, look it's Queer Eye," Chet said. "You know Chris. I get why he was hot for Eli. He always was well hung. Get it? Well hung?"

"Funny," Ryan said. He slammed his fist into Chet's jaw. "How's that for a punch line?"

Chet wiped his sleeve across his bleeding lip, "You're dead, faggot!"

He charged and landed a stiff hook. Ryan returned with a jab and a knee to Chet's gut. Ryan snatched a handful of his tormenter's hair and slammed his face into the wall.

Chris helped a dazed Chet to his feet. Chris removed his varsity jacket and the two started for Ryan who reached behind his back and aimed two semi-automatic pistols at the two jocks.

"Oh, my God!" Abigail cried.

I stepped in front of her. Goddard and Chet remained fixed where they stood, their complete attention on the two guns.

"You always got your boys protecting you like a little punk," Ryan said. "Well, let me introduce you to my boys. They go by the names of Smith and Wesson."

We marched into Tyler's old classroom. Inside we found Mr. Norrington, Trevor, Tonya and Owen bound and gagged with duct tape to the desks. Tonya whimpered and sobbed until she caught a backhand from Ryan.

"Shut the fuck up bitch," he growled.

Ryan leaned against the locked door and oversaw Chris secure Chet, Abby and me with a roll of duct tape. The idiot would do an exemplary job in securing my restraints. I surmise he wanted to make certain I was immobile in case the shooting began. Each of us sat at a desk. Students in the class of Students Pushed Too Far 101 where Ryan—who marched up and down the row—was no doubt about to educate us.

"I'm going to remove your tape from your mouths," he told us. "Any screaming or begging and the tape goes back on. That is of course if I don't decide to just simply blow your brains out."

"Where did you get the guns?" I asked when the tape was removed.

"A guy named Burke," Ryan said.

"When my dad is done with you, your sorry ass is going to be begging for the chair," Chris said.

"Promises, promises," Ryan said.

"Why are you doing this?" Abby said.

"I can't believe you just asked me that," Ryan said. "Hey, Goddard, why don't you tell your dimwitted girlfriend why I'm doing this."

Chris stared at the ground.

"I'm sorry about Elias," Abby said. "He was a friend of mine, but this isn't going to bring him back."

"Abigail is right," Norrington said. "Think about what you're doing young man. You are making a grave mistake."

"No, the mistake was not doing this much sooner," Ryan said. "Because this is obviously what it took to get your attention! But to answer your question, Abigail, each of you, with the exception of Noah, is here because you each played a role in Eli's death in one way or another."

I shut my eyes and released a heavy sigh, "Every time I look up, somebody is waving a gun in my face. I should've kept my ass in Atlanta."

"Ryan has lost it," Cal said crouched next to me. "You've got to get Abby out of here. And why the hell do you have that calm look on your face?"

"Because for once someone is trying to kill me for something I know has absolutely nothing to do with me," I said. "As long as Abby and I just sit tight, I don't see anything bad happening to us."

"Yeah because being around a crazy person with a gun always ends well," Cal cried.

"Go get Neely," I said.

"I'm not leaving you and Abby here."

"Cal!"

"Noah, I'm not leaving you two! Don't ask me to abandon the only two people I love. Not like this."

"I had nothing to do with Eli, Ryan," Abby said.

"Maybe not directly," Ryan said. "But you're Goddard's woman so that makes you guilty by association."

"Not anymore," Abby said. "We've been over for a week now."

"I don't understand why you're leaving me," Goddard said.

"Shut up," Ryan ordered. "We're focusing on me right now. Truth is Abby, I really wasn't expecting to run into you so I really haven't decided what to do with you one way or the other. So for now, your best bet is to sit there and keep quiet."

Ryan shoved a table in front of the door.

"What are you going to do?" Trevor asked.

"You bitches are about to stand trial," Ryan said.

"You think you're so fucking tough," Chet said. "You're just a sissy with a gun."

"Says the coward who always roamed in packs," Ryan said. "But that's how you always rolled. Big bad jocks so scared of a fair fight. You know I never understood why. What the hell did I ever do to you? What did I ever do to any of you?" He raised a gun. "ANSWER ME GOD DAMN IT!"

"Nothing," Tonya whimpered.

"Exactly," Ryan said. "Not a god damn thing. You know for the life of me I couldn't figure it out. But then I've had to deal with this shit my entire life so I figured it was the norm. When you get your ass kicked by your older brothers enough times, for being smaller or liking comics or playing chess and when your parents are always reminding you what a disappointment you are, after awhile you start to think you're a piece of shit. Finally, they just got sick of me and shipped me off to boarding school. But you know, that was probably the best thing they could've done for me."

He glared at Norrington. "I was so happy to be here. I was happy to be someplace where I wasn't treated like shit. I didn't care how boring classes were or how much homework I got. I never skipped class or did anything that would get me in trouble. Everything was perfect. Sure I didn't have any friends, but I got the chance to reinvent myself."

"Noah, you still have my pocket knife?" Cal asked.

I nodded.

"His back is turned," Cal said. "You can cut your bindings while he's not looking, maybe you can tackle him."

"Do you see the hardware he's packing?" I asked. "I'm the only one here he's not pissed at. I might be able to reason with him. If I startle him, he's gonna start shooting."

"For the first time, life was good," Ryan continued. "Grades were fine. Hell, I even got into baseball which is kind of ironic considering all the times my old man told me I was too weak for sports. Turns out all I needed to thrive was to get away from his toxic bitter ass. All was well until this asshole Goddard here went snooping through my things. He found that magazine in my closet. Because thanks to this shit-head, school life became a lot like home life."

Ryan smashed his fist into Chris's jaw.

"It started with the taunts: fag, queer, sissy, fudge packer, homo," Ryan continued. "Then there was the shoves, the trips, the knocking my lunch tray out of my hands, getting pushed down the flight of stairs. Couldn't stand up for myself because it was always at least three against one. And of all of the people who gave me shit," he turned to Chris, Chet, Trevor and Owen. "You four were always at the forefront. Never missing a chance to make my life a living hell.

But that wasn't enough, you had to humiliate me in front of everybody to the point that people were too scared to be associated with me or else they risk getting their asses kicked too. You know when you're constantly told that you're inferior, eventually you begin to believe it. After all, why would so many people hate me? Surely there must be something wrong with me. I can't tell you how many times I wanted to curl up in a ball and just die. But I didn't cry though. Because real men don't cry and just because I'm gay doesn't mean that I have to be a sissy."

He strode next to Norrington.

"And that leads us to the not so good headmaster," Ryan said. "You know I was actually stupid enough to go to this prick for help. But of course I should've realized that he didn't want to hear anything horrid about his precious football stars. Tell the class what you told me, Norrington."

The headmaster remained tight-lipped. Ryan placed the barrel of the gun to his temple.

"I said tell the class what you fucking told me!" Ryan yelled.

"I…I said that you needed to learn how to toughen up and be a man," Norrington said.

"So, tell me, Norrington, how am I doing so far?" Ryan asked.

"Noah," Cal said. "You got your cell don't you?"

"Cal, I can't exactly make a phone call," I said.

"Text for help," Cal said. "You can get to your phone without cutting yourself free. He's not paying you any attention. Go ahead."

I shifted my right leg and slipped my fingers into the right pocket of my cargo pants. I grabbed the phone and slowly pulled it out. I kept it underneath the desk. With Ryan's back turned to me, I muted the volume. I saw that I had several new text messages from Cassidy.

I've left a dozen messages. Neely and Vaughn haven't heard from you. Mr. Wong hasn't heard from you and I even stopped by Mr. Nolan's office who is really a cranky old man by the way. Where are you?

I quickly replied.

Me and Abby are held at gunpoint by Ryan in Tyler's room. Call 911 now!

I sent the message and sighed. Help would no doubt be on the way. Seconds later I received a reply.

So you're with Abby. If you weren't interested, you should've been man enough to say so. Not make up elaborate stories and stand me up.

I gritted my teeth and shook my head.

Woman, this is no joke. We are being held at gunpoint! CALL THE POLICE NOW!

Riiiiiiiiiiiiight. So answer me this. If you're being held at gunpoint, how is it you're able to text me right now?

I heard the click of a hammer.

"Fuck me," I mouthed to myself.

"I'm sorry," Ryan said. "Are we boring you?"

I placed the cell in Ryan's hand. Expecting to be shot, I was even more unnerved when he wrapped his arm around me.

"I get it, Noah," Ryan said calmly. "You're scared. You're one of the few people who was actually kind to me and didn't care what the others thought. You're just a victim of circumstance. Truth is I could let you go, but I actually need you here. You're my anchor at this point. You're the only thing keeping me calm right now. Just stay cool and I promise nothing bad is going to happen to you. Besides, I'm going to need you to tell them why I did this. Because you know they're going to try to blame it on rap music or video games or some shit."

"You don't know how much shit you're in," Chet said.

"Dude, shut the hell up," Owen said.

"Seriously," Goddard said. "Before he kills us."

"For what?" Chet said. "You heard him. He's going to kill us anyway. He might as well know that when he does, he's still going to be an AIDS-ridden fag only he's going to prison and is going to get raped by a bunch of black guys. And after that he's going to the electric chair."

"Okay, him you can shoot," Cal said.

"You don't get it do you?" Ryan said. "Once I'm done here, they can do whatever the hell they want. You already took the one person I ever gave a damn about."

"Oh God, you're going to whine about your boyfriend now?" Chet asked. "Or was he your girlfriend?"

Ryan stepped behind the teacher's desk and returned with the aluminum bat. With a gleeful grin on his face, Ryan repeatedly brought down the bat on Chet with unbridled fury. The girls wailed while Norrington and Owen pleaded for Ryan to stop. During the bedlam, I removed the pocket knife and began sawing through the duct tape. When Ryan struck Chet for the last time, the bound jock slumped in his chair, his face and body bloodied and busted. He whimpered and trembled in his seat. A satisfied Ryan ran a hand through his oily tousled hair.

"Don't you ever disrespect him like that again," Ryan said. "But since we're on the subject, let's talk about Elias Cole. Your teammate and friend. The one you assholes tried to kill. You know I was at the point of just biding my time until I graduated and got into a decent college and as fate would have it, he and I would wind up as partners in class.

"When he first came on to me, I thought it was a prank. When life stomps you down enough, you begin to expect the worse in everything and everyone. I figured he would keep things on the down low or would try to hide the truth from his friends. But that wasn't the case. He stood up for me and thought he could maybe get you guys to back off. You know he actually thought you fuckers would accept him if he came out to you all. I told him to just keep things discreet and wait until we left Hollowstone, but he insisted that he had nothing to be ashamed of and we shouldn't have to hide who we are. He thought his friends and family would accept him no matter what. My boyfriend, the idealist. That idealism got him killed.

"It must've eaten you alive that he actually stood up to you all. And when he kicked your asses that day in the hallway, priceless. But of course you couldn't let that slide. So being the honorable manly men you are, you decided to jump him like a pack of thugs. So one day you use this bitch here to lure him out to the middle of nowhere."

Ryan slapped Tonya again.

"And then you fuckers bash him and leave him for dead," he said. "And of course the cops don't give a shit about a gay kid getting bashed. Why the hell would they when even his own parents don't? When I went to go see him, he told me that he told his parents the truth. Eli told me that they threatened to send him to some reprogrammer to make him straight. Then they were going to sue the school for allowing this to happen and were going to ship Eli off to military school to make a man out of him.

"And my God, you should've seen Mr. Cole's face when he walked in on me and Eli. It took several doctors, orderlies and security guards to pull him off of me."

Tears flowed from his reddened face. Determined not to display any signs of weakness, he quickly wiped them away.

"I got a call from him," Ryan said. "The night he…He just said he was sorry and that he loved me and goodbye. And that's when I had an epiphany, I wasn't the issue. You were. Time and time again you got your rocks off on tormenting others and making them suffer. If it wasn't me, it would've been Eli or that old Chinese man or that girl."

"Wait, what Chinese man?" I asked.

"That's right," Ryan said. "That was before your time. The one that owns the bookstore in town. Wong, I think his name is. Goddard and his fellow Nazis used to enjoy vandalizing the old man's store. Then Wong went and started making trouble by going to the police and even Norrington. Isn't that right, Norrington?" He aimed his gun at the headmaster, "I asked you a question, sir."

"Yes," Norrington muttered.

"So, Goddard decided to teach Wong a lesson," Ryan said. "He and his boys got together one night, rode out to Wong's store and threw a Molotov cocktail through his window."

"Son of a bitch," Cal said.

I scowled at Chris who simply scoffed and rolled his eyes.

"It's amazing what you overhear when people think you're unimportant," Ryan said. "But here's the kicker, Noah. There was a hit and run that same night."

"He's crazy," Goddard said. "You can't believe him. He's lying."

"Lawretta Favreau," I realized.

"Yeah," Ryan said. "I saw the dent and blood on Goddard's car. When I read about the arson and the hit and run, I put it all together."

"You said it was a deer," Abby said to Chris. "You said a deer ran out in the road. You hit that girl? Oh, my God. Favreau. Her father killed Cal, because he thought he hit her. Cal's dead because of you!"

"Why didn't you go to the police?" I asked.

"Who do you think they would've believed?" Ryan said. "A senator's son or me? I don't get it. You fuckers have everything. Perfect families, money, beauty, privileges people can only dream of and yet, your souls are rotten to the core. You get some sadistic joy out of torturing people."

He marched to Trevor and shoved the gun against his face. Ryan unhinged his jaw and shoved the barrel into his mouth while I finished sawing the duct tape.

"Do any of you even feel any fucking remorse?" Ryan said. "DO

YOU?"

Trevor sobbed and we heard the drops puttering against the ground. A puddle formed around Trevor's feet.

"Now you know what it fucking feels like it," Ryan said. "But don't worry, I'm about to put you out of my misery."

He cocked the gun.

"No!" Owen screamed.

"Please you can't do this!" Tonya cried.

"Mr. Foster, you don't want to do this!"

"Shut up!" Ryan yelled. "The world is going to be better off without any of you. Now the question is who goes first."

"No, Ryan," I said.

"I know you of all people aren't going to defend them," Ryan said.

"Oh, to hell with them," I said. "They ought to be shot."

"Noah!" Owen cried.

"Oh, shut up," I said. "All of you brought this on yourselves. You made his life a living hell day in and day out until he finally had enough and snapped. What did you think was going to happen? And you Norrington, you did nothing because you were more concerned about your football team, your donors and this school's image, then protecting one of your students."

"How dare you—" Norrington said.

"No, how dare you," I said. "Ryan, I get it. I know exactly what you're going through."

"No," Ryan said. "You have no clue what I'm going through."

"Oh, no?" I said. "You just lost someone you loved. A piece of you has died. And what's worse is that no one seems to give a damn. I know exactly what you're going through. I've been going through it my whole damn life. First, I wonder if I'm cursed, because an act of God takes my parents and leaves me alive, because they died trying to protect me. Then I actually meet a teacher I'm fond of who gets murdered in cold blood. And then there was Cal. Cal was more than a best friend. He was practically my brother."

"I liked Cal," Ryan said. "He was always popular, but he never talked down to me. He always treated me like an equal."

"Keep him talking, Noah," Cal said.

"I thought it was cool when he invited me to that party," Ryan continued. "But he was cool like that. He was never embarrassed to say hi in class or anything. He was a great guy. And pretty hot."

Cal's large grin at the praise prompted me to roll my eyes.

"Crazy or not, the man can spot a winner," Cal said.

"Just let Abby go Ryan," I said. "I don't care what you do with me. She has nothing to do with any of this. Please, just let her go."

"Please," Abby pleaded.

Ryan glared at her, "You really can pick em."

"What?" Abby cried.

"You dumped Caleb for this piece of shit Goddard over here," Ryan said. "The same asshole who hasn't defended you in any way. Noah here has shown more concern for you then your own boyfriend. And yet Goddard still wasn't satisfied. Even though he had Abby, he still had Cal murdered."

"You're really crazy," Chris cried. "I didn't have anybody murdered. Favreau killed Cal."

"What are you talking about Ryan?" I asked.

"I was in town right before break," Ryan said. "I saw Goddard in an alley, he was paying off two shady looking guys. I heard him mention Cal's name."

"That's a lie," Chris cried.

I glared at Chris, "You son of a bitch. It was you."

"I didn't kill him!" Chris yelled.

"You better hope you don't make it out of this alive," I said. "Cause Ryan is going to be the least of your problems."

"Your boyfriend, the prince," Ryan said.

"I told you he's not my boyfriend," Abby said. "The only reason I left Cal was because Chris had to blackmail me into dating him."

"Shut up," Chris said.

"What's the matter?" Abby said. "Don't want your friends to find out how pathetic you really are? He ran to his sister and daddy and got them to talk my parents into forcing me to take him back! You think you've got shitty parents, Ryan? Mine can give yours a run for their money. Dad, the televangelist, threatened to throw me on the street if I didn't end things with Cal and go back to Chris." Abby no longer fought back the tears as she faced her ex-boyfriend. "You think Cal was the reason I left you. It was you! You're cruel to everyone, hateful, and controlling and you always criticized me. It was like I was never good enough for you. Cal just loved me for me. He never tried to change me and he always pointed out the good in me when I couldn't see it for myself. And you, you just can't help yourself to belittle me. Whether it was what I wore, or my weight."

"Is that what this is about?" Chris asked. "Is that why you're getting all dramatic and breaking up with me because I said you looked like you were getting a little thick?"

"THAT'S BECAUSE I'M PREGNANT YOU ASS!" Abby cried.

Silence fell upon the classroom. No one looked more horrified than Goddard and Cal.

"That's what you wanted to talk to me about?" I asked.

Abby nodded. "I found out about a week ago. I tried to talk to my parents. I figured since they make a living preaching about forgiveness and compassion, they would help me. You know what they said, that the ministry couldn't afford a scandal and either I get an abortion or they were going to throw me out on the streets like the whore I was. My father, the minister, Mr. Abortion Is A Sin was forcing his own daughter to have one."

"How?" Chris asked.

"How do you think?" Abby said. "I had sex and I got knocked up!"

"Well that settles who goes first," Ryan said.

He aimed the gun at Abby.

"Abby!" Cal cried.

I leapt from my seat and stood in front of her.

"Get out of the way, Noah," Ryan said. "Don't make me shoot you."

"What are you doing?" I asked.

"Sorry, Noah. Normally I'm an avid pro-lifer but there's no way in hell I'm allowing Goddard's demon spawn to be born," Ryan said.

"It's Cal's!" Abby cried.

"What?" Cal asked.

"What?" I repeated.

"It's Cal's," Abby sobbed. "I never slept with Chris. Cal's the only person I've ever been with. I swear to God. That's why Dad wanted me to have an abortion. He would've been thrilled if it had been Chris's. A murdering bastard for a father, sure. Cal, no way. They've taken everything of Cal's from me, but they aren't taking this. Please Ryan! I'm begging you!"

"Shut up!" Ryan screamed.

He scratched his temple with the barrel of his gun. He paced in circles before flipping over an empty desk.

"This isn't how this is supposed to work!" he yelled. "It was simple. You're all supposed to pay for what you did to me and Eli!"

"Young man, we can still get you help," Norrington said.

"You patronize me one more time and I'm going to shoot you first you old son of a bitch," Ryan barked.

"I did it," Owen said.

"What?" Ryan asked.

"Everything you said," Owen said. "I did all of it cause I hated you."

"What are you doing?" Chris asked.

"Clearing my conscience," Owen answered.

"Why?" Ryan asked. "What the fuck did I ever do to you?"

"I was jealous of you," Owen said. "Noah's right. What we did was fucked up, Chris, and you know it. Truth is Ryan, we aren't that different. I always liked comics and chess and stuff like you, but my dad told me that he wasn't raising some wimp and I needed to learn how to throw a football and be a man. Wanna know something funny? I don't even like football. I resented you. For all the shit you put up with, at least you got to be you. I didn't even have the balls to do that much. Whatever happens, I'm sorry."

Ryan gritted his teeth and trained the gun on Owen who simply lowered his head and braced for the inevitable. Gripping the gun with both hands, Ryan pulled back the hammer but his hands trembled.

"You're not a murderer," I said. "If you wanted us dead you would've done so a long time ago. You wanted to make us understand and it took you doing this to get our attention. This is a cry for help. I get it."

"They deserve to die," Ryan sobbed. "You know I'm right."

"I agree," I said. "But I don't think Eli would."

"God," Ryan sobbed. "I can't do anything right. I just…I'm tired."

"I know."

He placed the gun against his temple.

"NO!" I screamed.

I tackled Ryan to the ground. The two of us wrestled for the gun. He wasn't going to die. No one else was going to die. With a vice grip on the barrel, I managed to free the firearm from Ryan's grasp. Ryan shut his eyes and whimpered.

"It's okay," I said. "It's going to be okay."

Ryan laughed, "You know something, Noah. No one will ever be able to call me a sissy again."

The thick blanket around me couldn't keep me warm. Neither

could Abby who rested her head against my shoulder. We watched the police escort a handcuffed Ryan into a squad car. Ironically, I couldn't be angry with him.

In all honesty it was a miracle he hadn't snapped sooner. We were lucky. Things could've been worse than what they were, but it certainly didn't feel that way. Hollowstone had claimed yet another soul. Hollowstone. The name couldn't have been more apropos. The students were hardened stones and empty within. Ryan was right. They were damaged, the whole damn lot of them and one didn't have to look far to see why.

"Noah, I'm so sorry."

"Don't apologize Abby. I shouldn't have judged you. You've been through hell and I should've been there for you."

"Noah!"

Cassidy, Neely and Vaughn raced to us.

"Noah, I'm so sorry," Cassidy cried. "I thought you were giving me the brush off. I'm so sorry. I was scared I was never going to see you again."

"This day is getting crazier and crazier," Vaughn said. "First you, then Favreau."

"Wait, what about Favreau?" I asked.

"He's dead," Neely said. "Was killed trying to escape the jail."

"What?" I asked.

"You don't think Chris…" Abby said. "Cal and this guy Favreau. You don't think he actually... I know he's a jerk and hit and run is one thing but actual murder…"

That's when I spotted him. Being consoled by Phyllis, Chris gave his statement to a uniformed officer.

"Think what?" Neely asked. "What about Goddard?"

"Noah thinks Chris killed Cal," Abby said.

"What are you guys talking about?" Cassidy asked.

"Goddard killed them both," I said. "He had your brother killed, he had Cal killed."

"Whose brother?" Cassidy asked.

"Noah, you've got to tell the cops." Abby said.

"No," I said. "Not yet."

"Noah, Abby's right," Vaughn said. "Let them handle this."

"Cops are the ones who are in on this," I said. "I'll deal with Goddard myself."

Chapter Nineteen

I found Goddard slouched on a bench in the locker room. While I expected to find him cowering, I didn't actually expect to find him sobbing. If I didn't know any better I would've thought he was showing signs of remorse. But I knew better. To have remorse requires a soul.

"I thought I saw you slither in here," I said.

He quickly wiped the tears from his face, "What do you want, Scott?"

"You ever read the story of Cain and Abel?"

"What?"

"Of course you haven't. The Bible is holy and fatal to your kind. Cain and Abel is the story of two brothers. Cain, being the evil bastard that he was, grew jealous of Abel—the good brother—and murdered him in cold blood. I'm sure you can relate with Cain, seeing that you murdered your brother.

"Yeah, I know the truth. Cal was your half-brother. He rolls in here and basically shows you up. Your girlfriend chooses him over you. So you killed him. Oh, wait that's right, you couldn't even do that. You had to hire someone to do your dirty work. What I can't figure out is why you had Tyler murdered."

"I don't know what you think you know," Chris said. "But I'm going to say this for the last time. I didn't kill Tyler or Cal. Of course we'd both know I'd be lying if I said I felt bad about Cal."

He started to depart, but I blocked his path.

"And yet I just can't bring myself to believe you," I said. "I mean after all you do have a track record of hurting people just for the fun of it. Wong, Lawretta Favreau, Eli, Ryan, Abby. You get off on hurting people because it's the only time you don't feel like a sad little worm."

Chris clinched his fists, "You're really starting to annoy me."

"Then I'll get to the point. You've got two options. You can either turn yourself into the police or you can turn yourself into the police, after I've kicked your ass six ways to Sunday. Between you and me, I'm really hoping you opt for the latter."

"You know something. I've been wanting to do this since the first day of school."

He threw a sucker punch which I barely ducked. I landed a left cross. Chris staggered back, rubbing his smarting jaw.

"Thanks for choosing the latter," I said.

He tackled me into the wall. With a head-butt to his nose, I kneed Goddard in the gut and slugged him. Goddard returned with a punch of his own. I slammed my elbow into Chris's jaw, grabbed a handful of his hair and slammed his face into the lockers. The larger Goddard shoved me on top of the bench. He wrapped his meaty hands around my throat and squeezed with all of his might.

"Not so tough when Cal ain't around to protect you huh?" he chided.

Struggling and flailing, I managed to get my legs between us and I slammed my feet into his chest, propelling him across the locker room. Before he could recover, I speared him into a stall. I pummeled his face before dunking his head into the toilet.

"Not so tough when big sis ain't around to protect you huh?" I said.

Goddard managed to power his way out of the commode and we grappled and struggled out of the stall. The two of us traded punch for punch. My teeth clenched, I was incensed with a righteous fury. I finally discovered Tyler and Cal's murderer and nothing short of divine intervention was going to stop me from avenging them. He threw a punch which I returned with two of my own. I blocked another swing and landed a jab in his throat. Not giving him a chance to recover, I kneed him in the gut and planted an uppercut to his chin.

"Oh shit, fight!" Cal yelled, appearing in the locker room.

Goddard attempted to crawl for cover but a stiff kick to his ribs immobilized him.

"Kick his ass," Cal cheered.

I stomped on Chris's hands and repeatedly trampled him.

"Murdering bastard!" I cried. "COME ON!"

I straddled the whimpering coward and whaled on his head. His sobs and whimpering only heartened me to continue.

"Noah, wait," Cal said.

I didn't. Too long had Chris gone unpunished for his sins. I had no intention of showing him a modicum of mercy.

"MURDERING BASTARD!"

"Noah, you're killing him!" Cal screamed. "Noah, stop!"

I continued to bring my fists down on Goddard's face.

"DAMN IT NOAH STOP!" Cal screamed. "YOU'RE NOT A MURDERER!"

"Dad, please stop!" Goddard sobbed. "I'm sorry, please stop it. I promise I'll be good."

Shocked by the revelation that I had triggered some kind of traumatic memory and horrified by the realization of what I had become, I lowered my fist. The once proud and arrogant senator's son, laid curled in a fetal position, crying. Cal glanced back and forth between the two of us as if he couldn't decide which one to pity more.

Over an hour had passed. Neither of us had moved an inch. Our breathing labored, we sat in silence. Chris and I leaned against the walls, swollen and beaten. Both resembling two prized fighters who had just gone twelve rounds in a no holds barred grudge match.

"He just couldn't leave me alone," Chris said, breaking the silence. "Everywhere I turned, he was there. I just wanted him to go away. Why couldn't he just go away?"

"Is that why you hired those men to kill him? The ones Ryan saw you with?"

"They weren't killers," Chris said. "They were private investigators. I hired them to find dirt on Warner. Anything that I could blackmail him with just to make him leave school. I didn't kill him. I swear to God. I just wanted him to leave. If he was gone then maybe Abby would love me."

"And blackmail usually works so well."

"What the hell was I supposed to do? I was desperate. He just shows up out of nowhere and ruins my life. I find out I've got a brother who steals my girlfriend, fools everyone at school and wins over my father."

"What?" I asked.

"Oh, you should've heard the old man when he broke the news to Phyllis and me about Cal. He was so nonchalant. He told us that he fell to temptation and spawned a kid he didn't even know about and he decided to pay him a third of our inheritance. He wasn't fooling anyone. Cal had dirt on him. I think the only reason he told us was because he found out Cal was coming to school here."

"So your dad didn't want Cal dead?"

"Are you kidding me? He adored Cal. Took pride in the fact that the only person who ever beat him was his own son. Phyllis and I were under strict orders to steer clear of him. I figured whatever Cal had on Dad must've been big if he folded for him. I thought maybe if I could blackmail Cal, Dad would be impressed with me and would finally accept me. Dad never missed an opportunity to remind me of how much of a disappointment I was and that his bastard child was a better son than I'll ever be. I couldn't get away from Cal. He was the son that the senator always wanted."

He wiped away a trickle of blood from his busted lip. "I tried so hard to be like Dad and make him proud, but he made it clear that he'd rather have some trailer park gutter trash than his own son. His real son."

"The father you're so proud of is a rapist and a pedophile."

"What?"

"Cal's mom was sixteen, working in a diner. Your dad was in town, made a play and she refused him. He raped her and threatened to kill her if she told anyone. Cal by no means had an easy life. He grew up dirt poor not knowing who his father is while you and your sister lived a privileged life."

"Living with the old man was anything, but privileged."

"In any event, you're mad at the wrong person. Cal was the victim in all of this. And besides you can't blame him for all of the other people you've hurt. Wong, Ryan and Lawretta."

"She came out of nowhere. The fire caught so quick at Wong's store and we hopped in my car and shot out of there. We took one of the back roads to get back to the school, thinking we'd avoid the cops. She came out of nowhere….it was an accident. I thought I was dead for sure. I wasn't even afraid of the cops, but what Dad would do if he found out I screwed up again. I would've been dead if Phyllis hadn't covered for me and made everything go away. But it doesn't go away, does it?"

"Your dad's a monster," I said. "He's destroyed too many lives and has gotten away with it. You want to be better than your old man. Then do what he could never do and make things right."

Cal slouched on the bench, staring distraughtly at his brother. I forgot he was still present. I stood up and limped out of the locker room, leaving the two brothers alone. I believed Chris. To this day I don't know why. Perhaps it was because that was the first time Chris showed who he honestly was. And while he was a lot of things, he wasn't a murderer. Chris had more motive than anyone to kill Cal. The question begged if he wasn't the killer, then who was?

Chapter Twenty

It's astonishing where you find yourself when you've hit rock bottom. Some people turn to booze or pills. I turned to another source. Staring at my sneakers, I couldn't face Father Michael as I confessed everything—save for the supernatural business with Cal, Neely and my prophetic dreams—that had transpired over the past few months. Not facing Father Michael was probably the only way I could've finished. He was completely quiet throughout the confession. When I finished there was a long gap of silence.

I braced myself and prepared for the stern lecture about how God was disgusted with me. Preparing for the worst, I finally faced my priest.

"You poor soul," he said. "You've been through all of this and you've had to bottle it up."

"You're not mad?"

"Mad? Why would I be mad? You've been through hell and back. Most adults twice your age couldn't have handled what you've endured."

"Bad things keep happening to everyone around me. It'd be one thing if they happened to me. I think I could deal with that. But horrible stuff keeps happening to everyone I know and it always seems to be connected to me somehow. Cal, Mr. Tyler, Eli, Ryan, Abby, Neely…my parents.

"We weathered the worst of the storm. We stayed together and tried to survive. We thought we were safe and then…all that water. We were running but Dad got his foot stuck. I just remember him screaming to Mom, 'Get Noah to safety. If you stay we'll all be dead. Get Noah to safety.'"

I wiped the tears from my eyes and continued, "We left him there to die. I just remembered screaming for Dad but Mom carried me and ran as fast as she could. We got swept up in the water. Everything went black. Next, I remember, I was in a hospital. Never did find out how I got there. I thought it was over with my parents, but since coming here, now I'm not so sure."

"I didn't mention this to you before, because I knew how raw you were about Caleb's passing, but a few days after you two returned from Colorado, I found him sitting in the pews up front. He told me everything that happened."

"I've never really been all that religious," Cal said. "I know that's shocking for you to hear about me, Padre."

Father Michael snickered, "Of course, you're not. You only started coming to church to impress Abigail."

"That's not true…entirely."

"Please, I'm a priest, not an idiot. I had you pegged from the second you stepped into this church."

"Aren't you supposed to not pass judgment or something?"

"Your reputation precedes you. I can't tell you how many times your name was mentioned in my confessional long before I met you. And I wasn't always a man of the cloth. As infamous as your reputation is, I can certainly give you a run for your money with my former life."

"Padre, I'm impressed."

"Thank you. And while you are many things Mr. Warner, a good little church boy isn't one of them."

"I could be."

"No, Noah's the altar boy. You're the heathen."

Cal laughed. "I guess this is where you tell me I've been a bad influence on him, right?"

"On the contrary, I think you two have brought out the best in each other. Noah has come into his own in the short time I've known him and I suspect you're the main reason for that. And I don't think you would have turned here, if it wasn't for Noah's influence."

"Noah and Abby have always found some kind of peace in this whole religion thing. Just growing up I had to fight to survive and I knew no one from on high was coming to save me, so I had to save myself. I never really believed in God, no offense. I mean if it works for someone else, more power to them, but I've never really needed it."

"And yet here we are."

"I know. I guess with everything that's happened part of me is wondering what if there is more. I mean I've done the bad boy thing and it's been fun—good times—but I'm left wondering if there isn't more to life. It's like I'm missing something. I don't know. It sounds stupid, me saying all of this."

"No, you're at crossroads in your life and you're trying to find your way. There's nothing stupid about that. Your previous life was dire and I have no doubt that your hand was forced, but now you're in a place where you can put the past behind you and move forward. You've proven that you can accomplish a lot, so think of this as an opportunity for a clean slate and a new beginning."

Cal nodded, "I guess it's worth a shot. I'm not saying I'm going to be a saint because well, I'm me. But I can try to be a reformed me. Or, I don't know, maybe try to be a better man…if that's possible."

"My parents still can't believe that I became a priest so let me tell you, it's possible. Besides, by striving to be a better man, you're already one."

"And if I screw up?"

"It's called growing up. Learn from your mistakes and keep striving. You're going to get there. Bad boy or not, you're a good man, Caleb Warner."

"Thanks, Padre."

"We bad boys have to stick together."

I stared at my sneakers yet again. I was at a loss for words.

"I know a thing or two about good and evil," Father Michael said. "I've ministered to people from all walks of life. From political leaders to convicts. A few were actually both. I've also had to perform an exorcism or two."

"Really?"

"Another story for another time. The point is that I know a thing or two about evil and being cursed and you are neither of those things. That school has destroyed so many lives and God only knows how many secrets have been buried long before you arrived. I honestly believe you were sent here for a reason.

"Caleb was trying to turn his life around in spite of all of the hardships because of you. That poor boy might've killed those hostages tonight if you hadn't talked him down. Think of all of the other people you've helped since you've come to town. It's been a burden for you, I don't doubt that, but I honestly think you were sent here to set things right. A lot of wrongs wouldn't have been exposed if it weren't for you. God never gives us more than we can handle."

The phone rang from Father Michael's office. "I have to get that."

He patted my shoulder and departed. A crestfallen Cal sat in the front row. I limped down the aisle and joined my roommate.

"What a day, huh?" I said.

"I was going to be a dad. I was going to be a father."

"I know."

"We would've been fine. All three of us. We wouldn't have had to want for anything. Abby and I could've spent every waking moment watching our kid grow up happy. I could've been the father I never had. One more thing they took away."

"I don't know why this is happening. The more we find out, the more bizarre it becomes. We're going to get answers and I'm going to look after that kid of yours and Abby."

The harsh howls of the wind reverberated inside the church. The lights flickered.

"Something's up," I said.

Cal had vanished. I ventured towards the door. Any trepidation I would've normally had was long since gone due to the day's events. My hunger for answers long overrode any fear or better judgment. The winds finally calmed when I stepped on to the sidewalk. Not a soul was in sight…save for one. He leaned against the light post patiently awaiting me.

"You," I said.

Raphael greeted, "Hello, Noah."

"Raphael?"

He delivered a slight bow. "No doubt you have many questions."

"You could say that."

"I think it's time they were answered."

Though it was the dead of night, the angel possessed an aura about him; an effulgent warmth. I felt secure.

"Your priest is right," Raphael said. "You were chosen."

"Why me?"

"Because of the man you are and because of your great-grandmother. Her wisdom saved me. I've spent the last few decades trying to repay her whenever I could. Which is why it pained me that I failed her when she needed me the most."

"What are you talking about?"

"By the time we learned of the destruction in New Orleans, it was too late. While I wasn't able to protect your parents, I was going to move heaven and earth to keep you safe."

"You mean?"

"I was the one who got you to the hospital. And a moment doesn't pass when I don't regret not being able to save your parents or the others who perished."

I wasn't sure what I was supposed to feel at that moment. Any other time I probably would've broken down after hearing such news, but right now I didn't have the luxury. If Raphael was here, then it meant something major was going down. I needed answers.

"None of this is happenstance," Raphael continued. "Your fate. The others involved. It is all connected."

"So the dreams I've been having?" I asked.

"Prophetic dreams. Visions to aid you."

"So, I'm here to protect the herald?" I suddenly recalled the dream of Cal speaking at the rally. "But I'm too late. Cal's already dead—" And that's when it struck me. "It's not Cal I was supposed to protect, was it? That wasn't him in the dream."

"No. That would be his son. The one young Abigail Philips is carrying right now."

"So, the kid is supposed to be some kind of messiah or something."

"Not exactly. But he is destined to be a great leader who could bring about great change; perhaps as a president or a doctor or even a teacher."

"Why me and why not you? You're the big guardian angel. Why aren't you stopping all of this?"

"I'm afraid it's a bit more complicated than that."

"Try me."

"We are forbidden from interfering in crucial mortal affairs like this one, at least directly. To do so would tip off the other side. The conflict could easily escalate to a full-scale war and trust me, you do not want that to happen."

"So the cloak and dagger stuff keeps the peace and keeps the herald alive. But that's just it. He's still in danger, otherwise you wouldn't be here. And why are you here, if you're not supposed to interfere? Why did I keep seeing you and the other angels."

"We were there to watch over you. Because you're gifted with the sight, you were able to sense us. Even now, I am taking a great risk by contacting you like this but I would not have done so if it weren't of the utmost importance. We believe that the other side has a champion as well."

"Someone is going to try to kill Abby—the same someone that's behind all of this. Who is it? Who killed Cal?"

"That I do not know. The identity of this champion is being masked by a glyph."

"The guy in the cloak. He had a tattoo. Some demonic symbol. He was chanting to three other men."

"They were Fallen."

"What?"

"Fallen angels. In the dream what did they say?"

"They said something about stopping the herald at whatever cost. I couldn't see the guy—the Fallen, is it—they were talking to. It was dark and he was wearing a cloak. So this champion, he is behind all of this, Cal's murder, Tyler's murder and all of the others?"

"I believe so."

"So what happens now?"

"My brethren and I must leave and prepare. If the other side is moving against the herald, they may be preparing for a preemptive strike in case their champion fails. We must be ready."

"So, how am I supposed to get to the bottom of all of this?"

"I suspect you already have all the answers."

"The dreams?"

"Indeed. After all, it is all connected."

"What do I do, wait until I fall asleep again?"

"Who says you aren't dreaming now?"

Chapter Twenty-One

I groggily lifted my face from the pillow underneath me. Removing the blanket, I found myself stretched out on the wooden pew. My cell continued to rang. Neely's name appeared on the caller ID.

"Hello?"

"Noah? Oh my God. Where the hell are you? We've been trying to call you all night. I had to explain everything to the others. Pretty much everything. I omitted all of the supernatural stuff. But they know that Randy was my brother and that you and I have been investigating the murders."

"How did they take it?"

"Shocked more than anything. Abby couldn't wrap her head around it and Cassidy was beyond pissed. She went into vivid detail about how she's going to kick your ass for keeping this from her."

"Oh, joy. I'm sorry I didn't call you Neely."

"But you're okay?"

I suddenly remembered that the last time she saw me, I was en route to confront Chris, "Yeah I'm fine. I'm sorry I didn't call you back. It wasn't Goddard."

"Are you sure?"

"Yeah and we've got bigger problems."

I filled Neely in on everything that took place since I last saw her.

"Holy crap," she said. "It makes sense though."

"What do you mean?"

"Your dreams. Cal. Angels, demons, messiahs. And today. There's been a weird energy in the air. Skies, they've been gray," she said. "Something's going down. Whatever it is, it's not good."

"Is Abby with you?"

"Yeah she's fine. I talked her into crashing in my room. It seemed like a good idea, I didn't think she should be alone with everything that's happened."

"Thank you. Are you on campus?"

"That's also why I'm calling you. Classes were canceled for the next few days in light of the whole Ryan situation. A lot of people have cleared off campus. Unexpected holiday and all. Thankfully the library is open which is where Vaughn and I are. You need to get here now. There's something you need to see."

"What is it?"

"Vaughn finally hacked the hard drive."

"I'm on my way."

I found Vaughn and Neely in the far corner behind a row of shelves. Vaughn had his laptop open, judging by the horrified expressions on both of their faces, this wasn't good.

"Okay what's going on?" I asked.

"I wasn't sure if we should meet here Vaughn said. "This was too big. But Neely didn't want to be too far from Abby."

"I left her a note and told her we were here," Neely said.

"You decrypted the hard drive?" I asked.

"Oh, yeah," Neely said. "You're going to want to see this. There was a reason why Old Man Goddard was pissed when Cal stole his hard drive."

Vaughn rotated the computer. They were records. Detailed accounts of nefarious dealings with congressmen, senators, judges, and other high profile Washington officials. The records accounted everything from prostitution, bribery, extortion, even murder.

"This can't be real," I said. "This has got to be bogus."

"You said it yourself," Neely said. "Sen. Goddard would've done anything to keep whatever was on that hard drive from reaching the light of day. He's been involved with many of the dealings himself."

"So the senator had dirt on the nation's biggest leaders and was using it to further his own agenda," Neely said. "It's official. Politicians are the new high school girls."

"This was his personal black book," Vaughn said. "He's been in office for over half a century. That's why he had so much clout. He knew everyone's dirty little secret and used it against them. He was untouchable."

"Until one day, he gets sloppy and gets beat by his own son," Noah said. "That's why he never went after Cal. He couldn't take the risk of this stuff hitting the public."

"And when Caleb died and the info never came out…" Vaughn said.

"He counted his blessings and kept mum," I said. "Thinking his problem went away. I bet he's probably pissed that he didn't call Cal's bluff."

"What do we do now?" Vaughn asked.

Both he and Neely turned to me. Seeing that I was the one who had been in the center of this storm since the beginning, I was the de facto leader. We had just opened Pandora's Box. Where did we go from here?

"I'm not taking any chances here," I said. "Right now no one knows that we have the files. It's time to lower the boom."

"You sure you want to do that?" Vaughn said. "These are some really powerful people here."

"Vaughn's got a point, Noah," Neely said. "We're out of our league."

"The senator and his kind have gotten away with murder for years," I said. "Literally, if this is right. Never again. I'm not waiting for someone else to try and kill one of us."

"You sound like you've got a plan," Vaughn said.

"Yeah. A work in progress, but yeah," I said. "Vaughn, you're going to burn copies of those files. Then you're going to email them out to Vance and March. Neely, get Abby and pack a bag. We're getting the hell out of here."

"Why?" Vaughn asked.

"I think whoever killed Cal and Mr. Tyler might be after Abby and her son."

"Son?" Vaughn said. "You sound like you know for certain that she's having a boy. And how do you know someone's coming after Abby specifically? You're not into that psychic mumbo jumbo like Neely here, are you?"

"Honey," Neely said. "The occult is just one of my hobbies. Using my patronizing atheist boyfriend for kickboxing practice, is another."

"Shutting up, now," Vaughn gulped.

"Abby mentioned that someone nearly ran her over," I covered. "I'm willing to bet that wasn't a random driver. We pack a bag and head to the nearest FBI office. It's like you said Vaughn, this is going to cause a major storm. I want us clear. And maybe this will draw the killer out of hiding."

"And with federal protection, we'll be safe," Neely said. "Okay."

"So the four of us are about to be on the run," Vaughn said. "Cool."

"Five of us," I said. "Cassidy's a part of this now, too."

Neely and Vaughn nodded.

"So when do we leave?" Neely asked.

"Now," I said. "Go grab Abby, pack quickly and we're leaving. I'll call Cass and see where she is."

My cell buzzed once more. I flipped it open to discover I received a text from Cassidy.

"Speak of the Ice Queen," I said. I read the message aloud. "Car just died on me, Noah. Stuck on Lebanon Road, ten miles out past exit three. I've tried calling. Bad reception. I hope this text comes through. Can you please come get me?"

"That's in the middle of nowhere," Vaughn said. "What the hell is she doing out there?"

I called Cassidy's cell. It went directly to voicemail. I texted her back. We waited for nearly five minutes. Nothing.

"Noah, I don't like this," Neely said. "This could be a setup."

"If it is, they've got Cassidy," I said. "I can't take that chance. I've got to go."

"You can't go out there by yourself," Vaughn said. "I'll go with you."

"No," I said. "You guys get Abby and get the hell out of here. I'll catch up."

"Noah I'm not leaving you behind," Neely said. "Not after all of this."

"I can't let something else happen to anybody I care about," I said. "And as long as I know you guys are safe, I'll be good. I promise I'll be careful. I'm going to get Cass and we're going to meet up. Abby's kid is what matters here. Please, whatever you do, get them to safety."

"I don't like this," Neely said. "But we're going to play it your way. Please watch your back."

"I will," I said. "Hopefully, Cassidy is just stuck on the road and needs a lift."

"What are you going to do if it is the killer?" Vaughn asked.

"I'm going to end this."

Chapter Twenty-Two

Cassidy's blue Volkswagen Beetle sat deserted on the side of the road when I pulled up beside it.

"I don't like this," Cal said.

"That makes two of us," I replied.

In the distance, a deserted white plantation house sat on top of a hill. I drove up the stretch of gravel driveway. The manor appeared more derelict, the closer I drew to it. The rot permeated over the once ivory manor. It clearly had been abandoned for decades. The door was ajar, blackness pervading beyond the minor opening. I reached into the trunk and removed a tire iron.

"Something's off," Cal said.

"I know," I said. "I've got to find out what's happened to Cass."

"Not her," Cal said. "The air. Something's happening. Something feels weird."

He disappeared. Neely alluded to the same phenomenon earlier. If Cal was affected, then something major was happening on a higher plane. Completely alone, I braced myself and ascended the steps. The wooden planks creaked as I entered the house.

I decided not to call out for Cassidy. If she was in trouble and if someone was holding her, perhaps I could get the drop on them. The windows painted black, the only source of light emanated from the entrance behind me. I spotted a paint design in the middle of the floor. Peering closer, I realized they were actually sets of glyphs. Glyphs that weren't etched in paint but rather…blood. This was the killer's lair and like an idiot, I just walked right into a trap.

The door slammed shut. I could barely see in front of me, I raced for the door when two massive arms coiled around me and hoisted me off of my feet. I wildly flailed the tire iron. My weapon connected with the perp's head with a loud thunk. The strong arms slackened and I scrambled for the door. I reached out to the grab the door handle when I was tackled to the wooden floor. A needle pricked my leg. I struggled futilely but the attacker had me firmly pinned. My head spinning, the dim manor became a blur moments before everything faded to black.

Laughter echoed from Nanna's kitchen when I walked in with my newspaper.

"Hey son," Dad greeted running a hand over my scalp. "Grandma made us breakfast, again. Your plate is in the microwave."

"Thanks," I said.

"I still can't believe you are sixteen," Nanna said. "You think I'd be used to it by now, but kids are adults before you know it. I'm going to have to bake you a cake before you leave."

Mom tucked her long hair behind her shoulders. Her regal posture always reminded me of royal dignitaries.

"Mrs. Scott, you're absolutely going to spoil us," Mom said.

"Anissa, how many times have I told you, you're family," Nanna said. "Call me Ruby. Besides it's not every day I get to see my family. I have to give you some incentive to come visit me."

"We were excited when we found out that Noah's recital was going to be held here in Atlanta," Dad said.

"And you know I never miss a chance to see my grandson perform," Nanna replied.

"This could be a huge scholarship opportunity for him," Mom said.

"Are you nervous sweetie?" Nanna asked.

"Nah, I feel good about tonight," I replied. "At least I feel good until I get on stage."

"Noah, is looking at Remington University," Mom said. "They have an excellent music program."

"This scholarship could mean a full ride," I said. "And suddenly the nerves are kicking in."

I took my seat at the kitchen table and flipped open the newspaper.

"What's wrong, Noah?" Dad asked.

"These stories," I said. "All of the stories in the paper. Murders, hate crimes, suicides. They all took place at this school called Hollowstone. One guy got murdered in a hold-up."

"What is wrong with this world?" Mom asked.

I slowly turned the page. I gasped.

A message was etched in blood: YOU'RE NOT DONE YET!

"Noah," said a familiar voice. "Noah! Come on Altar Boy, wake up!"

My eyes fluttered open. Cal was crouched next to me.

"Thank God," Cal said. "Don't move. Don't make a sound. Stay still."

My head slowly stopped spinning. Lit candles were littered throughout the room. Judging by the demonic markings and glyphs on the wooden walls, I was still in the plantation house. The room was an attic littered with old spare furniture, most of which was still covered with white sheets. Across the room stood a man working at a table. Though his back was turned to me, he looked familiar. When he glanced at the doorway, I stifled a gasp. Luckily the thunderstorm outside muted my sounds. Across the room was none other than my teacher, Mr. Miller. I turned to Cal to confirm that I wasn't hallucinating.

He nodded, "That son of a bitch is the one behind it all."

I silently mouthed to Cal, "Where's Cass?"

"She's not here," Cal said. "I've looked everywhere. All right, Noah, when I give you the signal, you're going to shoot for the door and race down the stairs and get the hell out of here." Cal clutched his sides and doubled over. "Something's wrong. I'm fading."

"Cal."

"Never mind. Now, Noah while his back is turned! Run! Go! Now!"

I darted across the room. Miller turned around a split second prior to me spearing him over the table. I raced across the narrow hallway and scrambled down the steep flight of stairs. I drew closer to the door when it suddenly opened, causing me to stop mid-stride.

"You!" I finally muttered.

Phyllis hoisted her pistol, "You wouldn't be leaving us now would you, Noah? Because that would be very rude."

I didn't hear Miller come up behind me. He viciously twisted my arm behind my back and hauled me back upstairs.

Phyllis kept the gun trained on me while Miller secured my wrists and ankles with mounds of duct tape and rope.

"What do you think about the décor?" Phyllis asked. "My boo here is into the whole demonic stuff. Not really my scene, but, hey, I love a man with a kink."

When Miller finally finished, I couldn't move my arms or legs, much less make another escape attempt.

"This should keep you nice and immobilized," Miller said. "That sedative should've kept you under. You're a lot tougher than you look. Of course, I bet you get underestimated a lot don't you, Mr. Scott? Otherwise we would've seen you coming."

"Where's Cassidy?" I asked.

The two grinned at each other.

"She's fine," Miller said.

"You've been asking too many questions," Phyllis said. "Digging around places, you shouldn't have been looking."

"You killed my best friend," I said. "Why?"

Phyllis planted a deep kiss on Miller's lips. "Should we tell him, honey?"

"Why not," Miller said. "He's tried so hard to find out the truth. I think he deserves that much."

"Your 'best friend' was becoming too much of a pain in the ass," Phyllis said.

"He was your brother," I shot back.

"That mongrel was no brother of mine!" she screamed. "His whore of a mother took advantage of my father in a moment of weakness and our lives have been tormented ever since. He comes out of nowhere and takes a third of everything that my father sacrificed for me and Christopher. But that wasn't enough. He had to come to Hollowstone to lord it over us.

"Then he stole Abby from my brother. Actually that was probably the only noble thing Cal ever did for this family. What Christopher ever saw in that bitch, I'll never know. But that wasn't enough. Cal started sticking his nose in my business. That little stunt with the football team nearly got us busted."

I glared at Miller, "You're the phantom drug dealer. Of course. Who would know drugs better than a chemistry teacher? You're also the one who got the football team their steroids. You dealt to your own students."

"And why the hell not?" Miller said. "It's not like I get paid enough to deal with those spoiled rich snot nosed brats. If I can make some cash off of them, so much the better."

"Besides," Phyllis said. "My beau is quite the candy man."

"And that's why you killed Phelps?" I asked.

"Greg had a bit of a gambling problem," Miller said. "Though I'm sure you already know that. He was all too happy that I had the hookup on the steroids. He practically forced that shit on the team. We were winning games and he was winning bets. However, when we got busted, it all came crashing down for him. The cops were after him and so was his bookie. Phelps decided that somehow I owed him something. He threatened to go to the cops if I didn't front him some money."

"So you killed him," I said.

"How in the hell you found that corpse, I'm still trying to figure out," Phyllis said. She rolled up a piece of paper and walked to a dresser where lines of coke awaited her. "Even Phelps's death is on Cal's hands. But even then he wouldn't stop. Somehow you two wind up in Colorado and manage to fuck up what should've been a clean hit. I swear it's like he had ESP or some shit."

Miller flashed me a knowing glance.

"So, you two made Cal's murder look like a robbery," I said.

"We found out you two were back in town and we decided to move," Miller said. "Of course leave it to that bastard not to have his wallet on him."

"You used your wallet," I said.

"And wiped the prints," Miller said.

"Why did you kill Tyler?" I asked. "What the hell did he ever do to you?"

"Tyler found out about the two of us," Miller said. "He threatened to go to Norrington."

"That was a big mistake on his part," Phyllis said. "No one was coming between me and Wallace. Too bad Jason is dead or else he could've warned Mr. Stick-Up-His-Ass what a mistake that would've been." Phyllis snickered at the shocked look on my face. "We didn't exactly kill him, but we thought we'd give him a push."

"The little pansy got on my last nerve with his whining in my class," Miller said. "How can you be a mobster's kid and be such a spineless little pussy having nervous breakdowns? Yeah, we knew about that. He was always hiding under Cal's skirt. I was almost impressed when he grew a pair. The fucker caught Phyllis and me together in my classroom one night and thought he'd blackmail us. Told us to stop bullying him or he was going to tell Norrington."

"I switched his meds with something more….dynamic. He went off the deep end and killed himself. Courtesy of a bad batch of coke we made sure was sold to him."

Phyllis giggled, clearly pleased with herself.

"Your dad and Goddard, they didn't know about any of this, did they?" I said.

"Please," Phyllis said. "Christopher's a half-wit. Always running to me to clean up his messes, whether it was Abby or that little townie he ran over. My father is a great man but he had one fatal flaw. He was always looking for a son to carry on his legacy. Someone to be strong and capable like him. He kept expecting it out of Chris and he even had a twisted respect for Cal, but I was always overlooked. His first born. After all, daddy's little girl would never do anything naughty. She's supposed to be docile and demure and a dainty southern belle. But soon enough, none of that is going to matter. I'm going to be matriarch of the House of Goddard."

"Phyllis's old man is dying," Miller said. "Cancer. He's got a few weeks at best."

"And there was no way Cal or that bastard of his was going to inherit a cent," Phyllis said.

I glared at her with a mixture of horror and shock.

"I knew about Abby for awhile now," she continued. "She never knew but I was in the next stall when she took that pregnancy test in the restroom. She stormed out and I found the test in the trash. I knew that my brother was too dense to get laid so it had to be Cal's."

"You tried to run her over," I said.

"Yeah shoving her down the stairs just seemed too clichéd," Phyllis said. "Funny thing though, she's seemed to have disappeared but something tells me you know where she is."

"She's gone," I said. "I told her to get out of town. She's long gone from here."

"Yeah, but I think you know where she's headed," Phyllis said. "You're going to help us find her."

"The hell I will," I said.

"Oh, you're going to help us," Phyllis said. "You wouldn't want anything bad to happen to Cassidy."

"Where is she?" I asked. "Let me see her."

"Hold that thought," Phyllis said.

The crunching of gravel and the low engine hum announced the arrival of another party.

"Speaking of loose ends," Phyllis said. "Detective Foley is here for his final payment. He's no doubt gonna want a bonus for making Favreau's murder look like a jailbreak."

"I'll take care of it," Miller said.

"No honey, no sense in you having all of the fun," Phyllis replied. "I can handle this."

She tucked the gun behind her back and casually strode out of the room.

"She is quite the little spitfire," Miller said. "Phyllis may think my dabbling in the supernatural is just a hobby, but we both know better, don't we Noah?"

He pushed back the sleeve and brandished the glyph on his forearm, the very glyph that shielded him from being detected by Raphael and the other angels.

"I don't know what you're talking about," I said.

Miller laughed, "That's what I like about you, Scott. You're such a straight arrow that you can't even tell a decent lie. You're the one the Fallen warned me about. Tyler's knowledge about Phyllis and me wasn't the only reason I had him killed. I thought he was the champion your side sent to stop me. I found a text on the occult in his classroom."

I remembered. It was the book Tyler was going to give to Neely as a gift.

"With Tyler dead, I figured I had gotten rid of the opposition," Miller said. "But then Cal showed up and killed the hitman we hired."

I shifted my gaze.

"I'll be damned," my teacher said. "Cal didn't kill that guy, did he? It was you. He covered for you."

"The gun went off," I muttered.

"Like hell it did. That guilt is written all over your face. I have to say, Noah, you continue to amaze me. It didn't make sense that Cal would be on the side of angels. But you on the other hand. Then Foley told us how you kept snooping around. It all began to add up. You've been in the mix since the beginning, but with Cal around, no one thought to consider the meek little violinist. It's always the quiet ones."

"Why? What's in it for you? I get Phyllis, spoiled little rich girl and thrill-seeking psycho. But you? What do you get out of all of this?"

"Isn't it obvious? I get to sleep with a hot little meal ticket who's going to set me for life. And that's just the beginning. They got big plans for me."

"So what you sell your soul for power?"

"Sell it? I gave it away and gladly. See I wasn't born with a silver spoon in my mouth unlike your little classmates, Scott. Do you know what it's like to be dirt poor? Not knowing if you're going to eat from day to day. Or to see your father broken, because the factory he worked at shut down, because some rich prick decided to relocate the factory to a third world country for cheaper labor.

"And then to sit and watch your old man get drunk and depressed and bitter and use your mom as a punching bag until one day she stays down for the count and doesn't get up. You tell me Noah, where was your God then? Why didn't he come down and save me? If he's such a merciful God why didn't he show me any mercy when I prayed for help every god damn night? You tell me that.

"You wanna know the truth. God is corrupt. Satan saw into the truth of things, that's why he rebelled. Because he would rather rot in fire and brimstone than to serve some sanctimonious hypocrite.

"In order to survive, you have to take matters into your own hands. You learn to depend on yourself and take whatever edge you can find. These kids...I had no problems selling them drugs. Probably because part of me hoped a few of them would overdose. So weak and whiny. Too dense to realize how good they have it. They'll never have to want for anything and yet they're still ungrateful. Their parents made their millions off the backs of people like my old man just so their brats can leech off of society."

"And yet you're with Phyllis?"

"She sees things my way. She may play the role but she's a kindred spirit."

"Or she's playing you."

"Maybe, but this has been mutually beneficial relationship. You know for what it's worth, it's nothing personal, Scott," Miller said. "If I had any regrets about any of this, it's probably you. You're not like the rest of those punks. You don't walk around with a sense of entitlement because you know life doesn't work that way. All things considered, you're a decent guy. I get it. Your only crime is trying to do the right thing. It's admirable. I always liked you. Unfortunately, you just had the bad luck of getting sucked into his drama."

Three gunshots erupted from outside.

"And it looks like Detective Foley just received his final payment," Miller said.

Two more shots rang out.

"And his bonus," Miller added.

"You just killed a cop," I said. "Do you honestly think no one else is going to figure it out?"

"We chose him for a reason," Miller said. "Cops don't get any dirtier than Foley. He had his hands in some many shady dealings that by the time they realize he's gone, they're not going to know where to start searching for suspects. Assuming they even bother looking for him at all. Well time to go dispose of a corpse."

Miller reached into his jacket and removed a syringe. He grinned as he watched me struggle and pull against my bindings.

"Get the hell away from me," I cried.

"Don't worry Noah," he said. "It's just a little something to keep you relaxed till we get back."

He plunged the syringe into my arm. Almost immediately I became drowsy. Despite my efforts, I inevitably passed out while a grinning Miller stood over me.

I'm not entirely certain how long I was out. I slowly opened my eyes to a dark empty room. It was night, that much was clear. I kept my ears peeled for additional footsteps. Not hearing any wood creaking, I took it as a sign that Phyllis and Miller had yet to return from disposing of Foley's corpse. Or so I thought. The door creaked open. My body tensed as I braced for the worse.

"Oh, my God, Noah!" Neely cried.

"Neely, what the hell are you doing here?"

"I followed you. I figured something was bogus about that text."

"It's Miller and Phyllis. They're the ones behind everything. They killed Cal and your brother and the others. They still have Cassidy. I don't even know if she's still alive."

"Cassidy's fine."

"What?"

"She was in the common area this morning. Somebody stole her purse which had her keys and her cell in it. Must've been Phyllis."

"But Cass is fine?"

"Yeah, as a matter of fact we found her after you left. She's safe. She's actually waiting in the car."

"What? You two have to get out of here. Now. Go get help."

"I'm not leaving you here."

"If they catch you, we're both dead."

"Forget it Noah, we're getting out of here together."

"Where's Abby?"

"She's fine. Vaughn took her out of town, just as we planned."

"Neely, you got to do the same. Phyllis and Miller could be back any minute."

"I need something to cut you out of this tape."

"I don't think they frisked me."

"What?"

"My keys are still in my pocket. My switchblade might be in there too."

"Found it," she said.

"Neely, I'll be fine, you gotta go now. I'm only going to slow you down. Miller shot me up with something. It's mostly worn off but I'm still a little groggy."

"I'm almost done and we can both leave together."

"Neely….Neely."

"Damn, it Noah, I'm not leaving you."

I pointed my head and she turned around. Miller and Phyllis stood in the doorway. Miller's gun was aimed at Neely. I hid the switchblade behind my back.

"Looks like we're going to have to dig another ditch honey," Phyllis said. "We have a stray that needs to be put down."

Neely's left hand slipped into the side interior pocket of her corduroy jacket, fidgeting for something.

"So you two are behind everything," Neely said. "You killed Caleb Warner, and Phelps."

"And Favreau, Jason Finnegann and that pissant Tyler," Phyllis said a-matter-of-factly.

"You killed my brother," Neely said.

"Wait, Randy was your brother?" Miller asked. "He mentioned he had a kid sister."

"I knew there was something I hated about you," Phyllis said. "And look at you sticking your nose where it doesn't belong. Must be a genetic defect in your family or something. Too bad you didn't learn from your brother's mistake."

"You're dead, bitch," Neely said.

"Yeah, but the gun my beau is holding suggests otherwise," Phyllis said. "Give Randy my best."

Miller took aim. Neely braced for the worst. From behind, Cassidy smacked the gun from Miller's hand with a Maglite. The gun slid across the floor as Phyllis and Neely dashed for it. I quickly tugged at the remaining tape and rope.

Cassidy and Miller struggled over the Maglite. He inevitably yanked it from her grasp. Before he could strike Cass, I tackled him to the floor and pummeled him.

Phyllis reached for the gun, but Neely rammed her into the wall. She backhanded Neely. Before Phyllis could connect with another strike, Neely delivered a kick to her stomach. Neely landed a punch and a vicious elbow across Phyllis's face. Fueled with rage and cocaine, Phyllis savagely lunged at Neely. The two women grappled until the larger Phyllis slung Neely to the ground and raced for the pistol. Before she could grab it, Cassidy kicked the gun underneath a cabinet.

"I'm going to tear you limb from limb you worthless little whore," Phyllis hissed.

She pounced but Cassidy slugged the high school senior into a stack of furniture. Before Phyllis could recover, Neely bum-rushed her.

I continued to straddle my teacher, slamming my fists into his face. Running on instinct, Miller batted me off of him. He pinned me on my back, tightening his vice-like grip on my throat. Cassidy leapt on Miller's back, alternating between yanking his hair and clawing his face.

"Let him go!" Cassidy cried.

Miller flung her off of him. Clutching her side, Cassidy scooted backwards as Miller started for her. I clipped his legs from underneath him. Charged with pure adrenaline, I hopped to my feet and punted Miller's ribs.

Neely broke free of Phyllis's stranglehold with a mule kick to her midsection. She clutched the killer's wrist and flipped her on her back.

"Get up," Neely yelled. "I'm not done with you yet!"

I ducked a punch from Miller's massive fists and belted him in the ribs. I connected with his nose and, enraged, he tackled me to the ground. Mounting my chest, Miller's full weight kept me immobile as he clutched his massive hands around my throat and squeezed once more. Like fish on land, I gasped for air, but soon spots filled my vision. In final act of desperation, I retrieved my switchblade. I repeatedly plunged it into his side. The pain registered and he slackened his grip. Inhaling a huge breath, I stabbed Miller in his stomach, at least that's where I aimed. The destination was in fact a bit further south.

"AHHHHHHH!" Miller screamed, clutching his crotch. "AHHHHHHHH!"

I retracted the blade and flicked the lighter. I pressed it against Miller's sweater and watched as my teacher went ablaze. He screamed and flailed his arms and stumbled across the room. Between the wood and the random blankets covering old furniture, the fire spread beyond the murderer.

Phyllis swung wildly at Neely who parried her attacks. Neely jabbed away at her nemesis like a punching bag, before decking her with a spin kick. The blow flung Phyllis through a wooden table.

"Hey, Goddard!"

Neely swung the Maglite, hitting a grand slam across the killer's jaw. She stared over her foe who lay sprawled on the floor.

"Lights out," Neely said.

Miller squelched some of the flames. Severely wounded, his girlfriend unconscious and half of the room on fire, he crawled and limped out of the room. Neely aimed the gun at an unconscious Phyllis. She steadied her quivering hands.

"I ought to end you right here and now," Neely said.

"No!" I yelled. "She doesn't get the easy way out. She's standing trial for everything she's done. She's going to rot away for the rest of her life."

Neely nodded.

"We've got to get out of here," Cassidy said, "This place is about to go up."

"You guys tie her up with the duct tape, take her outside and wait for the cops," I said. "If she breathes wrong, shoot the bitch."

"Wait, where are you going?" Cassidy asked.

"I'm going after Miller," I said. "You saw how hurt he is, he couldn't have gotten far."

"Noah, you can't go after him alone," Neely protested.

"I'm not letting him slip away or giving him another chance to come after us," I replied. "Like I said earlier, I'm ending this."

I grabbed the Maglite and raced out of the room. In the hallway, I discovered a trail of blood on the ground leading to a staircase. I slowly moved up the creaking steps. The trail led me to a balcony, its glass door opened, almost inviting. I crept onto it. No sign of Miller anywhere.

Blood stains were smeared on the guardrail. I approached the edge and glanced at the six story drop into the dark abyss. Still no sign of Miller. From the corner of my eye I saw a blur. I dodged a poker that nearly connected with my shoulder. I hoisted the flashlight while

Miller raised the iron rod. The two of us circled each other like jungle predators readying for their killing strike. Police sirens blared in the distance.

"Hear that, Miller?" I asked. "The police are on their way. It's over."

"Gotta hand it to you, Scott, you've shown a lot heart," Miller said. "But now you're really starting to piss me off."

"That's funny," said a familiar voice. "I thought I was the only one who could do that."

Cal stepped out on to the balcony with us wearing his trademark smirk. While I couldn't put my finger on it, there was something different about him.

"You!" Miller growled. "You're dead! I killed you!"

"You can see him?" I asked Miller.

"You can't be here!" Miller yelled.

"Why not?" Cal said. "You took everything away from me. It's only fitting that I'm here to return the favor."

"How?" Miller asked.

"Dimensional shifts," Cal said. "That's what's been going on all day. One of the side effects of an angelic brawl on a battleground brimming with demonic energy. And in case you were curious Miller, your boys got their asses kicked. So no, they won't be coming to save you. Like Altar Boy said, it's over."

Miller's crazed eyes focused on me.

"You! It'll all end once I get rid of you."

Miller lunged at me with the poker. Though I blocked the strike with the flashlight, the guardrail gave way and the two of us fell over.

"Noah!" Cal screamed.

With one hand on the edge of the ledge, I dangled in midair while Miller clutched my legs.

"I'm not going alone," he said.

He yanked and struggled to pull me down with him. My fingers finally slipped. From out of nowhere, a pale hand wrenched my wrists and held on to me. Miller lost his grip and plummeted. His broken body lay lifeless on the ground. Moments later, it erupted into flames.

Looking up, I was shocked to find that my savior was none other than Cal. Using all of his strength, he pulled me back on the balcony. I gasped for air and leaned against the wall. The winds increased and flurries of snow descended upon us. All I could think was that

Newton was definitely going to need a new slogan.

"Cal?" I asked.

He grinned. "You did good, Altar Boy. You did real good. Thanks."

A flash emanated and everything faded to white.

Chapter Twenty-Three

"And one more," Lydia said.

"Again?" Vaughn asked.

"I promise this is the last one," Lydia said.

"You said that ten pictures ago," Vaughn joked.

"Oh hush," Nanna grinned. "The four of you look absolutely adorable in your caps and gowns. We need as many pictures as possible."

Cassidy, Vaughn, Neely and I scrunched in together and grinned once more as the paparazzis snapped away. Wong's bookstore was closed for a private party held in the honor of us esteemed graduates. Among the attendants were Vance, Cal's mother Cynthia, her husband Mitchell, Father Michael, Nate and Jared; a pair of fourteen-year-old twins Wong recently hired, Lydia, Abby and a squirming CJ.

"Good," Vaughn said when the camera flashes ceased. "I'm finally taking this getup off."

"You better not," Nanna said. "You look too handsome."

"I think someone is happy to see Uncle Noah," Abby said.

I took CJ in my arms. I beamed at the blond infant, even when he headbutted me in the mouth.

"Yeah you're going to be a hellion like your old man," I joked. "And for that matter you better watch out, Abby. The females will come a knocking."

"Too late," Abby laughed. "I can't tell you how many times we get stopped on the street because of the 'cute baby.' Oh that reminds me, Father Michael is going to christen him next week. I know you're getting ready with the move—"

"I'll be there," I said.

"Think you can play something?"

"Not a problem. So how is it living with Cynthia?"

"I thought it was going to be weird," Abby said. "But to be honest she and Mitchell have been a godsend. And they adore CJ and they both treat me like a daughter."

"Have you talked to your parents?"

Abby shook her head. "They made it clear they wanted nothing to do with me. But it's fine. I'm going to finish up school and I might look at taking some college courses."

"Well it's not like you have to work," I said. "You're set for life with Cal's inheritance."

"Yeah, but I think I want to do this for me," Abby said.

"I get that."

"And Cynthia and I were talking and we're going to use some of that money to open up shelters for single and expecting moms," Abby said. "We're going to talk to March next week."

"I think that's excellent," I said.

CJ beamed and clapped when Cassidy approached.

"Hello, Ms. Valedictorian," Abby said. "Congratulations."

"Thank you," Cassidy said.

"My beautiful and brilliant girlfriend here is going to be doing a paid internship at March's law firm this summer."

"That's wonderful," Abby said.

"Thanks," Cassidy replied. "She said she was impressed with me. She said I had the exact type of demeanor one needs to excel in the legal profession."

"She would know," I added.

"I loved your speech," Abby said.

"Thank you," Cassidy said. "I had been a nervous wreck for over a week. The only time I was able to calm down was when Noah—"

I cleared my throat. "Child present."

"Oh, yeah," Cassidy said. "Sorry."

"I was really touched by you using Cal's poem in your speech," Abby said.

"It was actually Noah's idea," Cassidy said.

"Thank you," Abby said. "Both of you."

CJ squealed at Cassidy.

"Hello, little guy," Cassidy cooed.

"Do you want to hold him?" Abby asked.

"I really don't do well with children," Cassidy said. "I'm not really the maternal type."

Abby handed CJ to Cassidy. Smiling nervously, Cassidy held the baby at arm's length as if it were an explosive on the cusp of detonating.

"She really wasn't kidding," I said.

Nearby Cynthia and Mitchell laughed as Father Michael shared an amusing anecdote. Across the room Neely squealed as Lydia showed her the engagement ring. Worried that his girlfriend was getting ideas, Vaughn cringed and a smiling sympathetic Vance patted him on the shoulder. Near the register, a beaming Mr. Wong and Nanna toasted.

"Nate," Wong called.

"Yes?" the fourteen-year-old said.

"Get Mrs. Scott and me some more punch and tell your no-account brother to get off the cell with his boyfriend and get back to work.

"Noah told me you could be quite the taskmaster," Nanna said. "You really make them earn their wages."

Wong chuckled, "Who said I was paying them?"

Nanna playfully slapped his arm. "You are bad."

"Excuse me, everyone," Father Michael said. "I thought it would be nice if we made a toast. Noah, would you do us the honors?"

All eyes were on me. There was so much I could say and at the same time I didn't even know where to begin. And as I matched gazes with each of the attendees, I recalled why each of them was important to me. It was then I realized what today's party was truly all about.

"To family," I said.

"To family," everyone repeated.

Spotting a familiar figure outside, I excused myself for a bit of fresh air.

"Nice toast," Cal said.

"Thanks," I said. "I don't exactly have your flare for words but I did what I could. Your son is growing."

"I saw him."

"He's definitely got your smile."

"Yeah. Let's hope he's got his mom's good sense to keep him out of trouble."

I laughed. "Here's hoping."

"What's wrong, Noah?"

"It's not right. You should be here for all of this. Your kid is supposed to grow up to be this amazing leader and you can't be there."

"I'm always going to be there," Cal said. "Maybe not in the way that I'd like but I'm gonna be a part of his life."

"You got cheated."

"We all do. I got no regrets. I lived each day to the fullest and I rocked it. Most people go through their entire lives dead. Besides, I got to live the American Dream. I died young and stayed pretty."

"I really don't know what I'm going to do without you around."

"You're not going to be in as much trouble that's for sure. But it's cool. Heaven ain't so bad. They don't like to party much but I'm working on changing that."

"So you got in, huh?"

"Yeah. Apparently there was some debate about it. But looks like I got bonus points for saving an altar boy. But I'm fine, giving the angels grief keeps me entertained."

"They are so going to kick you out."

"I'm going to be all right. And so are you. And that I have on good authority."

"Your lips to God's ears?"

"Something like that. And I know you. Noah, you're going to have an amazing life. You're going to have all of these awesome experiences and adventures. You're going to meet so many cool people and you're going to get to do things that even I never got to do. You got nothing to worry about. If you can survive Hollowstone, you can survive anywhere."

Up ahead, Raphael stood by a lamp post. He grinned and nodded.

"Looks like I gotta go."

"So is this goodbye?"

Cal brandished his trademark smirk, "Not by a long shot, Altar Boy."

Opening my eyes, I found myself lying in a hospital bed. Though sore and bruised, I felt more exhausted than anything.

"Noah?" Neely said. "Oh, thank heaven!"

"Hey, Neely. What happened?"

"The cops arrived shortly after you went after Miller. They found you unconscious on the balcony. Doctors think that with the drugs Miller shot you with, your body just gave out from exhaustion when you stopped running on adrenaline. You've been out for over a day."

"You okay? What about Cassidy?"

"We're both fine. She's been here the whole time. I finally talked her into going to the snack machine just to get some air."

"What happened to Miller?"

Neely shook her head. "They found his corpse charred. The cops think he was caught on fire and fell to his death."

"And Phyllis?"

"Behind bars where she belongs." Neely removed her cell from her jacket. "Gotta love the voice memo function."

She pressed play:

"So you two are behind everything," Neely said. "You killed Caleb Warner, and Phelps."

"And Favreau, Jason Finnegann and that pissant Tyler," Phyllis said as-a-matter-of-factly.

"You killed my brother," Neely said.

"Wait, Randy was your brother?" Miller asked. "He mentioned one time that he had a kid sister."

"I knew there was something I hated about you," Phyllis said. "And look at you sticking your nose where it doesn't belong. Must be a genetic defect in your family or something. Too bad you didn't learn from your brother's mistake."

"We got them, Noah," Neely said. "She's going away for a long time. All the money in the world isn't going to get her out of this. And Vaughn called. The FBI is looking at the files we turned over. They're going to be busy for awhile. It's finally over."

"Thank God."

"Any other prophetic dreams?"

"It's kind of fuzzy but I think I got a glimpse of the future. Any signs of Cal?"

Neely shook her head, "Maybe with everything being resolved, he was finally able to cross over."

"Probably."

Neely wiped the tears from her face. "I thought finding the killers and making them pay would make me feel better about Randy. But the truth is, no matter what happens to them, he's still gone."

"I know. Unfortunately I know all too well."

"Does it ever get easier?"

"Most days aren't as bad. But some of the few…all you can do is take it day by day. At least that's how I get through. Of course I wouldn't have gotten through this if it hadn't been for you. Thanks for having my back."

"Thanks for having mine."

Cassidy entered.

"Noah!" she squealed.

She wrapped her arms around my neck.

"Breathing….can't…" I gasped.

"Oh, sorry," Cassidy said.

"I'll get the doctor," Neely said.

I laid my head against Cassidy's chest. and relished her sweet scent. I closed my eyes and enjoyed her soft caresses across the side of my face.

"I was so scared I was going to lose you," Cassidy said. "And it would've been my fault. You were out there looking for me."

"They would've found some other way to get to me. None of that matters. It's over."

Cassidy removed her glasses and kissed me.

"I love you, Noah Scott."

"And I—"

The door slammed open as Mrs. Reeves rushed in.

"Mother?" Cassidy said.

"I get a message at the country club and I find out that my daughter is involved in a police investigation!" Reeves cried. "Do you have any idea how embarrassing that is?"

"Someone was trying to kill us."

"And what in the hell were you doing getting mixed up in this nonsense in the first place?"

"Did you not hear me?" Cassidy reiterated. "Someone tried to kill me."

"That's what happens when you hang out with gutter trash." Mrs. Reeves said. She scowled at me. "This is all your fault. I knew you were a ghetto rat the second I laid eyes on you. Cassidy, did you know your boyfriend is on scholarship at the school? What's the matter, couldn't find a nice inner city school to attend? Thought you were going to latch on to a rich girl and worm your way to someone's trust fund?"

"BACK THE HELL OFF!" Cassidy yelled.

Cassidy's outburst took both me and Mrs. Reeves aback.

"Who do you think you're talking to?" Mrs. Reeves asked. "I am your mother."

"No, you're not," Cassidy said. "You never have been. What you are is some bitter old shrew who uses her only kid as a punching bag just to feel better about herself."

"Honey, you think you're special because you found someone desperate enough to be with you," Mrs. Reeves said. "The joke is going to be on you when he leaves you in a lurch. Look at you. What do you think anyone would see in you?"

"He's not Dad," Cassidy said. "And I'm not you. Thank God. And whether or not it works out with him, I'm done with you." Cassidy opened the door. "Take care of yourself Sheila."

Flabbergasted, Mrs. Reeves shot icy glares at the two of us and stormed out of the room. Cassidy slammed the door behind her mother.

"Are you all right?" I asked.

"Surprisingly enough, yeah," Cassidy said. "Very cathartic. And something that needed to be done a long time ago."

A few days later Neely and I found ourselves in Norrington's office. Exchanging glances, neither of us had any idea why we had been summoned.

"Mr. Scott, Ms. Daniels, I know the two of you have had quite the year, especially with all of the tragic business that's happened," Norrington said. "And I was even more shocked to learn that Randy was your brother, Ms. Daniels. He was like a son to me."

"What's going on Mr. Norrington?" I asked. "Why did you need to speak to us?"

"The board and I met yesterday and we agreed that with all of the tragedy that has plagued the school this year, we need to heal and move on. However that's going to be difficult to do when Ms. Goddard's trial begins. Things are only going to get worse before they get better. The media is going to be hounding the campus nonstop. We thought it would probably be best for everyone if you two finished out at other schools."

"You're kicking us out of school?" Neely said. "Are you kidding me?"

"And after I saved you from Ryan," I said. "Why am I not surprised by this?"

"It must be painful for you two to remain here," Norrington said. "This way it's a fresh start for everyone."

"You're kicking us out of school because you're more concerned about this school's image?" Neely repeated. "You've got some nerve!"

"Ms. Daniels, please calm down," Norrington said.

"Yeah relax, Neely," I said. "Because we're not going anywhere."

"Excuse me?" Mr. Norrington said.

"Oh, you heard me," I replied. "We're planning on graduating from here and getting into a good college and nothing is going to interfere with that. So you, the board and Hollowstone's image can go to hell, but we're not going anywhere."

"Mr. Scott, I realize that you're upset but let me explain—"

"No, let me explain something to you," I said. "You should've thought this one through, George. Cal and I weren't just roommates. We were brothers. We borrowed each other's stuff all of the time. Clothes, CDs, DVDs. There was especially one DVD Cal let me watch one time. It was quite the comedy. A little sex tape of a certain headmaster literally caught with his pants down."

Norrington's face went white.

"Here's how it's going to play out," I said. "We're finishing school here. And if anything, and I mean anything, happens to me or mine, I don't care if it's so much as a cloudy day, Mrs. Norrington is going to be a getting a copy of the DVD."

"Who do you think you are threatening me," Norrington hissed. "You have no idea who you are dealing with, boy."

"And you clearly have no idea who you're fucking with," I said. "But let me explain it to you. I just spent the better part of a year going toe to toe with crazed gunmen, mobsters, hitmen, bookies, drug dealers, gang bangers, dirty cops, rapists, jocks, crooked politicians and two psychotic killers. If you honestly think you can succeed where they all failed, then bring it!"

And with that, Neely and I took our exits.

"Okay Noah," Neely exclaimed. "You are officially the new definition of badass! Norrington had the fear of God on his face."

"Yeah," I said. "But he was right about one thing. Things are only going to get worse before they get better. And with Phyllis's trial, a lot of stuff is going to come out."

"You think we need to give our families a heads up?"

I nodded, "It'll be better if they hear it from us."

"You're right. I am not looking forward to this. Dad's going to be pissed when he finds out the real reason I came to school here."

"Yeah, Nanna is going to skin me alive when she learns what happened. And I need to make a few trips before the trial starts."

"Where are you going?" Neely asked.

"I have to take care of some unfinished business."

Before leaving town I arranged a meeting at St. Joseph's. Upon arriving, I realized that my presence wasn't really needed. From the back of the church Father Michael, Mitchell and I watched a sobbing Cynthia Warner and Abby hug one another in the front pew.

"She's been beside herself since she got your phone call, Noah," Mitchell said. "I don't think I've ever seen her this happy."

"It's a wonderful thing you did here," Father Michael said.

I simply replied, "It just made sense."

"I can't do this," Cassidy said.

"You're going to be fine," I said.

"What if she hates me," Cassidy said. "In case you haven't noticed, people tend to hate me, a lot."

I smirked, "She's going to love you."

We pulled into Nanna's driveway. A glowing Nanna met me at the door with a warm hug and a kiss on my cheek.

"Nanna, there's someone I would like for you to meet."

A trembling Cassidy stepped from behind me and adjusted her glasses. She tucked a tendril of hair behind her ears.

"It's nice to meet you, ma'am," Cassidy said. "Noah has told me all about you."

Nanna grinned, "Well it's a pleasure to meet you."

Nanna listened attentively while I filled her in on most of the major details that happened over the past year. She showed no surprise, terror or fright when I explained the numerous times I was nearly killed. When I finally finished, I released a deep sigh. Seconds of silence passed. Cassidy and I studied her face, waiting for some semblance of anger or remorse. Nanna brandished an unnerving smile to Casssidy.

"Isaac was only a few years older than Noah when he brought home Noah's mother," Nanna said. "I knew she was the one because he never brought home any of his other girlfriends. Anissa was the most stunning thing I ever saw. Very poised and graceful, she was like a bona fide princess. And while I thought the world of my grandson Isaac, this was a girl who was out of his league. He hit the jackpot with her. When you two appeared on my patio. It was like déjà vu."

Cassidy and I exchanged puzzled glances.

"What about all of the stuff I just told you?" I asked. "You're taking this all pretty well."

"If you're lucky enough to live to be my age, you realize certain truths," Nanna said. "Fate is going to deal you certain cards and there's no getting around that. It could be a hold-up outside of a church. It could be losing a grandson and daughter to a natural disaster. It could be worrying about your great-grandson and hoping that he's in one piece nearly 300 miles away.

"You can't control the cards you're dealt but you can control how you play them. You're right. I could get upset or freak out or panic. Or I could focus on what's important. I thanked God when he protected me and my grandson from that mugger. And while that was a terrible experience, it reminded me that he's looking out for us. The most painful thing was to lose both of your parents in that hurricane. But even in all of that darkness, God still showed me some hope. He brought you home safely. Letting you go off to that school was difficult. But I knew it was the right thing to do. I knew this was your path. I don't have to worry because I raised a great-grandson who is strong enough to handle anything thrown at him.

"Knowing what I know now, would I have let you go? No, because no parent wants their child exposed to danger. But clearly you had a purpose for being there. There's a lot of people who wouldn't be alive if it weren't for you." She beamed at Cassidy. "And thank you for bringing my grandson home safely."

Nanna patted my arm and walked out of the kitchen.

"Everyone keeps saying I'm a hero," I said. "I don't feel like one."

"Most heroes don't," Cassidy replied.

Nanna was all too happy to put up Cassidy until I got back. I had two more trips to make. While my confession to Nanna had gone shockingly well, I knew that I wouldn't be so fortunate with my next stop.

I tracked Frank Finnegann to a pub in the middle of South Boston. Entering the dimly lit establishment in the afternoon, I found that the place was practically empty, save for the elderly bartender who polished some glasses and several large gentlemen located sporadically all over the bar. Finnegann himself sat in a corner booth, casually reading his newspaper. Armed with a manila folder, I was met with suspicious glares from the pub's patrons.

"Excuse me, Mr. Finnegann," I said. I slowly started for the booth but two large men blocked me.

"My name is Noah Scott," I explained. "I go to Hollowstone Academy. I was a recipient of your son's memorial scholarship."

Finnegann gave a slight nod and his two enforcers stepped aside. The reputed mobster extended a hand and I hesitantly took a seat at the booth.

"So did you have a wonderful year at the school?" Finnegann asked. "I can't imagine you did. I heard there's been a lot of crazy stuff happening down there."

"It was…enlightening," I said. "Which is why I'm here. It's about your son."

The warmth drained from Finnegann's hardened face. I braced myself and made certain I chose my words carefully.

"What about Jason?"

"My roommate Cal, Caleb Warner was best friends with your son. Cal frequently spoke highly of him."

"I remember him. He was there at the hospital the night Jason died. I was sad to hear about his death."

"In the process of investigating Cal's murder, I found out the truth about your son's death," I said. "Jason didn't die because of a relapse or because his meds stopped working. He was murdered. The same people who killed Cal are the ones who killed Jason. Your son learned the truth about the relationship between his teacher Wallace Miller and his classmate Phyllis Goddard.

"Unfortunately they knew about your son's mental history. They switched out his medicine with some other drugs and when he had the breakdown…they figured even if he told the truth about the two of them, no one would believe him. What happened to your son wasn't his fault. I can't imagine what it's like to lose a child. But I lost both of my parents when I was a kid and if someone had information like this, I would give anything to find out about it."

Finnegann stared past me in an almost catatonic state.

"No doubt you'll want to verify all of this for yourself," I said. "Here's everything I have. The last thing I wanted to do was come here and dredge up painful memories for you but I thought you had a right to know the truth about your son." I pushed the folder forward to the center. "For what it's worth, I'm sorry. From what everyone's told me, Jason was an amazing person."

Finnegann's gaze was transfixed on the folder. I slid out of the booth and quietly departed.

Finnegann's visit haunted me for the next few days. My mind still pondered on his mournful face while I waited in the visiting area of the Belladon Psychiatric Institute. I snapped out of my musings when the purpose of my visit entered the area. Ryan was a far cry from the visage when I last saw him. His hair shaggier, stubble etched across his face, his thin frame was slightly bulkier. His hazy eyes revealed a more rested mind, or perhaps one that was doped up, possibly both. In any event, this was the most peaceful I had ever seen him.

"So they're finally locking you up too," Ryan greeted.

"Yeah, they finally figured me out," I replied. "I brought a couple of graphic novels for you to read. I turned them in at the front desk. I don't know jack about comic books, but Cassidy thought you would like them."

"Tell her I said thanks."

"So how have you been? What's it like in here?"

Ryan shrugged his shoulders. "It hasn't been that bad. I spend most of my days going to therapy sessions and talking about my feelings, but it's cool. Everyone's nice and I've actually made some friends in here."

"How are things with your parents?"

"I wouldn't know."

"You mean…"

"You're the only visitor I've had."

"I'm sorry Ryan."

"It's okay. I'm actually better off. So what's been going on at Hollowstone? No doubt they're still talking about me going postal."

"Actually you no longer even rank."

"What?"

"You don't get the news in here do you?"

"No. What's been going on?"

I filled Ryan in on everything that transpired.

"Damn," Ryan said. "So it was Goddard, just the wrong one."

"Yeah. Chris turned himself into the police. He confessed to everything about the hit and run, the arson of Wong's."

"What?"

"And apparently when he arrived at the police station, Owen was there. He confessed to everything about Eli's bashing."

"That's….huh. It won't do any good though. The others involved will just lawyer up and get off scot free. But I guess it's better than nothing. I guess some good came out of that whole ordeal."

I nodded.

"Noah, can I ask you a question?"

"I think you just did, but go ahead."

"Why? Why did you always go out of your way to be nice to me? Why did you always try to reach out to me? Even now?"

"Cause I knew you were a wonderful person, even if you couldn't see it. I think you just needed someone to show you that. I'm glad Eli did. I'm just sorry I wasn't there for you more like I should've been."

"It seems kinda stupid to say this now but thanks. And I'm sorry."

"Just take care of yourself and get better. That's all the thanks I need."

As the trial drew near, Hollowstone became a feeding frenzy for the media. Obsessed with the mystique of a rich girl gone bad, the press depicted Phyllis more as a rock star as opposed to a stone-cold murderess. With Phyllis's brother under house arrest, the House of Goddard was depicted as celebrity gold. I feared that all of this media attention on the two of them might garner unwarranted sympathy with the jurors, especially when Sen. Goddard passed away.

Like a pack of rabid jackals, reporters circled the campus lawns, looking for any morsel of a scoop. More than anything they wanted to know what life was like in the school that was rife with scandal. Norrington eventually beefed up security which was one of the few sensible deeds he had done as headmaster. For all intents and purposes, campus became a prison. Going to work and church required planning an elaborate escape route.

The jackals finally backed off when they made the mistake of bombarding Nolan's Buick when he arrived for work. With microphones, tape recorders and cameras shoved in his face, my mentor fought his way out of his vehicle.

"So you're not going to leave, huh?" Nolan yelled.

He reached into his car and removed a paintball gun. With a maniacal grin on his face, he opened fire on the mob of reporters. The journalists screamed and fled while mercilessly pelted with yellow paintballs.

"I got your exclusive right here!" Nolan screamed. "You yellow journalist bastards!!!"

Faculty and students cheered Nolan on. Norrington's security finally wrestled the gun away from the short deranged music teacher, but not without being on the receiving end of punches and kicks.

"Next time I'm bringing the shotgun!" Nolan screamed.

Nolan started a trend and when other students followed suit, the press eventually backed off.

The trial began. Each day more insurmountable evidence was presented by the prosecution. However Phyllis wore an ever-present smile on her face. Something told me that her confidence went beyond the team of lawyers that surrounded her. It was as if she had a secret that the rest of us weren't privy to.

Almost as if she knew—not confident, but actually knew—she was going to be acquitted on all charges, in spite of the recorded confession provided by Neely, ballistics and the DNA evidence tying both her and Miller to the murders of Phelps, Cal and Foley alone. The prosecution had managed to track down the car that was used in Abby's hit and run attempt. One by one Neely, Cassidy and I took the stand and recounted the night in the manor and each of us identified Phyllis as an active and willing participant in the murder. This case couldn't have been anymore textbook. Yet the cockiness she exuded was unsettling.

The idealist within hoped she was the one being delusional or simply putting on a brave front, but the inner pragmatist suspected that she had a reason for maintaining such arrogance.

The defense team opted not to put Phyllis on the stand. Instead they paraded legions of psychiatrists, legal and expert witnesses who all claimed that this was solely Miller's doing, Phyllis's involvement was completely under duress and coercion. While the prosecution had already countered this with their team of expert witnesses, I repeatedly found myself studying the jurors' expressions. I was plagued with the nagging fear that Phyllis's absurdity of a defense was the excuse they needed to exonerate Cal and Tyler's killer.

Following the closing arguments, it took the jury five hours to deliberate. Sitting in the front pew of the courtroom, Vaughn, Neely, Abby, Cassidy and I anxiously awaited the verdict. One by one the jurors marched into the courtroom and took their appointed seats. The forewoman handed a parchment of paper to the bailiff who delivered it to the honorable Judge Henry Bonds. The wrinkled elderly man read the decision before he handed it back to the bailiff.

"Madame Forewoman, what say you," the judge said.

"In the matter of the murder of Caleb Warner," the forewoman said. "We the jury find the defendant Phyllis Goddard, guilty of first degree murder. In the matter of conspiracy of the murder of Randall Tyler, we find the defendant, guilty."

Neely and I hugged one another. The tears strolled down Abby's face. The forewoman read off the numerous lists of other indictments, Phyllis was found guilty on all charges. Bonds smacked the gavel to quell the commotion.

"Thank you, ladies and gentlemen of the jury," Bonds said. "This was a difficult and trying case and emotions no doubt are running high. However, the burden of proof was not met in this case and as such I cannot follow the verdict of the jury. Ms. Goddard, you are free to leave. Court is adjourned."

Bonds smacked the gavel and quickly retreated to his chamber like a rat scampering into a hole. The court was in bedlam, some cheering for the verdict while others screamed at the injustice. The bailiffs and the team of defense lawyers escorted Phyllis out of the courtroom. Basking in her victory, she tossed back her hair and placed on her designer shades, shooting both me and Neely a confident smirk.

"I should've killed that bitch when I had the chance!" Neely cried.

Vaughn clutched Neely's arms to halt her from starting after Phyllis. Cassidy consoled a sobbing Abby.

"He can't do that," Cassidy cried. "This is bull!"

I stood motionless while the anarchy continued around me. For in that moment, Hollowstone reminded me of the lesson that it had bludgeoned me with since the day I set foot on campus. True to Cal's words, it's about money and power. If you have enough of it, you can literally get away with murder.

And the evidence from Sen. Goddard's black book? The FBI got their hands on it, a few investigations and inquiries were done. A few midlevel officials resigned from their posts but only three arrests were made. The accused plea-bargained out of their ordeals and Goddard's black book was conveniently buried and forgotten. Most of the people listed in Goddard's files were still in power and they called in every resource and connection to keep themselves from facing any semblance of justice.

It was discovered later by Vance that Judge Bonds had received a sizable donation to his reelection campaign. After extensive digging, Vance traced the funds back to Phyllis Goddard. Of course his publisher wouldn't allow him to run the story. Having had enough of the hypocrisy and corruption, Vance resigned from the newspaper along with his fiancée Lydia to teach ethics in journalism at the University of Tennessee.

His final story? Phyllis Goddard was found murdered while vacationing in Spain. Her mangled body was discovered in her hotel room. Investigators never found any suspects but I surmise a certain Bostonian verified the intel I provided regarding his son's death.

Slowly, each of us tried our best to put the nightmare behind us. That became easier with our senior years which promised the end of our time in Hollowstone and new beginnings with college. One by one we each got our acceptance letters. Neely would be entering the hallowed halls of Harvard while Vaughn would be attending MIT. The two decided to backpack across Europe for the summer.

I procured a full ride at Remington University where I'd be doing what I love most, playing and studying music. Of course the biggest surprise came from Cassidy when she informed me that she would be studying law at Remington.

My final day on campus I stopped by Nolan's office. I tapped on his door.

"Mr. Scott," Nolan greeted. "Finally leaving us I see."

"Yes, sir," I said.

"And I have no doubt you're going to do me proud," Nolan said.

"Of course, sir. I wouldn't be getting in if it weren't for your letter of recommendation."

"That's true. My word does carry much weight. Though I'm sure you played your part signing your name on the scholarship and such."

I grinned. My mentor sat on the front of his desk. His feet dangled off the floor.

"I suspect you're going to make waves at Remington just like you did here," Nolan said.

"Yes, sir," I replied. "I'm going to practice and study that music like there's no tomorrow."

"I'm sure you will but that's not what I meant," Nolan said.

"Sir?"

"I've been teaching here for a long time now and I can tell you that most of the students who darken these halls are a bunch of ignorant trust funders. When I first saw you, I had a feeling about you. I knew you were going to shake things up without even trying.

You haven't gone unnoticed around here Mr. Scott.

"You've weathered trial after trial and in the end you've stood strong. You're an extraordinary young man and you're just what this school needed. Thank you for reminding me why I got into the teaching profession. Of course every future student of mine is going to have an impossible standard to live up to now."

I shook Nolan's hand.

"Oh, I also have a gift for you," I said.

I handed him a DVD.

"What is this?"

"Oh just a little insurance policy, should Norrington ever step out of line."

I gazed at the school one last time. Memories of the past three years overtook me like a current. Each one poignant and bittersweet. Finally, I hopped in the Charger and threw on my shades.

"All right Cal," I said. "This one's for you."

And with that I sped off and left Hollowstone for the last time.

I decided to try my hand at writing and took a few creative writing courses during my freshman year at Remington. This prompted me to pen my experiences about my time at Hollowstone:

Funny thing about the truth. No matter how deep you bury it, it's always there for someone to uncover. I never told anyone about my time in Hollowstone until now. If there's one thing Caleb taught me, it's that there are some stories that must be told.

About the Author

Dennis R. Upkins was born and raised in Nashville, TN. A voracious reader, a lifelong geek and a hopeless comic book addict, he knew at an early age that storytelling was his calling.

Receiving an academic scholarship, Upkins graduated from the University of TN at Chattanooga with a BA in English. After working as a reporter for a local newspaper for a few years, he moved from Tennessee and relocated to Atlanta, GA where he procured a BFA in media arts & animation from the Art Institute of Atlanta.

In addition to writing, Upkins is also a freelance artist and a digital photographer. His artwork and short stories have appeared in a number of publications, most notably Drops of Crimson. And his audio short, Stranger Than Fiction, can be found at Sniplits.com.

Upkins regularly critiques and analyzes the representation and the portrayal of minorities in comics and media as a regular contributor to arsmarginal.wordpress.com and prismcomics.org.

When he's not out saving the world and/or taking it over in his spare time, Upkins's hobbies include drawing, photography, rollerblading, martial arts and of course creative writing.

CPSIA information can be obtained at www.ICGtesting.com
Printed in the USA
LVOW012102290911

248441LV00019B/81/P

9 781463 504373